Let Not The Deep Swallow Me Up

Andrew McCarthy

First published by Three Ships Publishing in 2019
threeshipspublishing@aol.com

A CIP catalogue record for this book is available from the British Library

ISBN 9781696337052

Let not the floodwater overflow me,
Nor let the deep swallow me up;
And let not the pit shut its mouth on me.

Psalm 69. V15

Contents

The Fishing Trip

Every night when I go to bed, I hear Mum downstairs. She puts the dishes away, and then she makes a cup of tea and talks to Dad. I don't know what she says, but Dad never answers, of course. Sometimes she puts the radio on. I like to hear the music coming up the stairs. It's hard to hear properly, so I try to guess which song is playing. After a little while, Mum gets Dad ready for bed. I hear her taking the sides off his wheelchair - that sharp, metallic noise - then the bumping as she pulls him up and gets him onto the bed. Then it goes quiet as she puts his pyjamas on. She can't get him upstairs any more, so he sleeps down in the front room. He has a special bed from the hospital, one that he can't fall out of. When Mum comes up, she always puts her head round the door to check on us, and then she goes into her room, leaving a light on at the top of the stairs for my little sister, Ellen. Ellen's been having these bad dreams, you see - nightmares - and she can't get to sleep without a light on. When Mum tucks Ellen in, she tells her that it'll help if she thinks of her favourite thing before going to sleep. Ellen hasn't told Mum what her nightmares are about, but she's told me.

*

It all started with the fishing trip. I'd planned to go on my own, but Ellen caught me packing my gear into my rucksack and said she'd tell Mum unless I let her come too. I didn't really mind, because Ellen's no trouble, and so I said she could, but that she'd have to get up early the next morning and, if Mum asked, pretend that we were going to the park. She promised not to give us away - 'Cross my heart, hope to die' - and sat on the bed to see what I was packing. I told her that everything was ready apart from the bait, and that we needed to get that while Mum and Dad were out.

'Mum takes Dad out for a walk after tea, doesn't she?'

'Yes.'

'Well, that's when we'll get the worms, then. The bait. We'll dig them up from the garden.'

And that's what we did. As soon as they'd gone, we went out to the shed to get Dad's spade. Nobody goes in the shed any more. Dad used to spend a lot of time in there, making things. He liked to carve things out of wood. It was his hobby before he got ill. When Ellen was little, he carved her an ark and all the little animals to go inside. Now the shed's just full of rubbish. I found Dad's spade, and an old tin can with some nails in it. I emptied the nails out of the tin and gave it to Ellen.

'Hold onto that. C'mon, we'll have to be quick.' It had rained during the afternoon, and the soil was dark and soft and easy to dig. Ellen stood behind me with the tin can. 'Keep an eye out for Mum and Dad, won't you? If Mum catches us she'll know we're going fishing in the woods.' Ellen didn't answer, but she nodded when I looked round to check she'd heard.

I pushed the spade deeper into the soil and it made a scraping noise against the grit and chalk. After a few minutes I saw a fat, brown worm poking out from one of the clods of soil. I leant the spade against the fence, bent down and tugged the worm free. I held it up to show Ellen and then dropped it into the bottom of the tin can. She frowned.

'Ugly! Worms are ugly, aren't they? Not like flowers or birds. Do you think God made ugly things, Adam, as well as beautiful ones?'

I took the spade and carried on digging. 'I suppose he must have done, mustn't he?'

'Why would he want to make something as ugly as worms, though?'

'I don't know. So we can catch fish with them, maybe.'

Soon the tin can was half full of worms. I sprinkled some soil over them and put a piece of cloth and a rubber band round the top of the can so they wouldn't spill. I put the spade away, and we went inside and hid the worms under my bed. When they got back from their walk, Mum sat Dad in front of the fire, like she always does, and rubbed his hands to warm them up.

*

The next morning, I think Mum guessed we were up to something. 'I don't want you two playing in those woods. It's not safe. And no fishing in that pond either, Adam. Do you hear?'

'We're not going to the woods, Mum. We're going to the park – that's all.' Mum was too busy trying to spoon some breakfast into Dad's mouth to argue. When we eat, she ties a big tea towel round his neck, and feeds him. The food dribbles down his chin and makes a mess of his clothes otherwise. Every morning Mum dresses Dad in a clean shirt and a jumper or cardigan. She gives him a shave and combs his hair and moustache so that he always looks

2

smart. There was a time when Dad was able to write notes to say what he wanted, but then his hands stopped working, like the rest of him.

'That's it, down it goes – fresh eggs, those.' She wiped his mouth and took a sip of her tea. 'And you'd better keep an eye on Ellen. Don't let her wander off anywhere.'

'Yes, Mum. I will. She'll be all right. I'll take care of her.'

*

After breakfast, Aunty Jean came round. She looks after Dad, and us too in the school holidays, while Mum goes out to work. Mum has a job at Mr Jensen's pet shop in the town, where she cleans and helps out. Mr Jensen used to have a circus, and Mum says he's been all over the world.

'Right, your Aunty Jean's here so I'll be off. You remember what I said about those woods?' Mum wheeled Dad to his favourite spot, where he can see out of the back window, and put his brakes on. She kissed him on the head, buttoned her coat and looked in the mirror. She took her lipstick out of her handbag, put some on and readjusted her hair. She went into the yard, where Aunty Jean was closing the gate and waving to us through the window. They talked for a few moments before Mum unlocked her bicycle from the drainpipe and was gone.

*

'Mornin', kids. How's the big man today?' Aunty Jean put down the bag she was holding and sat in the armchair beside Dad. Dad just blinked and twitched. 'Nice mornin'.' She pulled a newspaper out of her bag and started to thumb through it.

'You two off out, are you?'

'Yes, we're going to the park.' Ellen turned and smiled at me. 'Aren't we, Adam?'

'Yes, that's it – the park.'

'Just us two, then.' Aunty Jean opened her bag again, took out a packet of cigarettes, put one in her mouth and lit it. 'Well, you have a nice time, and here...' – she rooted in her bag again – '... Get yourselves some sweets.' She took out her purse and handed me some money. I thanked her and we went upstairs to collect my rucksack and rod, and the worms from under my bed. We crept back down the stairs as quietly as we could, and out of the front door. I heard Aunty Jean call out, as I closed the door behind us.

'Have a nice time – and be home for your tea or your mother'll be cross.'

I opened the letter box and shouted back that we would.

*

The sun was climbing up over the sooty chimney pots. The sky was misty, but I could tell it was going to be a fine day. Ellen asked if she could carry the worms, so I handed her the tin can and we set off down the street. When we got to the railway bridge, we climbed over the fence into the horse fields. The mist was beginning to lift, but it was still hard to see to the other side of the fields where the woods started. The grass was silvery and wet with dew, and the horses glistened and steamed in the sunlight. You could see their breath, too, in the cool morning air. They stooped, chewing at the grass, and then lifted their heads to look at us as we passed. A big, black crow sat and cawed at us from one of the fence posts. The further we walked, the more clearly we could see the trees through the mist, and then we saw the little gate and the pathway through the woods to the pond. There were coils of barbed wire along the top of the fence, and the gate had a painted wooden sign nailed to it that said, 'Private – Do Not Enter'.

'What if somebody comes, Adam? What'll we do if somebody comes?'

'No one will come. Don't worry. No one ever comes.'

*

It was dark in the woods. We could only just see the sky through the trees. It was still and quiet too. The wood pigeons cooed now and again, and the leaves and the bracken crunched and snapped under our feet as we walked.

'There's a funny smell, isn't there?' Ellen pulled a face and giggled. 'It smells like wee.'

'The woods always smell that way. It's probably the ferns, that's all. C'mon.' We carried on walking through the trees.

'Why does Mum say the woods aren't safe, Adam?'

'I don't know. She thinks we might get lost or have an accident, I suppose.'

'It'd be easy to get lost, wouldn't it? Without this little path.' Ellen handed the tin of worms to me and stretched out her arms like a tightrope walker. I followed behind her.

'The woods aren't so big. You'd soon find your way out.'

She stopped, turned and looked at me, still with her arms out. 'I don't think I would. Don't leave me, will you?'

I smiled and patted her on the head. 'I won't leave you. Don't worry.'

*

There was no one around when we got to the pond. The water was thick and dark and still, and we made our way to a spot where there were fewer trees, setting everything down on a little, flat bank that was one of my favourite places to fish. I untied my rucksack and took out everything that we'd need: reel, floats, hooks, shot and some bread groundbait I'd mixed in my room the evening before, after digging for the worms. I'd made some beef spread sandwiches as well, and I gave Ellen one of these to eat while I fitted my rod together and set the line.

'Dad made me a rod once, from garden cane and chicken wire, and a ball of twine for the line.' Ellen took a bite of her sandwich and watched my fingers work. 'He used to take me down to the towpath on the canal. The water was so dirty and smelly you'd never think fish could live in it. But they do. I caught my first fish there. It tugged at the line, the float bobbed under the water and I lifted it out. It looked like a jewel, Ellie. There's nothing like catching a fish.' I tossed some of the groundbait into the water, took the rubber band and the cloth from the tin and plucked out one of the worms with my thumb and forefinger. 'Dad used maggots sometimes – he reckoned that some fishermen put them in their mouths to warm them up so they'll wriggle more. The fish like that.'

I pressed the hook through the middle of the worm and got ready to cast. I made sure that Ellen was well out of the way and that the line wouldn't get caught up in the trees. The rod made a whipping sound, and there was a plop as the float landed, sending ripples across the still water. The hooked worm floated on the surface for a moment before it sank with the weight of the shot. The float stood bolt upright and still on the surface of the water as the ripples disappeared, and the water settled again.

'Will Dad ever get better, Adam?' Ellen finished her sandwich and threw the crust into the water. I didn't answer and we sat down, side by side, at the edge of the pond.

*

We didn't talk for a while. It was nice, just being able to sit there quietly, watching the float and waiting. You can forget everything, watching that little float, waiting for it to dip beneath the water. If you look at it long enough it's hard to tell if it's moved or not, if there's a bite or not; if there is, you have to strike at just the right moment. The birds were singing noisily in the trees, and Ellen spotted some little frogs hopping along the bank. She laughed as they tripped and tumbled back into the water.

'There are some bramble bushes by the fence there. Why don't you go and pick us some?'

Ellen jumped up, and I pointed to where the brambles were, and told her to take my coat and put them in one of the pockets. When she put the coat on it was far too big, so I rolled up the sleeves for her and off she went. I watched as she crouched down and carefully picked and examined the brambles, talking quietly to herself as she did. She gathered up a handful and carefully placed them in the coat pocket, and then another. A blackbird landed on the ground a few feet away from her and she offered it one, but it flew up into the trees. After a few minutes, Ellen came and sat back down beside me. She took my coat off, pulled a crumpled handkerchief from her sleeve and laid it out on the ground. Then she scooped the brambles out of the coat pocket a few at a time and placed them gently on the handkerchief.

I laughed. 'Well that's quite a haul you've got there!'

She straightened up and smiled with satisfaction at the little pile of brambles. 'Isn't it just?' She looked down at her hands which were stained dark purple with the fruit. She licked them, rubbed them together, and tutted when she saw that her palms were still smeared with the purple juice.

We each ate a sandwich, and then the brambles, and just as I was about to reel in the line and put out fresh bait, Ellen shouted, 'Look! It's gone! The thing's gone under.' The float had dipped under the water, but I could still see it, being dragged along just beneath the surface. I took the rod and struck, and I felt the line tighten. 'Have you got one? Have you got a fish?' Ellen was jumping up and down with excitement.

'Yes, I think I've got one.' I reeled in the line carefully. I could feel that there was no need to let it run, that the fish wasn't big enough and I could bring it straight in. 'Could be a tench, or a bream!' I exclaimed, and Ellen clapped and shouted as it came up out of the water and spun and twitched in the sunlight.

'We've got a fish! We've got a fish! Are we going to eat it, Adam? We could light a fire and cook it for dinner.'

I put down the rod and took hold of the fish. It was a roach. The hook came away easily from its lower lip. 'Of course we're not going to eat it. It's too small, anyway.' I showed Ellen the fish and she stroked it with her finger. It was a plump, silver little thing with orange eyes and fins, and although it was small it was slippery and hard to hold on to. Its head was sharp, like the head of an arrow, and its mouth gaped, sucked and gasped for air. 'Better put it back.' I bent down and loosened my grip, but before my cupped hand reached the water, the fish flipped itself free and, with a little splash, was gone.

'Doesn't the fish feel anything, Adam? Doesn't it hurt it?'

'No, Ellie, they don't feel anything.'

'But how come?' Ellen gazed down into the water, looking for the roach as the silt cleared.

'Well, I think because their blood's not warm like ours. Cold-blooded things don't feel anything.'

*

Ellen held the tin can while I took off the rubber band and the piece of cloth and picked out another worm. She watched as I put the worm onto the hook and cast the line out into the water again. I passed her my coat to sit on, and I sat on my empty rucksack.

'It's nice when nobody's here, isn't it?' I balanced the end of the rod on a log that was poking out of the water, and leant back on my elbows.

Ellen was stripping the leaves carefully from a branch. 'Mmm, it's very quiet.' She collected the leaves into a neat pile and started to launch them, one by one, onto the water. 'When you used to go fishing with Dad, what did you talk about?'

'Oh, I can't remember. All sorts, I suppose.' The leaves drifted and spun further and further out, and Ellen watched them, pointing and directing them with the stripped stick.

'Was Dad funny? Did he make you laugh?'

'Yes, sometimes he was funny. He used to paddle his feet in the canal, in the summmer, and tell me the names of all the different birds we saw.' Ellen was very young when Dad first got ill. It's a shame, because she doesn't remember what he used to be like.

The sky was clearing, and the sun was beginning to break through. The water didn't look so thick and dark any more, and at the edge of the pond I could see to the bottom, where there was a school of tiny fish nosing at a cloud of dark, green weed. Ellen watched her leaves disperse across the pond and then she lay down on my coat and gazed up into the branches of the trees.

*

It was a while before we spoke again. Eventually Ellen sat up, took her stick and started to poke at one of the brambles that had rolled onto the ground. 'How big is the biggest fish in this pond?'

'Oh, I don't know. A pike, I suppose, could be nearly as big as you.'

Ellen laughed and lifted the squashed bramble with the end of her stick. 'What does a pike look like?'

'Well, they're sort of slimy green, and they've got big jaws like a crocodile, and teeth, and fat green bellies.'

'A fish with teeth? What, like a shark?'

There was a gentle breeze, and the line had started to drift towards the weeds at the edge of the pond. 'Well, sort of.'

'Does a pike have cold blood like a roach?'

I gestured to Ellen to take the rod. 'Yes, I think all fish have cold blood.' As she took hold of it and sat back down, I told her to be careful to reel in the line if the float got too near the weeds, and she promised she would. I threw out more groundbait and sat up on the fence behind her. Ellen kept her eyes on the float, which was already starting to drift over to the weeds again.

'What if the float goes under? What if I catch a pike?'

'Don't worry. I'm right behind you – I'll see it. Just watch those weeds.'

*

On the other side of the fence there was a wheat field, with red poppies growing beside the path that ran all the way round it. The wheat was swaying in the breeze, the sun had finally burnt away the early morning mist and the sky was clear and blue, apart from two swallows. The sun felt warm on my back and shoulders, and I closed my eyes and listened to the swallows screeching. When I opened them again, Ellen was still holding the rod and watching the float, which had drifted even further towards the weeds.

'You'd better reel in a bit.' I jumped down from the fence. 'Just turn the handle – carefully, mind.' She did as I said and the line tightened, bending the end of the rod down towards the water. The float dipped and disappeared under the surface and then popped back up again as she let go of the handle. She stopped and looked at me.

'Have I got a fish?'

I let her keep hold of the rod, but I moved in closer, ready to take over if she couldn't manage. 'I don't know. Try again.' She turned the handle of the reel again, but the same thing happened. 'No, I think it's stuck on something.' I loosened the line and we left it for a minute, to see if it would free itself. Then, together, we pulled the rod upwards and reeled in again. The float burrowed and weaved slowly through the water and, as it came closer, I could see something trailing behind and beneath it – the thing that our hook had snagged itself on. At first it looked like a plastic carrier bag – a pale, distorted shape just beneath the surface of the water. Each time we stopped, it sank back down into the blackness beyond the sun's reach. But then each time we pulled at the rod and reeled the line closer, there it was, towed in the float's wake, closer and closer to the water's edge.

'OK, you keep going and I'll see if I can get it in.'

Ellen carried on pulling and reeling, while I took off my shoes and socks and rolled up my trousers. I stepped into the freezing water and reached for the line, which was close enough now to be able to swing whatever it was that we'd caught onto the bank. I took the rod from Ellen and pulled and swung in one movement, slipping as I did and falling backwards into the shallow water just short of the bank. I jumped up quickly, trying to catch my breath and recover the rod, which I'd dropped as I fell. It was floating at the water's edge. I grabbed it with one hand and turned to see what it was we'd landed. I looked at it and then I looked at Ellen. She stood staring at the thing on the ground beside her.

*

It was only a moment before I realised what it was. But the strangeness of it made me search in those few seconds for a less terrible explanation. Could it be some strange species of pond life or vegetation that I'd never come across before? Or an animal that had died, found its way to the bottom of the pond and then been fed on by pike until it was impossible to identify? But no, this thing, that we'd disturbed and dragged up through the weeds to the surface, was a hand. It had been severed cleanly just above the wrist, revealing two knuckles of shocking white bone. It must have been in the water for quite a long time, because it was bloated and swollen, mottled and discoloured like a deep bruise. The fingers and thumb were resting limply on the ground, the blackened nails sunk deep into the flesh around them. A string of slimy pondweed was wrapped round one of the fingers like a ring. Neither of us spoke. We just stared at it, for how long I don't remember. The swallows plunged and screeched overhead, and Ellen gripped her stick, looking as if she was thinking about poking it.

Ellen was the first to speak. 'What shall we do?'

'I suppose we'll have to tell someone.'

She took a step back and stood beside me. 'Who do you think it belongs to?'

'I don't know.' I picked up my coat and put it on.

'Do you think the rest of him is down there?'

'I don't know, Ellen. But I think we'd better go.'

I started to pack the fishing gear away, wondering if it was right to just leave the hand where it was. An animal might come and carry it off. 'We'd better cover it up with something and go.'

Ellen bent down and picked up her handkerchief. 'Maybe we could use this?' It was stained with juice from the brambles and didn't look big enough to cover the hand.

'Yes, perhaps. It's not very big though. We could put a stone on top of it so it doesn't get blown off, I suppose.'

We walked over to the fence and I found a small stone. I took the handkerchief, placed it carefully over the hand and put the stone on top, to hold it in place. The edges of the handkerchief didn't reach the ground, but the hand was mostly covered. 'There, that'll have to do.'

Ellen handed me my bag, and I told her to walk on ahead, as far as the gap in the fence, which led back into the woods. When she was gone, I lifted a corner of the cloth. Ellen had left her stick behind, and I poked at the hand with it. The flesh wasn't as soft as I'd expected, but the stick still left a shallow dent in the skin.

*

On the way home, I wondered if whoever the hand had belonged to was still alive; maybe they'd survived some terrible accident? Like Ellen, I wondered if the rest of the body was still down at the bottom of the pond? What if there'd been a murder? I thought about telling Aunty Jean what had happened, but I guessed she'd probably tell mum and we'd get into trouble. I wondered if we should ring 999 and tell the Police, but in the end I thought it was best not to do anything, to just keep quiet, say nothing.

We went and sat in the park for a while and Ellen played on the swings. Afterwards we went home, and I put the fishing gear in the shed so that Aunty Jean wouldn't see it when we went inside. 'You all right? You look white as a sheet.' She was making a pot of tea in the kitchen, another cigarette hanging out of the corner of her mouth. Dad was still by the back window. 'Seen a ghost, 'ave you?' We put the radio on, and Aunty Jean made us all a cup of tea.

*

We haven't spoken about it since. I think Ellen would like to tell Mum, but I told her we'd get into trouble if she found out we'd been to the woods. Ellen doesn't like this secret, though, and I know it's the hand she's been having nightmares about. She told me. She dreams that she's back at the pond looking for it, but when she gets to the place where we left it, it's gone. She says she knows it's moved by itself, but she doesn't know where it is; whether it's hidden in the bramble bushes, or the wheat field, or maybe back in the water. And then she dreams she's in the water, in the middle of the pond, and she's trying to swim back to the bank but she can't, and she knows she's going to sink to the bottom of the pond and drown. She says there's someone on the bank, watching, but she can't tell who it is. She tries to shout to them for help but they don't seem to hear. There's been nothing about it in the newspaper yet. Perhaps it's still there, underneath Ellen's handkerchief. I thought about going back to check, but I decided not to. I suppose someone else is bound to find it in the end, and perhaps then Ellen's bad dreams will stop, eventually.

Magnolia's Ark

Magnolia finds herself standing at the top of the stairs, staring down into the blackness of the hallway. The last thing she remembers is lying in bed, her tired eyes tracing the scrolled pattern on the bedroom wallpaper, like contour lines on a map she'd thought, as she felt herself drifting towards sleep. She can't remember waking up, or pulling back the covers, or stepping into her slippers, or walking from the bedroom to the stairs. She can remember nothing, except the wallpaper, and that feeling of being lost before sleep comes. It's cold. Magnolia feels her skin tightening beneath her nightdress, and her legs growing heavy with the awareness that she's no longer sleeping. She's not curled up in bed as she should be, drifting on the ocean of sleep, but is instead stranded on the landing, her toes poised at the very edge of the first stair. She reaches out to steady herself and, gripping the banister, finds its solidity reassuring, as though she half expects her hand to pass through it, ghost-like, into nothingness. She rubs her eyes and looks around. It's dark and still, and the house seems strange – an unfamiliar landscape.

In front of her, overlooking the stairwell, hangs a picture of a mountain and a lake painted by her mother. The picture seems unnaturally bright in the darkness, and Magnolia can clearly make out the icy summit of the peak, the blue sky above it and the still, dark waters of the lake beneath. She turns her head and looks across the empty landing to the closed door of the darkroom. Magnolia is a photographer. She photographs people – mostly portraits of smiling family groups. Next to the darkroom is the entrance to her bedroom. The door is open and she considers going back to bed. She imagines seeing her mother and father lying in the bed instead of her, as she had done all those years ago, when she was a child – running her finger along the wall and feeling the strange texture of the scrolled paper. The next door along leads up to the roof terrace which overlooks the beach and the sea. She checks that it's locked.

*

As Magnolia's eyes grow more accustomed to the darkness, the hallway below emerges. She can make out the parquet tiled floor, and the front door with its bullseye glass pane. On one side of the door stands the plaster figure of a naked woman that she bought at a car boot sale. On the other is the telephone table. She listens for the faintest echo of a ring, wondering if it was this that brought her to the top of the stairs. But there's only silence.

Magnolia puts a hand to her forehead and adjusts her footing. She decides to go downstairs and make a cup of tea. She treads carefully, still holding the banister, and descends to the hallway. Through the door's bullseye glass she sees a distorted pool of light coming from the security lamp mounted on the side of the house. The darkness beyond is thick and heavy. She wonders how far out the tide is. She turns and walks along the passage into the kitchen, where she flicks on the light and goes to fill the kettle. She makes the tea and goes into the sitting room, where a large hulk of driftwood is still glowing in the grate. She sits down in the rocking chair beside the fire, and gradually feels the last traces of sleep and disorientation ooze from her.

*

Magnolia finishes her tea. She gets up and walks across the room to a sliding glass door. She pulls it open and enters a spacious annexe made of glass. She looks out, but can see nothing except for a few paving stones illuminated by the security lamp. The stones are part of a path which leads to the front of the house and ends at the roadside. On the other side of the road is the pebble beach and, further out, the sea. Magnolia often dreams that the house is surrounded by the sea, like an island or a boat. It's an ark, the waves lapping against the weatherboarding, its bulk creaking, and pitching gently to and fro. The glass room is sparsely furnished. In the corner there's a small wooden chair with an old Polaroid camera on it. To the left, hung on the main house wall, is a battered cuckoo clock which isn't working, and in the centre of the room there's a large leather trunk.

The trunk used to belong to Magnolia's grandfather. She gazes at its stained tan hide and withered straps, its rusted ribs and worn edges. She walks over and touches it, feels the roughness of the leather encrusted with salt. The trunk contains Magnolia's collection. She collects things that people have discarded or lost. The things she's collected have not been acquired, but salvaged, and the trunk in which they're kept is Magnolia's ark. Of course, there are bits and pieces from the shore, but Magnolia knows that things can be washed up all over the place, not only on a beach. A suede mitten with a bus ticket inside it left on a park bench, a child's tiny shoe abandoned in a tray of oranges in a grocer's shop, a fountain pen she found in a telephone booth, a little wooden lion she picked out of the gutter on a busy street one morning; these are just a few of the things Magnolia has collected, wrapped carefully in tissue paper and placed in the trunk.

Magnolia glances at the camera on the wooden chair. She's been thinking about photographing each of the items in her collection and compiling a catalogue – a catalogue of the things to which she's brought salvation. For this is how she thinks of her collection; she's saved these everyday things from the deluge, and not only the things themselves, but also those to whom they belonged. She often marvels at this alchemy, at how things can be transformed. She marvels too at the trunk, which she likes to think of as being invested with a magical energy. As a baby, Magnolia had slept in the trunk. Her mother had filled it with sheets and warm blankets and placed it, instead of a crib, beside her bed. Just like Moses, Magnolia had always thought, in his caulked wicker basket in the bulrushes. And now it's Magnolia's ark, the ark of her covenant. The covenant between God and Magnolia is that sometimes things can be saved – they can occasionally, in some mysterious way, be unlost, just as her grandfather's trunk was.

*

Magnolia never met her grandfather. She couldn't remember being told about him either, but somehow she'd picked up the story. Her father had been born in Germany, where her grandparents had lived before the war. They were a poor, Jewish family, living on the edge of the Black Forest. Her father was just a small boy when his mother became ill. His own father was a religious man and visited the synagogue every day to pray for her, but within three months she was dead. It was then that he decided to gather together the few belongings they had and take his son to England, where he had a cousin, so that they could begin a new life there. The boy was sent on ahead while his father got together enough money to pay for his own passage. Several months later, Magnolia's grandfather was able to set sail for England, and was looking forward to being reunited with his son. But he was never to arrive. The ship floundered in a storm and he was lost. His trunk was washed ashore several weeks later, and eventually found its way to the cousin who'd taken in her father. Magnolia could remember wondering, as a child, how long her grandfather's trunk must have taken to dry out, and what her father must have felt when he first opened it and saw his drowned father's belongings, of which only the once brightly painted cuckoo clock could be salvaged – that and the ring, of course; the three gold bands of the Russian wedding ring that his dead mother had worn, and that his future wife would wear also.

*

Not only was Magnolia's father an orphan, but he also grew up knowing that whatever family he did have back in Germany had been murdered during the war. He alone was saved. He was the only survivor. When he left school, he found a job as a clerk in an insurance company. He did well, and after a few years was working in the City, calculating loss, measuring it and setting it down on paper. It seemed fitting. He was nearly fifty when he met Magnolia's mother, who was almost twenty years his junior. She was young, beautiful and quite different from Magnolia's father. He was self-contained and measured, while she was spontaneous, disorganised, and restlessly energetic. Magnolia sometimes wondered how two such different people could ever have come together.

As a child, Magnolia knew little of her father's work. She knew only that he was gone when she woke and was rarely home before she went to bed. Even when he was at home, he would often be working, and when he wasn't, he was still distant and unapproachable. Magnolia couldn't call to mind what his face looked like when he smiled, or the sound of his laugh, and she could only remember him hugging her once in her life. He would sit at the table in the glass room, which was always known as the 'glass house', his back to the ocean, his ledgers and papers piled neatly round him. Magnolia remembered the cuckoo clock hanging on the wall in front of him, the little bird popping out but making no sound. He'd silence it, to prevent it from breaking his concentration while he worked. When the glass house was empty Magnolia would sneak in. There was a telescope in there, on a stand, that she liked to play with. Sometimes she would turn it the wrong way round, look through it and laugh as the room, the beach and the sea all shrank and stretched away from her. But more often she liked to look out at the tiny, glinting ships moving slowly across the horizon.

*

Magnolia's mother filled her time obsessively with a long succession of hobbies, all of which were embarked upon with ferocious intensity but none of which lasted longer than a few months. Although it was perhaps her mother's brief flirtation with photography that had proved to have the most important influence on Magnolia, it was the gardening phase that she remembered best. Their garden was to the rear of the house, but was in fact nothing more than dry shingle, flint and paving stones, amongst which her mother managed to nurture a sparse array of prickly plants and shrubs, and a few delicate flowers. Only a wooden fence and a gate stood between the garden and a stretch of common land that was littered with broken bottles, smashed concrete and bricks. Their house had originally been intended as one of several which would be built on the land, but for some reason the others were never started.

When Magnolia recalled her mother, she often pictured her standing by the kitchen window, her sunglasses resting low on her nose; wearing a bright headscarf, striped Breton top and tight, three-quarter length trousers. She'd stand and survey the garden briefly, a cigarette held awkwardly in one hand and a trowel in the other, tutting and complaining to herself at the latest horticultural casualties. And then she'd toss her cigarette over the fence and once again set about feverishly trying to make the garden fertile, poking at the hard, dry ground with her trowel.

*

When she was growing up, Magnolia loved looking at old photographs of her mother and father together, just after they were married. There were some of them dancing together at their wedding, one of them sitting beside a river with a picnic, one in which they were standing arm in arm outside the Post Office Tower in London, and some taken while they were on holiday in Spain, the year before Magnolia was born. They looked happy in these pictures, and in love, but somehow, Magnolia thought, not themselves. She didn't recognise them.

Magnolia would often think of her childhood and try to remember those times when the three of them were together. It was a silly thing to recall, but what stood out were the evenings they spent sat on the sofa watching television. Those evenings were rare, but they always made her feel safe and secure, and happy. She'd sit between her mother and father, listening to the wind and the rain outside and the crackling of the fire in the grate. And she'd imagine that they were the only three people in the world, the house surrounded by the sea. She wanted to lay her head in her mother's lap, or snuggle close enough to her father to hear his heart beating. She wanted to hear their voices too, speaking kind words to each other, and to her. Sometimes Magnolia would write down secret messages and questions for them. She'd write these on strips of paper and tuck them into the cushion straps beneath the sofa: 'I love you, Mummy' or 'Am I good, Daddy?' As they all sat there together, she used to wonder if they might find them, and what they would say if they did.

*

It was a hot August day when Magnolia found out that her father was leaving. She was sitting quietly in the corner of the sitting room, watching her mother paint. It was the picture of the mountain and the lake, and her mother was copying it from a book propped up on a table beside her. She carried on stabbing the picture with her brush, and tutting occasionally as she told Magnolia that her father would be moving to the city, that they couldn't all live together any more. Magnolia knew what this meant.

She went upstairs and sat in front of her mirror. She looked at herself, thinking how ugly her freckles were, and how unlike her mother's beautiful, shiny black hair her own mousy brown curls were. That was the night she crept into their bedroom, running her finger along the wall and feeling the strange texture of that scrolled paper. She saw them sleeping and thought how strange it was that they could sleep together in the same bed, even though they'd decided to live apart. She wanted to sneak into the bed between them, but knew that she couldn't. Instead, she returned to her own room, took a small tissue paper parcel from under her mattress and opened it. The three gold bands of her mother's wedding ring seemed to glow in the darkness.

*

Magnolia's father had given her mother the ring on the day of their marriage. She'd taken it off once, to show Magnolia the interlinking bands, and she'd told her then how precious it was. She'd said it had come from far away and been lost at sea, and then miraculously thrown back into the world, unlost. She'd slipped it onto Magnolia's finger for a few moments before taking it back, telling her that it wasn't something to play with. Magnolia had been filled with joy by this simple gesture.

Which was why it had seemed so strange to her that day, a few weeks before her mother had told her that they'd no longer be living together, to see the ring lying next to her mother's cigarette packet on the kitchen windowsill. When she saw it, Magnolia had assumed that her mother must have removed it before she began weeding in the garden, not that she normally did. But as she strolled through the shingle beds, and between the prickly plants and exposed flowers, there seemed to be no sign of her mother. Magnolia longed to try the ring on again. She walked back into the kitchen and looked into the passage. She listened for any sound coming from the sitting room, but there was nothing. Her father had been in the glass house with his ledgers and paperwork most of the day. She went back into the garden and opened the gate. It was a hot day, and she wondered if her mother had perhaps gone to the café on the common to buy a bottle of lemonade. She looked across the common and towards the beach, but still there was no sign of her. As she turned, she checked the roof terrace, but it too was empty.

She waited, every few minutes scanning the common and the beach for her mother and at the same time listening for the sound of her voice from inside the house. Perhaps she'd gone upstairs to lie down. She knew that she'd be in trouble if the ring wasn't where her mother had left it when she returned, but the desire to feel it on her finger again was so great that she simply couldn't leave it there. She picked it up carefully between her thumb and forefinger and she ran. She ran out of the garden and across the common, knowing that she had to get as far away from the scene of her crime as she could, and as quickly as possible. As she ran, she felt her heart pounding. Then tears begin to well in her eyes until, breathlessly, she found herself laughing.

*

Where the common met the beach, grassy scrubland gave way to a few gritty dunes, forming natural shelters. It was difficult to see these from above. Magnolia jumped down into one of the dunes, the hand in which she held the ring still closed tightly in a fist. She leant back against the compacted sand wall of the dune and looked up at the cloudless blue sky, then out across the pebbles towards the sea, which was still and calm. Steadying herself, and trying not to think about what she'd done, Magnolia looked down at her clenched fist, which was now held so tightly shut that she could feel nothing inside it. She felt a sudden rush of panic as she imagined opening it to find the ring gone, and she wondered whether she might somehow have dropped it as she ran across the common. So she held up her fist and opened it, slowly, until she could see, there in the middle of her palm, the three bands of her mother's golden wedding ring. She was sure that she could feel an energy passing from the ring and into her. Still holding it in her hand, she looked towards the sea again. It was so vast, and so deep, and yet this tiny golden ring had been lost out there and found again. It had been saved. As Magnolia slipped the ring onto her finger, she thought about her grandmother and her grandfather, and she knew that she would never part with the ring, that it would always be hers.

That night Magnolia woke standing at the top of the stairs. She rubbed her eyes and looked down into the blackness of the hallway, and as she did, she had the feeling that someone was looking at her through the bullseye glass pane in the door.

*

It was the only time that Magnolia could recall her mother crying. She looked everywhere for the ring, day after day, searching through drawers and cupboards and crawling round the floor on her hands and knees. She conducted a fingertip search of every square centimetre of the house, and Magnolia lost count of the number of times she saw her running her hands down the back and sides of the sofa cushions, or removing them and gazing at the sofa's carcass, incredulous that the ring could not be found. But of course, it would never be found. The curious thing was that her mother never asked her if she'd taken it. Magnolia was sure that she would, but it seemed it never even occurred to her mother that she might do such a thing. She asked Magnolia if she'd seen the ring, and she wondered out loud if someone might have crept into the house and stolen it, but she never considered Magnolia a suspect.

Magnolia saw how sad her mother was, but in time she came to feel that the ring had truly been lost and that she'd played no part in its disappearance. One morning when she went downstairs for breakfast, she found a curled slip of paper on the kitchen table with one of her secret messages written on it. 'I love you, Mummy', it said, but her mother never mentioned it. Magnolia could tell that her father was angry that the ring had been lost, though he didn't say anything. He locked himself up in the glass house and closed the blinds.

*

A few days before Magnolia's father left, her mother started to take photographs with the Polaroid camera. She wandered round the house taking pictures of each room as if she wanted to capture things as they were, before it was too late. She took one from the top of the stairs, looking down into the hallway, and she let Magnolia watch as the image emerged slowly through the white emulsion print. She seemed so sad, and Magnolia felt sorry for her. Her father spent a lot of time on the telephone that week. He'd rush to answer it whenever it rang. Magnolia noticed that her mother ignored it, even if she was nearby.

Around that time, Magnolia remembered having a nightmare. She dreamt that she was standing at the top of the stairs, staring down into the hallway. She wanted to turn round, to turn away from the stairs and run, run up onto the roof terrace where she was sure there would be sunlight and air. But she couldn't move, couldn't even avert her eyes from the stairs and from the blackness of the hallway. She knew that there was something down there, but she couldn't tell what it was. She sensed only a presence, a dark, malevolent presence moving through the house, searching for her. Only as she waited, she realised that this presence wasn't inside the house at all, but outside. Through the darkness she could see the glint of a huge, distorted eye, blinking, peering in through the glass in the door, and as a blast of hot breath suddenly funnelled from the ringed nose of this unnatural, monstrous face and condensed across the glass, she knew that the eye belonged to a gigantic bull. It was out there, pawing the ground and snorting around the house, seeking entry, and Magnolia knew that it had come for her. She could smell and taste the hot breath from deep inside its lungs, and she could hear the beating of its massive heart growing louder and louder.

*

Magnolia saw her father once a month. He'd drive down from London and take her out or sometimes, during the school holidays, take her to his flat for a few days. She remembered how bare and empty the flat had seemed at first, with hardly any furniture. But she liked the view from the window, the Thames winding serpent-like through the city. It looked lost, she thought, almost as if it shouldn't be there. After a few such visits, her father introduced her to a girlfriend, Moira. Magnolia was struck by how remarkably like her mother Moira looked, though perhaps a little younger. They might have been sisters.

Moira was introduced simply as 'a friend from work', and the three of them went out to the cinema together. It was the first time Magnolia had been on the Underground. She found the low vaulted ceilings, the grimy fluorescent lights, the stale air and the crush of commuters unnerving. And as she stood on the platform, looking into the sooty blackness of the tunnel and listening to the screeching approach of the train, she felt herself beginning to panic. It rose up in her like a feeling of nausea, the kind of nausea you feel when you know something terrible is going to happen, or has already happened. She imagined the bull she'd dreamt about beating its way through those dark tunnels. But Magnolia sensed, too, that there was something glorious about the Underground, about the strange, impersonal intimacy of so many people crowded together beneath the city, all knowing where they were going, and all moving with such purpose to their destinations.

Moira cooked them all a meal. She cooked rabbit, and as they ate, Magnolia hardly spoke, although it wasn't her intention to be rude. Her father was silent throughout, and eventually Moira gave up on both of them. The meal was concluded in silence, punctuated only by the chink and scrape of fork on plate and, just as her father poured himself another glass of wine, the sudden burst of cuckoo calls from the clock that hung on the wall above his head. Magnolia hadn't enjoyed eating the rabbit; somehow it tasted of earth.

Magnolia stayed at the flat that night. She was about to go into the bathroom to wash her face and brush her teeth before bed, when she caught sight of her father's reflection in the mirror of the bathroom cabinet. She stopped and watched as he stood there, staring into the mirror. He didn't move for several minutes. Finally, he began to stroke his forehead with his fingertips. As he did so, he mumbled something to himself. It was one word, a word that sounded to Magnolia like 'lost'. Later, when she was in bed, he came to say goodnight. He knelt down and hugged her, but Magnolia felt awkward and uncomfortable. She wanted it to be over, and as she lay there in his arms, she thought about her mother's wedding ring, which she'd brought with her. It was wrapped in its tissue paper parcel, beneath her pillow.

*

Magnolia picks up the Polaroid camera and looks through the viewfinder. She pans around the room as she once did as a child with the telescope. She contemplates the camera's antique magic, its ability to capture a moment and represent it immediately. Finally, she trains the lens onto the trunk and presses the shutter button. It clunks, and the flash illuminates the glass walls and ceiling for a second. The camera wheezes into silence as she puts it back down on the chair in the corner. She doesn't wait to see the image develop, but returns to the trunk, kneels and unbuckles its leather straps. As she does so, she finds herself thinking about the family who had come to her studio for a portrait the previous month. A man, his wife and their two teenage children had sat for what turned out to be a rather unusual portrait. They brought with them a photograph of a young girl, and the man explained that this was their youngest daughter, who'd died in a boating accident the year before. He asked if it might be possible to superimpose her image onto their portrait, so that it would include the whole family. And so they positioned themselves in front of the marbled screen, leaving a gap between the two living children, an absence which Magnolia was to fill later with the image of their dead sister. When the portrait was completed, she wondered why she'd never received such a request before.

Magnolia lifts the lid of the trunk and removes layer after layer of protective tissue paper to reveal the assortment of parcels containing the items in her collection. Even though it's small, she knows exactly where to find what she's looking for. She slides her hand down the side of the trunk and eases her way through the paper until her fingers recognise the tiny parcel. She retrieves it carefully and closes the trunk's lid. She can't remember the last time she held this particular parcel in her hands, and as she places it on top of the trunk she remembers her panic that day in the dunes, when she imagined opening her fist to find it gone. She unwraps the neatly folded tissue paper and flattens it. In the centre of the paper lies the ring, no different from the day when she took it from the windowsill and made it her own. She feels its energy, just as she had that day, and though she's tempted to place it on her finger, she knows she mustn't.

They're gone now, her mother and father. They are lost. But the ring is saved, and through it they too are unlost. The ring, to which the past still adheres, is their salvation. She wraps it up again and places it back inside the trunk. Then she refastens the straps and returns to the sitting room. She sits beside the fire, closes her eyes and listens to the sound of the sea. The tide is coming in. She feels the gentle pitching of the house and the slap of the waves against the weatherboarding. She imagines going back upstairs, stepping through the door on the landing and onto the roof terrace, into the bright sunshine and clean air. She sees the mighty ocean all around the house, blue and calm, and high up above her head she sees a bird, a dove descending gently through the cloudless sky, holding the ring in its beak. And as the dove alights, Magnolia sees that her mother and her father are sitting in the sunshine, smiling, holding hands and beckoning her. She joins them and, as she rests her cheek on her mother's hand, she feels the sweet coldness of the three gold bands restored at last to her finger.

The Fall

The sudden beam of light flashed through the darkness only moments, it seemed, after Jess had fallen into the earth. It exploded above him, and from it came a voice. 'Jess ... Jess ... Jess!' At first the voice boomed and echoed, and then it was close, like a whisper at his ear or inside his skull. It drifted in and out of another sound, a sound that resonated through him, through his head, his limbs, his fingertips. Was it the intonation of a bell, or was it Pete's finger stroking the rim of that beer glass? 'Jess! ... Jess!' The voice called again, more urgently this time, like his mother's voice calling him first thing in the morning to get out of bed. But he knew from the blackness, from the earth against his cheek and from the position of his crumpled body that this was not his bedroom. 'Jess! ... Jess!'

As Jess became more aware that the voice was calling to him from above, the still point of light that it came from began to swing crazily and he was fully awake. He could feel his body suddenly swelling with pain and panic. His temples began to throb, there was something digging into his ribs - perhaps a root - and his hands and his bare legs stung where he'd grazed them on the rocks as he fell. He seemed to be the wrong way round, his feet pointing up towards the light and his head down at the bottom of the hole. He was suddenly filled with an urgent need to get out, to climb up to where the light was, a lantern swinging from a clenched fist - and the voice too. He tried to move but that just made things worse. It was as if the black earthen walls were contracting around him, as if he were being swallowed. He tried to stretch towards the light, but as he did so he could see that his arm was not where it should be, and was twisted at an unnatural angle. He looked up again, squinting into the painful brightness, and it was then that his dad's face loomed into focus and a hand reached down towards him.

'C'mon, Jess. Wake up, boy. Give me your hand. I can reach you, son.' Jess looked up at his dad's face, helplessly. He managed to turn himself slowly, and struggled onto his knees, surprised that his twisted arm didn't hurt more. He held up his other arm, and his dad took hold of it, gripped tightly and pulled. 'That's it, Jess. I've got you now. Up you come.'

*

The moor was littered with old mine shafts. Most of them were sealed with blocks of stone, or iron plates, but this one must have been broken open, or left for some reason. Over the years it had become partially covered by grass and heather, but then Jess's foot had plunged into the small, black aperture that remained and he'd fallen down, fallen through the ground, hitting stone and root and hard, black earth. His mam was always warning him to be careful and not to wander too far. She said there were poisonous adders on the moors, and hidden bogs that could swallow a boy like him in a matter of minutes. But Jess hadn't been looking where he was going. Jess had been running, his eyes full of tears, running away from home. Except that it wasn't home really, not any more. One minute they were eating their Christmas dinner, a family, and the next, Pete was shouting through their letter box, a stream of words spilling out of his mouth, Mary holding her hands to her ears, Dad rushing towards the door and Mam screaming at the top of her voice. Screaming, but not loudly enough to drown out the words, not loudly enough to stop them. And then Jess was running, his eyes full of tears, running away from home.

*

The story Jess's mam had told him was a lie. She'd told it over and over again, hundreds of times, until Jess knew it by heart and knew, too, that he was special, a gift from God. They went to chapel every Sunday, and as they walked across the dewy paddock, Jess and his mam would often have the same, well-rehearsed conversation. 'You're a special boy, Jess. You're special because you came to us from God.' She'd squeeze his hand and smile down at him.

'Was I born of the spirit, Mam?' This was something Jess had heard the Minister say in one of his sermons.

'You weren't born of our flesh, your Dad's and mine - that's true enough, but we love you all the same.' And then came Jess's favourite part. 'It was Christmas Day when you came to us, and a single bright star shone over the chimney that night. That's how it was, wasn't it, Dad?' She always turned to Dad, inviting him to confirm the truth of what she was saying, and he'd nod silently, usually arm in arm with Mary.

Jess loved Christmas, and every year he listened to the story of the nativity with fascination, imagining it in every little detail. In his mind's eye, their front room was transformed into a rustic stable scene. There was a scattering of straw on the carpet, an open window framing a single brilliant star, and a donkey standing tethered to one of the drawer handles on the Welsh dresser. And then there was Jess himself, lying quietly in the straw, and his mam and dad wearing robes and funny cloths round their heads, kneeling beside him with the three, bearded wise men bearing their gifts, all of them bathed in a golden light. Mary was there too. She was one of the shepherds.

*

Jess had once heard Mam say that Mary was 'young for her age'. Mary was twenty-three, but at the same time, she wasn't. That's what Mam said anyway. Jess didn't quite understand; Mary seemed fine to him, and he loved her. She'd often come into his bedroom on a Saturday morning and tickle him, or put the radio on and share her toast with him. Sometimes they'd go down to the canal together and feed the ducks after chapel, and Jess liked it when Mary washed his hair for him in the bath on a Sunday night. Best of all was the ghost game, which they played on Friday evenings when Mam and Dad went out to their fellowship meeting.

Jess used to look forward to it all week. No one else knew about the game, and the rules were simple. They'd always begin by putting the wooden cross that hung at the top of the stairs into the immersion heater cupboard, taking out one of Mam's fresh white bed sheets at the same time. Then they'd close all the curtains in the house and switch out the lights. They had to decide who was going to be who, but Mary was usually the ghost, with Jess having to try and get upstairs to the cross, and safety, before Mary captured him. The game sometimes went on for an hour or more. Jess would find a hiding place downstairs while Mary put the bedsheet over her head, wrapped it round herself and set about trying to find him. The sheet, and the fact that the ghost could only walk, while Jess could run, meant that the odds were kept fairly even.

At the bottom of the banister rail there was a turned wooden cap on top of the newel post, with a coiled serpent carved into it. Jess would sometimes stand beside it and try to locate the serpent's head with his finger as he listened for Mary moving around upstairs. Sometimes Mary trod on the creaky floorboard in Mam and Dad's room and Jess had worked out that, if he was lucky, he could get from the bottom of the stairs to the immersion heater cupboard and seize the cross more quickly than Mary could get there from the creaky floorboard. Once or twice he timed it perfectly, sprinting up the stairs as soon as he heard the creak. They played the ghost game every week, without fail. Until Mary started going out with Pete, that is.

*

Pete was a couple of years older than Mary, and at first Mam had been dead against it. Jess remembered Mary sulking at the kitchen table, shovelling her tea round her plate and then stomping off upstairs, slamming every door shut behind her on the way. There were arguments too, Mam shouting at the top of her voice that Pete had no business knocking about with a girl like Mary. Dad didn't like arguments, so he didn't get involved, preferring to sit in his armchair reading his paper, or trying to. For a while Mam stopped Mary from going out, but Mary still managed to see Pete. She got a job in a local charity shop, sorting donations and serving customers. Pete worked for an engineering firm in an old mill down by the canal. It wasn't far from the shop, so they'd meet up at dinner times and after they'd finished work. Things got worse at home until eventually, after a couple of months, a truce was called, Mam deciding that it might be better to play along, but keep a close eye on the pair of them. She invited Pete round for tea.

Jess remembered him walking into their front room, scrubbed and shaved, in a shirt and tie and a pair of new corduroys. He'd even brought a bunch of flowers for Mam, as a peace offering. It was obvious, though, that Mam wasn't won over. Pete was the biggest person Jess had ever seen. He was tall, but he was broad and heavy, too, and he seemed to fill the front room, blocking out the light from the bay window. He had a cauliflower ear that fascinated Jess – he couldn't keep his eyes off it. He stared so much that Mam glared at him and trod on his foot under the table when they were eating. Jess noticed that his dad kept staring at it too. After they'd eaten, Jess went to watch television in the front room, while Mary and Mam washed up. Dad had taken Pete to the outhouse, where he was showing him the bench lathe he'd just bought.

'See, Mam? Pete's all right, isn't he? There's nothing wrong with him, is there? He's nice. Just because his mam and dad don't go to chapel, it doesn't make him bad.'

'No, well, maybe not. But he is ... older ... isn't he?'

Mary shook her head. 'Not much, Mam. Not much older. That doesn't matter, does it? It doesn't matter to me.'

Mam didn't answer at first, and they carried on with the washing up, but she always had to have the last word. 'A few years

28

makes a big difference. Like it or not, you're still a girl. He scrubs up well and doesn't speak with his mouth full, I'll give him that, but he's a man! And you know – you ...' Mam broke off from what she was saying, closed her eyes and took a deep breath to calm herself. They carried on with the washing up in silence, and Mam watched Dad and Pete out in the yard. When Mary went upstairs, Jess heard Mam muttering under her breath as she watched them. 'Brute.'

*

The last time the two of them had played the ghost game was when Mary told Jess about Mr Murgatroyd. The Murgatroyds were a family that had lived in the village many years ago. There were dark tales about them, especially about Mr Murgatroyd, who it was said had murdered his wife and son. The game hadn't taken very long on that particular evening. Mary had found Jess hidden under the telephone table in the hall. She'd pulled him out, covered him with the sheet, and tickled him until he screamed with laughter and begged her to stop. Afterwards, they sat together in the dark, both of them under the sheet.

'You know what they say he did, Jess?'

'Who?'

'Mr Murgatroyd.'

Jess giggled. 'Mr Murdertroyd.'

'Who?'

He giggled again and repeated, 'Mr Murdertroyd.' Jess didn't know exactly what Mr Murgatroyd had done, but the name, and the play upon it, he'd heard at school.

'Yes, Murgatroyd. Murdertroyd. They say he killed them. He killed his wife and his little boy. Chopped them up and put them in the canal.'

Jess leant his head on Mary's shoulder, and she began stroking his hair. He could feel the moistness of his breath on the bed sheet as it touched his cheek. 'How did he do it, Mary? How did he kill them?'

Mary stopped stroking his hair and her hand came to rest on his shoulder. 'Don't know. But they found them in the water, or bits of them, anyway. In the canal.'

*

Jess knew Pete was going to cause trouble. He knew it every time he looked at the nativity picture in his Bible. Mary had brought the Bible home from the charity shop and given it to Jess as a present. It was a children's Bible, full of stories from the Old and New Testaments, and there were pictures in it too. On the two centre pages there was a picture of the nativity. Jess loved it. The scene was just as he imagined it. He thought that some of the people in the picture even looked a bit like Mam and Dad and Mary, although he couldn't say whether the baby Jesus looked like he had when he was that tiny. Only there was something wrong with the picture. It was one of the wise men. Everyone knew they were old men with beards. But here, in this picture, one of them had a face that was too young, and it was a face that Jess knew. It was Pete. Or at least it was the spitting image of Pete, and he was standing there, grinning like an idiot at Joseph's shoulder. Why, he even seemed to have a cauliflower ear.

Jess didn't show anyone else the picture, especially not Mary. She didn't have time for anyone but Pete, and she wouldn't have a word said against him. She didn't play with Jess any more. She'd stopped coming into his bedroom on a Saturday morning to tickle him or to listen to the radio with her toast, and she never took him down to the canal to feed the ducks, or washed his hair in the bath. Even the ghost game stopped when Pete was allowed to come and help Mary babysit on Friday nights, while Mam and Dad went to chapel. Pete would sit on the couch with Mary while Jess sat in Dad's armchair, and they'd all watch television. Pete and Mary would sometimes go into the kitchen to make a cup of tea, and Jess would hear them whispering and laughing. Mary usually took Jess up to bed early, before Mam and Dad got back. They always kneeled together beside his bed and said the same prayer.

> *Lord keep us safe this night.*
> *Secure from all our fears*
> *May angels guard us while we sleep*
> *Till morning light appears.*

Then Mary would kiss him on the forehead, say good night and go back downstairs.

One night Jess couldn't sleep, so he got out of bed and crept onto the landing. He sat at the top of the stairs, and listened. He could usually hear the television, but on this occasion everything was quiet. As Jess sat waiting and listening, he heard a strange sound, a ringing sound like a bell, except that it was a continuous, unchanging sound, and it didn't fall away as the note from a bell would. Then it stopped, and there was the sound of laughter and clapping, and Mary's voice. 'It goes right through you – right through. Do it again!'

And then there was silence for a moment, until the sound started up again. Jess tiptoed down the stairs and, making sure not to be seen, peered through the crack in the door to the front room. Mary was kneeling on the floor, holding her hands to her lips, as if she were praying, and Pete was on the couch, crouching over the coffee table, moving his finger round the rim of an empty beer glass. His tongue was poking out of the side of his mouth and his eyes were fixed, unblinking, on the glass. Jess noticed a cigarette lodged behind Pete's cauliflower ear, and a bottle of his dad's Mackeson stout next to the glass. The sound filled the room, and Jess felt it vibrate through him. He stood breathless, waiting.

*

Pete coming round on Christmas Day and shouting through the letter box had something to do with them all playing the ghost game together. Jess didn't know what, but something had happened that night. It was a Friday night, and Mam and Dad had gone off to chapel as usual. Pete was different when Mam and Dad weren't there. He sprawled on the couch and put his feet on the coffee table. He drank Dad's beer and tried to order Jess about and tease him. 'Go on, Jess. Get us another of your dad's bottles. And a piece of that mince tart your mammy made.' Jess sat in Dad's armchair. He glanced at Mary, who looked away, and decided to ignore Pete. Pete persisted. 'Oh c'mon, Jessy, you're not sulking, are you? Sulking because you can't play your ghosty game?'

Jess felt his cheeks begin to burn and the tears well up in his eyes, but he was determined not to cry. Pete laughed, and put his arm round Mary. She nudged at him with her elbow. 'Shush, Pete. Don't tease him. Don't be mean.'

Jess wanted to run out of the room, to get away from both of them, but he couldn't. He couldn't show them that he was bothered by Mary's betrayal, couldn't draw attention to his shame. Pete and Mary didn't speak to each other for a while and Jess wondered if Mary was cross at Pete for teasing him, or for letting it slip that she'd told him about the ghost game. He wondered what else Mary had told Pete. At that moment, he hated her. Eventually Mary nudged Pete again, and they got up and went into the kitchen. Jess could hear them talking, but not clearly enough to hear what they were saying. After five minutes or so, Mary came back in. 'We're going to play, Jess. We're all going to play together. The game.' Jess could tell that she was finding it hard to look him in the eye as she spoke. Pete was standing in the doorway, grinning at him.

'That's right, Jess. Sorry, little fella. I didn't mean to tease, did I, Mary?' Pete looked as though he was going to start laughing, but Mary didn't turn round. She was staring over Jess's shoulder at the television.

'Pete's going to be the ghost, Jess. Him against us. C'mon.'

Jess and Mary went upstairs. They put the wooden cross in the immersion heater cupboard and took out a clean white sheet for Pete. They went downstairs, and Mary told Pete the rules. 'Once the lights are out you can put the sheet on and count to fifty. Then you start looking for us. And remember, you can't run.'

'Right oh.' Pete smiled at Mary. 'I'll have you in no time.'

Mary switched out the lights, and Jess ran and hid in the kitchen porch. Then it went quiet. He thought Mary had gone upstairs, because he could hear the creaky floorboard in Mam and Dad's bedroom, but he didn't know where Pete was. He sat under the shelves in the porch and didn't move. He didn't move for a long time, because he was determined that Pete wouldn't find him. Then, he heard a bump upstairs. He tiptoed through the front room and into the hallway. He could sense that there was no one around, so he started up the stairs. But something was different. There must have been a light on somewhere, because he could see the patterns in the wallpaper and on the stair carpet, and he could see the carved serpent on the newel cap at the bottom of the banister rail. And then, there was Pete, standing at the top of the stairs with the white sheet in his hands.

*

The next day, Jess knew that something was wrong, that Mary and Pete had had an argument or something. Mary didn't get out of bed, and Mam kept shouting up the stairs for her to come down, but she wouldn't. Jess thought about telling his mam that they'd been playing the ghost game the night before, that Pete had gone home early and that Mary had come downstairs with red eyes as if she'd been crying. But he thought it probably wasn't such a good idea. Even if Mary had betrayed him, he felt sorry for her, because now she seemed upset. Eventually, Dad went upstairs to see her. When he came back down, Mary was with him. They sat together on the couch and Dad unfolded his newspaper and started to read. Mam tutted. Jess didn't like Mary being strange. He didn't like things not being normal. It made him feel anxious and scared. He wanted to say something to her, but she seemed far away. She just sat there, next to Dad, and stared blankly at the newspaper.

*

'I've a good mind to saw the thing off. A serpent indeed. What kind of a thing is that to have in a God-fearing house like this? I ask you!' Jess's mam was always going on at Dad about the carved serpent. She wanted him to make a new banister rail to replace it. 'And you've no excuse now you've got that lathe. It'll take you no time at all.' But Dad said that he liked the serpent, that it was probably very old and that, anyway, it was a reminder that there was a serpent even in Paradise. Mam tutted and called him a heathen.

On Christmas Eve, Jess dreamt about the serpent. He was excited about opening his presents the next morning so, to make himself extra tired, he was reading his Bible. Eventually the words on the page started to squirm around, so he stopped. He turned to the nativity picture in the middle of the book. He gazed at it and then he closed his eyes and tried to imagine his own picture: the front room with the scattering of straw on the carpet, the open window and the star, the donkey and the crib. Jess saw himself as the baby, lying in a manger, his mam and dad as Mary and Joseph, with their strange robes and the cloths on their heads, and Mary in the background, as one of the shepherds. But try as he might, he couldn't stop Pete from creeping in. Each time Jess pictured it, there he was, standing grinning at Dad's shoulder.

Eventually Jess decided to put the picture out of his mind, and soon he was asleep. He dreamt that he was standing at the top of the stairs. It was dark, but there was a light on in Mary's room, behind him. As he looked down into the hallway, Jess could sense that something was different, something was wrong. He stared hard into the darkness trying to work out what it was, and then he realised it was the carved serpent on the newel cap at the bottom of the stairs. There was something not right about it, and as he stared Jess realised what it was. The serpent was moving. It was unravelling itself from the tight wooden coil in which it was usually imprisoned, slithering off the turned globe and twisting itself round the stair spindle and down. Jess watched, unable to move as the serpent continued to unwind.

Finally, he turned and ran across the landing into Mary's room. Mary was standing by the window combing her hair. Jess shouted to her, but she couldn't hear him. He noticed that there was someone in her bed, but that the sheets were pulled up to the bedhead so he couldn't tell who it was. There was no sign of life from the shape in the bed, except for the slightest movement of the cotton sheet where the mouth would be. Jess could tell it was the movement of someone breathing. He shouted again and again, but Mary just kept staring out of the window. He turned to go, but as he stepped back out onto the landing everything was suddenly black, and he was falling, falling through the blackness. He was falling through space, a huge, empty space until, just as suddenly, the falling sensation stopped and the blackness began to tighten round him. He could feel the breath being squeezed from his lungs, the blackness constricting his body. And then he realised the terrible thing that had happened. He was inside it. He was inside the serpent.

*

It was the same ritual every Christmas Day. They all went to chapel first thing. They came back, and Mam started on the dinner while Dad lit the fire. Then, once Mam had put the goose in the oven and peeled the vegetables, they all sat down and opened their presents. They watched the Queen's speech on the television and then they ate their dinner. Mam always made a point of announcing that as well as being Christmas Day, it was also Jess's birthday, and before they left the table there'd be a chorus of 'Happy Birthday' and an extra little present for him.

Mary had been a bit more like her usual self as Christmas had approached, and she seemed to be enjoying helping Mam with the dinner, laying the table and making sure that everyone pulled a cracker with everyone else. After they'd sung 'Happy Birthday' she jumped up and kissed Jess on the cheek and gave him a big hug. He blushed, and asked if he could leave the table. Mam nodded and started to clear away the dishes. Jess sat down next to the fire and jabbed at the glowing coals with the poker. He shovelled on some more, and as they crackled and smoked, and burst into life, he thought of Pentecost and the tongues of fire. He felt his knees and his face getting hotter and hotter as the fire began to blaze once again, and he felt happy. He always felt happy when they were together: Mam, Dad, Mary and himself. He sometimes imagined everyone in the village disappearing and leaving just them, perhaps the only people anywhere in the whole world, living happily in their little house, together, forever.

It came without warning. Piercing through the crackle and spit of the fire, the chink of crockery in the kitchen, Dad's gentle snoring and the quiet voices on the television. The sudden squeal of the letter box opening in the hall, and then Pete's voice, shouting. He was shouting through the letter box, a stream of words spilling out of his mouth. At first nobody could understand the slurred, guttural noises that were filling the hall and the front room, the kitchen, the whole house. But then, certain words began to emerge more clearly, and Jess heard them repeated again and again, sometimes in a different order, but all connected. 'Mary'...'Jess'...'Mammy'...'Jess'...'Mary'...'Mammy...' There were gaps between the words to begin with, gaps filled with noise, and other words, words that would help to make sense of it but that Jess couldn't make out. And then it came, like a sudden presence into the room, the thing that Pete was shouting. And Jess understood, and Mary was holding her hands to her ears, sobbing, and Dad was lurching out of his chair and across the room towards the front door, and Mam was screaming, screaming at the top of her voice, screaming, but not loudly enough to drown out Pete's words, not loudly enough to stop them. And Jess was running, out through the kitchen, across the yard, over the fence and away. Jess was running, his eyes full of tears, running away from home.

*

'That's it, Jess. I've got you now. Up you come.' Jess didn't recognise his dad. He didn't recognise his mam either, as she burst through the wall of people from the village who were gathered round him. One of them was Mr Finch, the butcher, who was holding the swinging lantern in one hand and gripping his dad's shoulder with the other.

'Lay him down. Lay him down, I say! Something might be broken.'

There were other voices too, but they kept slipping away, lost in the sound of Pete's finger stroking the rim of that beer glass. Jess could feel his head being cradled in his dad's hand, and he could see his mam's face. She was crying. Jess closed his eyes. He closed his eyes and wondered where Mary was.

Let Not The Deep Swallow Me Up

The other evening I dreamt about Clarence. I often do at Christmas time, when he's in my thoughts even more than usual. I was dozing in my armchair in the parlour, when he walked in through the kitchen. He came over to me and took my hand in his. I got up from my chair. At first I just stood there, not daring to move, frightened in case he disappeared. He looked just the same. He didn't speak. He just looked at me and smiled – almost laughed – like you do when something wonderful has happened. Slowly I reached out my hand to touch his face, to make sure he was real, and as I did he drew me closer. I felt his arms around me, and then his breath on my face as our lips touched, gently. I rested my head on his chest and, as I felt it rise and fall, I listened for the beating of his heart. I closed my eyes, and we stood there for a long time, silently, together again at last. I felt so happy, but then there was a change, a sudden awareness that it wasn't Clarence who was holding me, but a stranger. I kept my eyes tight shut, too afraid to lift my head and look, too afraid of what I might see. The darkness was frightening too, though I realised that it was that very darkness I was clinging to, and not Clarence at all. And then I felt tears on my face, and I was awake, sitting in my armchair, alone, the clock ticking on the mantelpiece. I lifted my hand to wipe the tears away and looked around. But of course the room was empty, and Clarence was gone.

*

'Halibut.'

'What? You're having me on!'

'No, truly. Halibut.' Clarence smiled, and winked at her. 'Don't you like it?'

'Well, it's fitting for a fisherman, I suppose, but it's not what you'd call a common name, is it? Clarence Halibut?' Grace laughed, and put her empty glass down on the bar.

'Well it's the truth. Cross my heart, hope to die.' Clarence stubbed his cigarette out in the ashtray and swilled down the last dregs of his beer. 'And I suppose I should look on the bright side – it might have been Halibut Clarence!' They both laughed, and Clarence took his wallet from his breast pocket. 'So anyway, how about I buy you a Christmas drink and tell you all about it?' He grinned, and gestured towards the bar.

'My friends are over there. I should be getting back really. I was only going to the ladies' room.' Grace looked over her shoulder and smiled at the group of young women sitting at the other side of the bar.

'They seem pretty happy as they are. I'm sure they'll not miss you for half an hour. How about it?' Clarence pointed to an empty table by the window, overlooking the harbour.

'I don't suppose one drink will do any harm.'

Clarence bought the drinks – a pint of bitter and a port and lemon – and they sat down. 'Anyway, I don't know *your* name yet, do I?' He took a beer mat from the table behind them and carefully placed Grace's port and lemon on it.

Grace put her handbag down and picked up her drink. 'It's Grace. But you don't get out of it that easily. C'mon, Halibut. Let's hear it.' Grace sipped her drink, folded her arms and sat back in her seat.

Clarence laughed, took out a tin of tobacco and started to roll himself another cigarette.

'It's my dad's fault. He won't have it in the house. Cod, haddock, coley, mackerel, kippers, crab – you name it, we eat it – but never halibut.' He took a drag on his cigarette and blew the smoke over his shoulder, away from Grace.

'So why's that, then?' Grace smiled, waiting for a punchline.

'Well, Dad always says halibut's the king of fish. It's big is a halibut. Big, but gentle-looking, sort of sad, and it swims deep down, where the water's dark and cold. It can live for years – not just two or three – I mean twenty or thirty. But the thing about the halibut is it mates for life. Imagine that. A fish that mates for life. And if its mate gets netted, it follows, swims up out of the deep to get alongside it. Won't leave it, you see. Course, that means it's usually done for, too. Anyway, my dad thinks that's wonderful, and he'd rather never land halibut if he can avoid it. When my mum was pregnant with me, he used to stroke her belly and call me Halibut, so there it is. First name Clarence. Middle name Halibut.'

Grace smiled and continued to sip at her port and lemon. 'You're having me on.'

She liked him. He told her about the trawler he and his dad had bought so they could crew it themselves and land their own catch. And he talked about the lifeboat, and how he'd recently joined his dad on the crew. She thought it was sweet that he was so proud of following in his dad's footsteps. They talked on, and joked and laughed, until Grace remembered her friends. 'I'd better be getting back, Clarence.' She finished her drink, picked up her bag and got to her feet.

Clarence stood up too, and pulled her stool aside. 'Right, well it's been nice chatting to you, Grace. Very nice. And happy Christmas!'

'Yes, it has been nice. You too, and thanks for the drink.' She smiled awkwardly, turned, and was about to head back to her friends when Clarence took her arm gently.

'Grace, your surname's not Darling is it, by any chance?' He laughed at himself and let go of her arm.

'Darling? No. Why?'

'Oh, never mind. Another time. But anyway, listen – perhaps we could go out sometime, somewhere. In the new year?'

Grace laughed. 'Yes. I'd like that.'

*

I keep some of Clarence's things in an old wooden jewellery case in the sideboard. The day after I dreamt about him, I decided to take them out – it's something I do occasionally, and always at Christmas. I lifted the case out of the sideboard carefully, and put it on the parlour table. It has a little key which I keep behind the clock on the mantelpiece. I took the key, opened the case and began emptying out the contents. First, a small bottle of Clarence's aftershave. I took off the lid, put my finger over the top of the bottle and tipped it upside down, so that there would be just enough lotion on my fingertip to rub onto my wrists and my neck. Then his watch, which I set and wind each time I take it out. His latchkey. His leather wallet with the photograph inside of the three of us by the old lighthouse on the pier, Peter in his pram. A tortoiseshell fountain pen he treasured but rarely used. His wedding ring. A little packet of the telegrams he wired to me when he was out at sea. On the top of these is his first after we were married: *Thinking of you always Stop Home soon Stop Love the happy Halibut Stop.* The last Christmas card he sent me – he always gave me a Christmas card. I put this one out on the mantelpiece every year. And finally, two more things. A small brass pocket compass with a lid and a chain loop, and a brown envelope containing a brightly polished gold medal hanging from a dark blue ribbon.

I picked up the compass, and pressed the little button on the side carefully to open the lid. Inside, the compass rose looked as though it had been hand-painted, with the cardinal points marking the distance from true north. The delicate magnetic needle trembled and, as I held the compass in the palm of my hand, I turned it carefully to align the direction of the needle with the point marking north on its face. I put it down gently on the table. Then I picked up the brown envelope, slipped my fingers inside it and took out the medal. I held it by the dark blue ribbon and laid it on the table beside the compass. I ran my forefinger over its surface. Three figures aboard a small boat, pulling a fourth from the waves. And the inscription, *'Let not the deep swallow me up.'* I put the things back into the case one by one, all except the medal. I locked the case with the little key and put it back into the sideboard. I sat back down and looked at the medal, and the face of the figure being drawn from the water. I'd always known that Clarence would have wanted Peter to have it, but somehow the time had never seemed to be quite right.

*

Grace held Peter tightly in her arms as they mounted the narrow staircase to the bedroom. It was Christmas morning, two days after Peter had been born, and this was their first visit to see Clarence's parents. Clarence walked ahead of her, turning as he reached the bedroom door. 'Are you all right?'

Grace nodded and looked down at Peter, who was still sleeping.

'I know this is difficult, love. Seeing Dad like this. If you need to go back downstairs, it's fine.'

Grace reached out a hand and gripped his. 'I'll be fine. Don't worry. Go on, open it.'

Clarence opened the door carefully and entered the bedroom, stooping under the lintel to avoid banging his head. Grace followed with Peter.

Inside, the atmosphere was warm and cloying. Clarence's dad was propped up in bed, his eyes closed and his mouth open. His face and hands were a sallow, jaundiced colour, like fragile parchment that might easily disintegrate. Clarence's mum was downstairs. She'd been nursing his dad for weeks, and the doctor had said that it was just a matter of a few days now. Clarence sat on the edge of the bed and put out a hand to touch his dad's. 'Dad? You awake? It's Clarrie.'

His dad slowly opened his eyes and took a moment or two to focus. He smiled. 'Hello, son.' His voice was barely audible – little more than a breath. He glanced over at the night table beside the bed and pointed weakly at a water jug with a tumbler on top of it. 'Some water, son, please.'

Clarence poured water into the tumbler and gently helped his dad to lift his head and drink. His dry lips sipped at the water, though he hardly seemed to take any, and sank quickly back into the pillows.

'Is that better, Dad? Do you want some more?'

'Better. No more, son.'

Grace stood behind Clarence, by the window. She looked out across the rooftops, and watched the gulls swooping and hopping from chimney to chimney, gutter to gutter. Further down, beyond the rooftops, she could see the harbour. It was quiet, and as full of moored boats as you'd ever see it. She noticed one small blue boat entering the harbour and thought of her mother, who always told her to count little blue boats sailing into the harbour when she couldn't sleep, or if she was worrying about something. She turned and watched Clarence rubbing his palms on his thighs awkwardly, unsure of what to say. She felt uncomfortable, not just for Clarence, but also because somehow it didn't seem right for her to be here in this sick room, where death seemed so close, with Peter, who was so small and new.

Clarence touched his dad's arm gently. 'So, how have you been getting on, Dad?' His dad didn't answer, but winced with pain as he opened his eyes and tried to lift himself up on the pillows. Clarence looked across at the pill bottles on the night table. 'Mum's been doing a good job, looking after you.' His dad nodded, and coughed weakly. There was silence for a few moments as his breath slowly returned.

'She's a lifesaver is your mother. Look after her, won't you?'

Clarence didn't respond.

It was only a few days since they'd last seen him, but so much had changed. Not least, Peter had been born, but at the same time Clarence's dad had deteriorated. Grace could see it, and she could see that Clarence could too. He looked shocked and upset by how much worse his dad's condition had become. Everyone had known for several months that he was not going to get better, but this was perhaps the first time that they could truly see it and feel that his death would not now be long.

'So look, Dad. Here he is. Our beautiful new baby boy. We're calling him Peter. Peter James'. Clarence had suggested James, after his dad, and he and Grace had agreed to it as a middle name.

His dad seemed to notice Grace for the first time. She stepped towards the bed and passed Peter carefully to Clarence. 'Watch his head, love.'

She took the old man's hand and kissed his forehead. 'How are you, Dad?'

He nodded. 'Better for seeing you, love. And this little one.' He seemed suddenly more alert at the nearness and the newness of Peter. Peter had woken up too. Clarence moved closer to his dad and held Peter so that he could see him. 'Look. He's beautiful isn't he, Dad? Your first grandson.'

His dad smiled. 'Ah, he is that. My little Halibut.' Peter didn't make a sound. 'A boatman in the making.' Grace knew it was foolish and wrong of her, but as she watched, her discomfort grew and she wished that she could take Peter back downstairs, away from this. Clarence's dad closed his eyes again and sank back into himself. Grace took Peter from Clarence and went back to the window. She held him close and nuzzled the top of his head. Clarence rested a hand on one of his dad's and watched him closely. A vein throbbed weakly on his temple and a tiny muscle twitched involuntarily just below his cheek. There was a long silence before his dad opened his eyes again, and met Clarence's bewildered gaze. He lifted his hand slowly and pointed. 'I've something for you, Clarrie. In the drawer there.'

Clarence pointed to the night table. 'What, in here, Dad?' His dad nodded, and closed his eyes again. Clarence pulled open the little drawer and took out a small brown envelope. He looked at his dad, and then across to Grace, as if seeking permission to open it. Grace nodded to him. Clarence eased the envelope open with his thumb and forefinger, stopping to look up at his dad when he saw what was inside. 'Ah, but Dad! This is yours. I can't take this. I ...' He lifted the small, round object out of the envelope carefully and laid it in his upturned palm.

'It's no good to me, is it? My father gave it me, and I want you to have it.'

At first Grace thought it was a pocket watch. Clarence got up from the bed and moved towards her, holding out his hand to show her the object. 'Look, Grace. It's Dad's compass.' It was an old brass pocket compass. Grace looked, as Clarence opened its lid to reveal the painted face with the letters *N, E, S* and *W* inscribed on it, and the little needle which, she noticed, pointed out of the window and towards the harbour.

Grace touched Clarence's arm. 'It's beautiful, darling.' As Clarence clipped the lid shut, it seemed to glow in the half-light of the room.

Clarence sat on the edge of the bed again and took his dad's hand gently. 'Thank you, Dad. I'll treasure it. Always.'

His dad smiled, and nodded at Peter. 'And give it to him one day.'

Grace smiled at Clarence as he looked across to her, closed his hand round the compass and placed it in his breast pocket. She watched his dad's eyes close and then turned and looked out of the window once more, over the rooftops and down to the harbour. She looked for the little blue boat, but it was gone. Again she knew it was wrong, but she wondered how soon she might be able to leave the room, without its seeming thoughtless or upsetting Clarence.

*

In her dressing gown, Grace stooped over the fire, trying to revive the cinders in the grate. She could hear the wind blasting down the chimney and around the house, and the rain and sleet lashing against the window. She picked up the tongs, added a few pieces of coal to the fire, and put them back in the scuttle. As she crossed towards the kitchen, Grace stopped to switch on a small lamp that stood on a table in the corner of the parlour. She pulled her dressing gown more tightly round herself as she entered the brightly lit kitchen where Clarence was zipping up a bag and putting on his heavy reefer coat.

'You should go back to bed, love. I don't know how long we'll be. I might not be back until morning.' He fastened his coat and held her arms, kissing her on the forehead.

'I can't sleep when I know you're out there, can I? Peter will be waking for his feeds in any case. I'll keep a fire going, and I can doze in the armchair till you get back.' She kissed him, and went to fetch the hip flask she'd filled with whiskey while he was getting dressed. 'Have you got everything?'

He nodded back and, smiling, took the flask from her and put it in his pocket.

'That's it, all set. I'd better get off.' He moved towards the door quickly, then turned back to kiss her again. 'And when I get home I'll cook us bacon and eggs – how's that?' Grace smiled, they kissed each other again and Clarence opened the door. A blast of wind, freezing rain and sleet struck Grace, taking her breath away. Without looking back, Clarence slammed the door shut and was gone.

Waiting for Clarence to come home was something Grace was used to. He was out at sea all the time on his normal fishing trips. She didn't mind waiting then, waiting for the sound of the kitchen door opening and his voice filling their little house with his 'Hallo! Hallo, love. The Halibut's home.' Or for the careful opening of the sideboard and the chink of a bottle neck on the rim of a glass, if it was late and she was in bed, now with Peter sleeping soundly in the Moses basket beside her. She loved the smell he brought in with him, the smell of the ocean, and she loved that first sight of him, his dark hair ruffled and uncombed, his cheeks smooth and ruddy, his eyes smiling as he blew into his raw, chilled hands. His reefer coat would be open, and the overalls and boots underneath glistening with dried fish scales. Sometimes he'd come in with a tray of freshly caught fish wrapped in newspaper and ice. But 'the boat' was different. The knowledge that the sea had put somebody in peril, and that Clarence was going out there, into a life-threatening situation, made for a different kind of waiting, a waiting full of anxiety and fear, even more so now that she was waiting with Peter, too.

Grace turned out the kitchen light and went back into the parlour. Weak, papery flames were flickering in the grate, and she sat down in the armchair and watched them as they struggled to take hold of the coals. She decided to get into bed. She knew she wouldn't be able to sleep, but she didn't want to sit and listen to the noise of the wind and the rain. She'd feel safer there, waiting for Peter to wake for his feed. And then she'd try and sleep, hoping that before she knew it, they'd be sitting round the table in the kitchen, the sound of Clarence's voice and the smell of coffee and bacon and eggs filling the house again. As she entered the bedroom she looked at Peter. He was still sleeping peacefully. She watched his chest rise and fall, and she listened to his breathing. She adjusted the curtain at the window, not wanting the light from the lamp post in the street outside to disturb him. She slipped carefully into bed and pulled the covers up to her chin. She could see the imprint of Clarence's head in the pillow beside hers. She closed her eyes, and pictured a little blue boat sailing into the harbour.

*

I always spend Christmas with Peter and his family. Peter's a nurse, and works at the local hospital. That's where he met Maria. They were married in the same church as Clarence and I, and now they have a daughter, Lisa, who's nine years old. Peter came in his car to collect me on Christmas Eve. He laughed when he saw my bags. I'd only packed one small overnight case, but there were two others – much larger ones – filled with presents I'd wrapped the night before. 'Blimey, Mum, you're giving Santa a run for his money this year!'

It had been raining earlier in the day, but the rain was quickly turning into snow, and large wet flakes were falling heavily as we drove round the harbour. The town could be surprisingly busy at Christmas time, now that it had become something of a holiday destination. As the fishing had declined, so the number of second homes and holiday lets had increased.

When we arrived, Lisa came running out into the snow to meet us. She was so excited. Maria was waving from the door. Peter took my bags from the boot and we all went inside. The house was filled with the smell of the roasting meat that Maria was preparing for our evening meal. The Christmas tree and the decorations were all up in the living room, and there was a welcome fire roaring in the grate.

'Only one more sleep to Christmas, Granny Gracie – one more sleep!' Lisa helped me with my coat, took my hand and showed me the tree and the presents underneath. 'Look at all the presents! There are some for you too. Shall I show you?' I laughed and said that she could show me once I'd caught my breath. I told her I had some presents to put under the tree as well.

We had a lovely evening. Maria had cooked beef, which Clarence always liked on Christmas Eve. We ate, and then Lisa showed me which of the presents under the tree were for me and helped me put out the ones I'd brought. We watched television and

I combed her hair for her. Peter and Lisa put a little plate on the hearth, with a mince pie, a carrot, and a glass of sherry on it. 'For Father Christmas and Rudolf,' explained Lisa. When Lisa went up to bed I read her a story, but she couldn't lie still and listen because she was so excited. 'I don't think I'll be able to get to sleep, Granny.' I told her to keep her eyes tight shut and count little blue boats sailing into the harbour. She frowned, and snorted, 'Little blue boats?' I laughed and tucked her in.

Later, I sat with Peter and Maria, and we watched more television and had a drink. After a little while Maria fell asleep on the sofa, so Peter turned the television off and we sat quietly, gazing into the fire. Peter got up and looked out through a gap in the curtains. 'It's pretty awful out there, Mum. The snow's turned back to sleet. No white Christmas this year.'

I said that was a shame, but at least we wouldn't be snowed in. Peter sat back down in the armchair opposite mine and we continued watching the fire. I had the little brown envelope with the medal inside it in my handbag, down on the floor beside me. I'd decided to give it to Peter. I'm not sure why this seemed to be the right time, but it did. I wasn't sure what to say, either, but as we sat there together beside the fire, listening to the wind, I found myself reaching for my bag, opening it and taking out the envelope. 'I have something for you, Peter.' I held the envelope out to him. He looked surprised, but he reached across and took it.

'Oh yes. An early Christmas present, is it?'

'Not exactly. It was your dad's. It was given to your dad. A medal, for gallantry.'

Peter looked puzzled as he held the crumpled envelope in his hands, and as I watched him open it, I suddenly thought that it should have been in a nice presentation case, and how foolish I was to give it to him in that grubby old thing. I felt as if I'd made a terrible mistake, and I almost wanted to take it back from him. When he slid his fingers into the envelope, it was as if I was in that terrible sick room again, watching Clarence's hands reveal his dad's compass, while I held Peter safe in my arms.

'Goodness. This is quite something.' Peter lifted the medal out of the envelope by its dark blue ribbon and held it in his palm. 'So this was given to him, after – after the accident?'

'Yes. That's right. Posthumously.'

'Yes, of course.' Peter held the medal up close to examine it. Three figures aboard the small boat, pulling a fourth from the waves. 'Let not the deep swallow me up.' He spoke the words out loud. 'Sounds like something from the Bible. One of the Psalms.'

'Yes. It's their motto, too. The lifeboats.'

'Ah, right. I see.' He continued to look down at the medal, frowning. He leant forward, picked up the glass of sherry from the hearth and sipped at it. 'Well, it's a very special thing. Thank you. But I don't understand. Why haven't I seen it before? Why didn't you show it to me before?'

Our eyes didn't meet. He continued to look at the medal, and I turned to look into the weakening flames of the fire. 'I don't really know, Peter. I know I should have done, but somehow I couldn't.'

Peter drank the rest of the sherry and put the glass back down on the hearth. 'But then, we've never really spoken about Dad much, have we? I mean, there are so many things that we've never really spoken about aren't there?'

And he was right, of course. As he was growing up I'd told him about Clarence, but it was only after Lisa was born, and I saw how he and Maria behaved with her, that I began to realise how distant I'd been with Peter. But most of all, I knew what Peter meant about Clarence's death. That we'd never spoken of it, or of how everything in our lives somehow pointed back to that terrible event, like a compass needle set to true north.

'Why is that, Mum. Why have you never talked about Dad? I mean really talked about him?'

'I don't know, Peter. It's not that I didn't want to. But I wanted to keep you safe from it all, I suppose.'

Our eyes met, finally. 'Little blue boats eh, Mum?' I didn't mean to, but I looked away, back into the fire.

*

It seemed only a few moments since she'd been thinking of the little blue boat sailing into the harbour, when Grace awoke to the sound of Peter's crying – and to another sound. As she pulled back the warm bed covers and stumbled towards the Moses basket, she felt the cold night air grip her. She took Peter in her arms and drew him close to her. She could hear the storm outside, but worse – the howling and whistling of the wind, and the rain lashing at the window. And then, quite suddenly, she remembered Clarence's absence from the house. In those first moments of her wakefulness he'd not existed to her, but now his not being present with them flooded her consciousness. She had no idea of how long she'd slept, only that it was still night. Where Clarence might be at this precise moment and Peter's insistent crying wrestled for her attention. But there was something else, something that had prompted her waking. She listened for it. At first there seemed to be nothing, but then it was there again, a knocking sound that she recognised immediately.

She moved onto the landing and stepped carefully down into the darkness of the stairs, holding Peter tightly. Their closeness and her movement seemed to soothe him, and his crying stilled to a continuous grizzle. As they descended she heard the banging sound again; somebody was knocking on the kitchen door. Grace could feel her heart pounding too. It would be Clarence. He would have forgotten his latchkey. She imagined him on the other side of the door, rooting through his pockets for it and cursing his stupidity, ready with apologies, a hug and a kiss and promising hot coffee, bacon and eggs.

As she passed through the parlour, Grace looked towards the clock on the mantelpiece, but it was too dark to see what the time was. Reaching the kitchen, she turned on the light and stared at the door. She was listening for Clarence's voice, but there was still only the sound of the wind and the rain. If only the terrible wind would stop. She walked towards the door and turned the key in the lock, wanting to feel the cold night air and the wind and the rain on her face, and wanting to bring Clarence in from the storm, into the warmth and the light. But as she opened the door it was a stranger in uniform who stood there, wearing an overcoat with bright silver buttons and a peaked cap bearing an embroidered insignia. He looked at Grace and took off his cap. The wind swept his white hair across his forehead and he pushed it back and said something that Grace didn't hear. She stepped aside to let him into the kitchen and then closed the door behind him.

The man put his cap on the kitchen table and invited Grace to sit down. He asked if he could help her get anything for the little one. Peter was quieter now, but Grace knew he'd cry again if he wasn't fed soon. She knew she was staring at the man, and she knew too that he could have come for only one reason. As they sat, and he spoke, Grace still didn't hear him, although occasionally there were words which she found making pictures in her head. He must have done this so many times before, used many of the same words, even, though they weren't really necessary, of course. Grace knew. She didn't need to hear. She knew from his silver buttons why he'd come.

*

It was Clarence who first caught sight of the flare glowing unsteadily in the blackness, a faint star of distress. But no sooner had it swung into view than it was gone again, lost as the boat tipped steeply back down between two waves. The conditions were as bad as any he could remember, the wind and rain gusting force nine, the sea heaving and plunging, gigantic waves and spindrift sweeping in huge plumes, ocean and sky one great maelstrom. The casualty was a small fishing vessel, the *Grace Darling*, which was reported to be taking on water and about to sink. On board was a crew of just two, George Lamberton and his son Simon, both of whom were known to Clarence and the other boatmen. Flannagan had set a course for the vessel's last known position, the coastguard having reported that communication with her had been lost and that it was likely she'd already sunk.

'This is impossible. If she's gone down already there's no chance.' Parry was right. It would be a miracle if they located anyone in the water in such poor conditions.

Spooner shook his head. 'There's just no visibility, is there? There's nothing out there.'

Flannagan wrestled with the wheel and stared ahead, unblinking. 'Well, let's get closer first and see if she's down. She might still be afloat.' They called him Helmsman Hope with good reason, thought Clarence.

As the boat plunged on, they all knew they were getting close to where the *Grace Darling* should be, and each of them peered into the blackness for any sign of the vessel or her crew. Clarence glanced across at Flannagan, Parry and Spooner, wondering how long they could all keep hoping, when suddenly the sky was lit up by another flare, brighter and nearer this time. A moment later, Spooner shattered the concentrated silence, his face incredulous as he gesticulated wildly and shouted, 'She's there! Christ almighty! Look, twenty metres dead ahead, low in the water!' And there she was, just visible in the orange glow of the flare.

'Get the lamp on her, now!' Flannagan barked the order at Spooner, and the searchlight exploded into life, its beam stretching across the deck and out into the blackness – illuminating the stricken boat ahead of them. The boat was barely above the waterline, her bow rising and falling with each great swell and her stern sinking lower by the minute as two small figures worked desperately to keep the sea at bay.

'Bloody hell! Look at that! They're bailing, with fish boxes by the look of it!' Clarence still doubted that they could reach the boat before it went down.

Flannagan continued down-sea, passing the *Grace Darling* and leaving her to starboard. Once past, he altered course to starboard, into-sea, and approached her again. 'Right, we'll approach the starboard side with our port shoulder, yes?'

As they closed in, Clarence could see the two men struggling with the fish boxes; how they'd managed to stay out of the water in these conditions he couldn't imagine. They were now close enough to the boat for the men to be able to see them approaching. One of the figures stopped bailing, threw aside the fish box and started waving his arms over his head. As he did, the stern disappeared beneath the water, and suddenly both men were gone.

*

Clarence pulled on his gloves and stepped out of the wheelhouse onto the deck, followed closely by Parry. The sudden explosion of noise and the freezing water lashing his face stunned him momentarily, taking his breath away. Rooting himself to the pitching deck, Clarence gathered himself, wiped the stinging water from his eyes and nose, and moved forward. The deck tipped and tilted in front of him, and the spindrift hit him with such force that he wondered how long he'd be able to keep his footing. He continued to move forward cautiously, turning every few steps to check that Parry was still with him, and then struck out towards the edge of the deck. He could see the *Grace Darling*, half submerged in the water and, as they reached her port shoulder, he could also see the two men, who'd somehow managed to grasp one of the boat's lifelines. Clarence could hear their voices shouting over the wind's howling, and the boom of the sea hitting the boat's hull. The broken waves crested along the *Grace Darling*'s port side and covered the men in a wake of boiling white foam. Each time a wave struck, Clarence wondered whether they'd still be holding onto the line when its wake subsided.

He knew that they'd have to work quickly, and that the only way to save the two men was to drag them aboard. Fortunately, the lifeboat was still tipping in the swell, and ploughing low enough into the water for them to try and haul the men in. They wouldn't be able to hold on to that line for long, so the only option was for Clarence and Parry to take a man apiece. Clarence turned and shouted into Parry's ear. Parry understood, and immediately set about positioning himself level with the lifeline and wedging himself against the deck rail, in readiness to grab Lamberton senior. Clarence then moved into position. He could see, even through the blinding spray, that Simon was closer to him, and that he was shouting something, but he couldn't make out what it was. He wrapped his right arm round the deck rail, took off his left glove and waited. The boat tipped upwards, hit an oncoming wave and crashed down again as the wave broke against its hull. The line slackened, and Simon was swept up almost level with Clarence. For a second they were close enough for their eyes to meet, but then the wake of the broken wave covered them, and they were both submerged in the frozen water. Clarence reached out his hand to grab hold of Simon. He held his breath, waiting for the boat to rise again. As it did so, water streamed from his hood, and from his ears, his nose and his mouth. He coughed and spluttered, and repositioned himself so that the deck rail remained locked in the crook of his arm. He looked down at his bare hand. It hung loose and empty, and as his vision cleared he saw that the lifeline which both Simon and his father had been clinging to hung loose also. They were gone.

But as the boat levelled itself and the wake of bubbling foam passed, Clarence spotted Simon emerging from the black water, struggling not to slip beneath the boat. He could see that Simon was exhausted, and that he could barely lift his arms above the water, let alone swim for a lifeline. Clarence glanced back at Parry, who was sprawling on the deck with George Lamberton. Somehow, he had managed to grab him round the neck and hold on to him long enough for them both to be washed on board as the boat raised itself back up out of the water. Clarence struggled to move closer to Simon, desperate to try and reach him before he was sucked under the boat or swept out into the blackness. He released his arm from the deck rail, wrapped his legs round one of the stanchions, and reached down towards him, knowing that if another wave struck them it would be too late. As he did so, there was a sudden swell, and Simon was swept up towards him, his head hitting Clarence full in the face. Clarence was aware of a warm sensation in his mouth and nose, and the iron taste of his own blood, but he felt no pain; he was too focused on Simon, who was holding him round the waist and trying desperately to clamber up his legs to the deck. Clarence grabbed him by the groin and levered him upwards. He felt Simon's heaviness weighing on him, growing heavier and heavier the nearer he got to the deck until, with one last great effort from each of them, he was swung to safety.

Clarence hung over the edge of the boat, frozen, exhausted and disorientated. He could feel nothing, and had no sense of his own body. Parry grabbed hold of Simon's arm, and the pair scrabbled along the deck. Clarence knew he had to get himself back up quickly, so he pushed his legs against the side of the boat and tried to swing his arms and grab the deck rail. But each time he tried, he grew weaker. Then the boat began to tip again, up and back, up and back, slowly, before plunging steeply downwards, and Clarence felt something give, something sharp strike his face. He was falling, falling fast, the cold, black sea hurrying to meet him.

*

I woke up but it wasn't morning. It wasn't Christmas morning. It was still pitch dark, and the middle of the night. At first I had no idea where I was. I looked around and waited for some fixed point to emerge that would make sense of my surroundings. But nothing seemed familiar. I looked towards the place where my window should have been, and for the light from the lamp post further down the street coming in through the gap round the curtains. But there was no window, no light. And where the door was meant to be, again there was just blackness. It was only as the moments passed and sleep ebbed fully away that I remembered I wasn't at home, in my own bed, but in Peter's spare room, and that it was Christmas Eve. As I lay there, and felt wakefulness take hold, I knew I wouldn't be able to get back to sleep again. I remembered giving Peter Clarence's medal, and what he'd said about us never having spoken about Clarence, and the hurt in his eyes, the hurt that had always been there, and that I might have seen, had I only looked more closely. But how could I have done? How could I have looked closely into the depths of my son's hurt if it meant that he might see my own?

The wind had dropped, and it was silent and still outside. I thought I might get up and make a cup of tea, but I didn't want to wake Lisa. Another couple of hours and it would probably be light, and it would be Christmas morning.

*

'She was a lighthouse keeper's daughter, and a heroine. Grace Darling, the patron saint of all boatmen.' Clarence and Grace are making their way back down the winding, narrow stone staircase of the old lighthouse on the pier. It's a cold, January day, the first they've spent together.

Grace turns her head but continues to descend, one careful step after another. 'And what did she do, this Grace Darling, to become the darling of you boatmen?'

Clarence laughs. 'Well, she saw a ship, during a storm. It was running aground and breaking up on the rocks, and, knowing that there wasn't enough time to fetch help, she ran down to the jetty, untied a longboat and rowed out into the storm, towards the stricken ship. There was wind and rain and icy sleet, and huge waves were battering the boat, but she just kept going. She refused to give in. Her mind was made up to save the crew on board that ship. She pressed on through the storm, exhausted but determined, and eventually she reached the ship. And then, somehow, she found the strength to pull those sailors, one by one, out of the frozen water and into the boat, and row them back to the safety of the shore. It was a miracle, and they say that every time a lifeboat's called out, the ghost of Grace Darling goes with it.'

As they spiral down through the darkness, they feel a draft of cold air moving up the staircase. Even through the thick stone walls, they can still hear the wind. Grace feels Clarence's hand brush her shoulder, and as she reaches up for it, their fingers touch and slowly intertwine.

'Goodness, Clarence Halibut! All this going round and round in the dark. It's making me dizzy.'

They stop. 'Let's rest for a moment.' Clarence squeezes alongside her and they sit side by side on the cold stone step. He takes her hand again. 'So, will you be my Grace Darling ... Grace ... darling?'

Grace laughs. 'I can hardly see you, Clarence. Clarence Halibut. It's so dark in here. I'll have to imagine you.'

She reaches out her hand to touch his face. She feels his arms around her, and his breath close as he draws her nearer, and then his lips gently meet hers and they kiss as the wind howls outside. She rests her head on his chest. She can feel it rising and falling as he breathes, and when she holds her breath, she hears the beating of his heart. Grace longs for them to stay close like this. They kiss again, and Clarence gets up. 'We'd better keep going. We don't want to get locked in, do we?' He takes her hand as she steps down. He follows close behind her. A few more circling steps and Grace sees a faint shaft of light stretching up the stone stairway from the entrance below. They make their way down carefully, Grace longing to see the daylight and Clarence's face again.

The wind whips the tears from her eyes as they descend the last few steps into the light.

The Birthday Weekend

Tim had a picture in his head. A foetus, floating in a jar of formaldehyde. It was the same colour as the nicotine stains on his fingers, but was glowing like one of those lampshades in the book he'd been reading about Nazi doctors. He'd been trying to draw it, and had an idea he'd like to paint it, but on an enormous scale, and give it to Carrie as a present. He could hear her. She'd got up very early and was padding quietly round the bedroom, carefully opening cupboards and drawers, packing things into a large holdall so that everything would be ready. She thought he was still sleeping, but he wasn't. He had a headache, and his mouth was dry and stale from too many cigarettes, too much acidic red wine. He was delaying opening his eyes, thinking about the foetus again, and about what Carrie had planned.

Carrie hadn't told Tim where they were going. It was a surprise she said, to celebrate his birthday. She was trying so hard. She'd cooked them supper the previous evening and had even baked him a cake with candles. She said she'd arranged everything. 'But come on, where are you taking me?' he'd asked. 'You have to give me a clue at least. Coast or countryside? I won't know whether to take my bucket and spade or not.'

'Look, I'm not telling you. You'll just have to wait.'

*

Tim feigned waking. He stretched and yawned loudly, and rubbed at his eyes. Carrie was putting towels into the holdall. 'Morning, sleepy head.'

He screwed up his face, stretched and yawned again. 'Morning.'

Carrie went into the kitchen. Tim could hear the kettle being filled and the cutlery drawer rattling open. He reached under the bed and fumbled for his watch, which was inside one of his shoes, and his book. He put on his watch and thumbed through the pages of the book, half-listening to Carrie in the kitchen. He'd been reading about the experiments that were carried out on twins at Auschwitz by Josef Mengele – the 'Angel of Death'. One twin was often used as a control, while the other was exposed to injections of chemicals and deadly diseases, organ removals and amputations. There was careful monitoring of whether the torture of one twin affected the other, although in most cases both were killed in the end.

Carrie came back with coffee and he put the book down. She didn't like him reading it. She said it was sick. He thumped the pillow and sat upright. She handed the cup to him and kissed him on the forehead. 'Happy Birthday.'

Tim smiled. 'Yes. Thanks.' He sipped at the coffee as Carrie went over to the dresser, sat down and started to put on her make-up. Like the rest of Carrie's flat, the bedroom was ruthlessly spartan: untreated wooden floorboards, the simple pine bed, a stripped dressing table with a matching stool which slotted under it. No adornment, no clutter. Tim straightened the white cotton duvet cover and contemplated spilling a little of his black coffee onto it. Carrie kept a supply of covers in her airing cupboard. Tim often told her the place was like a hospital.

'So, what about my presents?'

'Presents later. No time now. You'll have to get up soon. We've got to get off.'

'Yes. OK. How are we getting there?'

'The car, of course.'

Tim nodded, and picked up his book again. He could see Carrie in the mirror, putting on her moisturiser. She glanced back at him, and then went into the garden. Tim was glad she'd gone. He didn't like her watching him get dressed. He drank his coffee and smoked a cigarette, then got up and put on his clothes.

*

When Tim was dressed, he washed and then joined Carrie in the kitchen. She was putting sandwiches into a cool bag. 'Do you want some breakfast?' Tim shook his head. 'We're pretty much ready to go then, I guess?'

Tim nodded. He went into the bedroom to fetch his camera. He picked up his book and his shoes as well, and went back to the kitchen. He put his camera and his book into the holdall, zipped it closed and then sat down at the table to put on his shoes. Carrie took the holdall, the cool bag and a large bottle of water and put them by the front door. Tim put on his coat and looked round the kitchen. Nothing was out of place. The stainless steel sink and drainer were clear, and the worktops were glistening with a sheen of moisture where Carrie had just wiped them. He noticed how white the concrete floor seemed. Carrie must have painted it again. She sometimes did this last thing at night, with white emulsion, if she thought it was starting to look grubby. She said it was therapeutic. The table was clear too, with just a small blue vase of narcissi in the centre. Such delicate little things, thought Tim, with their pale lemon flowers and golden coronas. Carrie reappeared with her coat on, and locked the French windows that led out into the garden. 'Right. C'mon then. Let's get this show on the road.'

*

Carrie put the holdall, the cool bag and the bottle of water on the back seat of the car, while Tim got into the passenger seat and put on his safety belt. When Carrie opened the driver's door and got in, Tim noticed that she was holding something in her lap. It was a box-shaped, brown paper package, with a red ribbon round it, and a bow. 'It's one of your presents.' Carrie held out the package for him to take. 'It's just something small. There are others, but I'll give you those later. This one's a kind of clue, too.'

Tim looked down at the package and took it from her. He knew that Carrie would have put thought and time and effort into it. She always did. 'Oh right. Thanks. Lovely wrapping.' He unwrapped it carefully as Carrie watched. Inside the paper was a box frame holding a carefully constructed arrangement of beachcombed objects: a delicate whorled shell, a piece of smooth driftwood and a globe of white stone with a hole through the middle of it.

'I hope you like it. You found the stone. Do you remember? You said it was meant to bring good luck.' She held out her hand and touched his arm gently. 'A stone with a hole through it like that?'

He turned towards her and smiled awkwardly. 'Yes. I remember. The hag stone. It wards off the dead. And nightmares. It's nice. Thanks. Seaside, then?'

'Seaside. Yes.' Carrie turned the key in the ignition and released the handbrake, and they set off. Tim screwed the brown paper and ribbon into a ball and dropped it into the footwell. He turned the box lazily in his hands and wondered how Carrie could have failed to see what else the stone might represent. A stone with a hole through the middle. He wondered if she might be planning on taking him to Lyme Regis. She often talked about going back. He was curious, but he didn't want to show it. He put the box frame on the back seat, closed his eyes and dozed. Carrie turned on the radio to fill the silence.

*

Tim had found the stone on the beach at Lyme Regis. It had been their first weekend away together, not long after they'd met. Carrie's mother had died the previous year and Carrie had talked a lot about her, and about the summer holidays they'd spent at Lyme when she was a child. Tim had arranged the trip as a birthday present for her. They'd stayed in a guest house called the Old Monmouth. It had seen better days, and they seemed to be the only guests. They ate breakfast on their own each morning in a dark, oak-panelled dining room. Then they explored the town, hunted for fossils on the beach, swam in the sea and walked out along the great stone Cobb.

'I should stand at the end like the *French Lieutenant's Woman.*' Carrie laughed and danced ahead of Tim, her arms wide, reeling in the sunshine. It was a hot, still day and the Cobb snaked out from the bay, which was packed with holiday makers basking in the sun, eating chips and ice creams. It was uncomfortably busy, and they'd set out along the Cobb to get away from the crowds and in the hope of a cool sea breeze.

Tim followed, and reached out a hand for Carrie's. 'Who's she, then?'

'The book, you know. I'd need a cloak, though, and some stormy weather. All this sunshine would never do. I can't believe you haven't read it – you should. It's very romantic. You like romance, don't you?'

Tim frowned at Carrie and tutted. 'No, not really.'

Although it was early in their relationship, he'd already taken to closing down certain topics of conversation. It irked him that she took pleasure in things they didn't share – things she knew, that he didn't. At breakfast she'd told him that Oscar Wilde had stayed at the Old Monmouth, and that he'd carved his name into a windowsill in one of the rooms. She'd talked about Jane Austen, and pointed out the Assembly Rooms where she attended a ball. And when they'd visited the town's little museum, she'd shown him a doll, in one of the glass cases, that the painter Whistler had given to a local child whose portrait he'd painted.

They walked to the very end of the Cobb and sat with their legs hanging over the edge of the wall, looking out to sea. There were two ships, far out on the horizon. They sat quietly, holding hands, and watched as the ships moved slowly towards each other. 'This is so lovely, isn't it? I'm so happy, Tim'. Carrie leant across and kissed him on the cheek. 'Thank you.'

'It is lovely. It's a shame we can't stay longer.' Tim released Carrie's hand as he felt his own growing moist with sweat. 'Has it changed a lot, since you came here when you were little?'

'Yes and no. I completely recognise it. All of it. But at the same time, I don't. Like when you dream that you're in a particular place. You know it's that place, but it just isn't.' Carrie slapped the palms of her hands down onto the rough stone Cobb. 'I remember this, of course. I always had to walk straight down the middle of it because I was scared I'd fall off the edge and into the sea.'

They kissed and lay back on the warm stone. Tim felt the heat of the sun on his face, and thought about Carrie as a child, in this place. After a few minutes, he heard voices coming towards them and he sat up. A boy and girl were making their way along the Cobb. The boy was carrying a fishing rod. Tim got up and held out his hand to Carrie. 'C'mon, let's head back. We can walk along the beach.' He pulled her up. They kissed again and set off, hand in hand. The boy and the girl giggled as they passed.

They walked down onto the beach, away from the busy seafront and towards the cliffs. They gazed up at the great ledges of blue lias stone and beachcombed for fossils. Tim picked up a stone with a hole through the middle of it and handed it to Carrie. 'It's a hag stone. They're sacred. It'll protect you from evil spirits.'

Carrie took the stone. She placed it on her ring finger and laughed.

*

The long, straight road into Dungeness was flanked on either side by great sweeping plains of desert-like shingle and scrub. Tim could see the sea on one side, and on the other a complex of huge, rectangular white buildings and towers, about half a mile inland. There were houses scattered across the flat landscape too, low-slung wooden shacks with corrugated iron roofs, strung together by pylons and telegraph poles. Straight ahead of them stood a black lighthouse.

Tim had spotted a sign at the side of the road as they drove in. 'Dungeness. Wow! What a place! Bleak.' Carrie had often talked about Dungeness and said that they should visit.

'I thought it was time. It's a very special place. You'll like it.'
Tim looked across to the complex of buildings that he'd assumed was some kind of industrial plant.

'So, what exactly is that?'

'It's the nuclear power station.'

'What, out here?'

'Yes.'

The weather had deteriorated. The sky was heavy with one great, slow moving continent of leaden cloud, and there was a powerful wind that Tim could feel buffeting the car. The power station was illuminated with tiny star-like lights that pierced a mist which seemed to hang over the place, despite the wind. It reminded Tim of a factory or a hospital, and made him think of the Nazi doctors. He imagined the entrance, an iron gateway bearing those words, *Arbeit macht frei.* And he thought of Vera, one of the twins in his book, who described visiting Mengele's laboratory and being confronted by a wall of human eyes – blue, brown, green – staring at her, like a collection of butterflies, she said.

Carrie pulled the car into the car park of a pub, The Pilot. The car park was empty, and the pub was closed. Shame, thought Tim – he quite fancied a pint. He settled for a cigarette instead. When they got out of the car the wind hit them. They walked to where the beach started, just beyond the car park. The beach was hard to walk on, and was dotted with clumps of sea kale and bursts of blackthorn and yellow flowered broom hugging the shingle.

Further along the shore Tim could see a cluster of little wooden boats and fishermen's shacks. Beyond these stood the lighthouse, and he watched as the pulse of yellow light flashed and disappeared, flashed and disappeared again. He took out his camera and lined up a shot of the power station. He'd never be able to capture this light, he thought. There was something odd about it. Everything seemed to be illuminated by a strange nicotine glow that reminded him of that foetus floating in the jar of formaldehyde. Carrie had gone ahead. She was already combing for shells and stones. He called her name, but she didn't hear him. He could barely hear himself above the wind, but he could feel her name resonating through him. He could hear the sea too, the sound of the waves crashing onto the shore and the backwash receding over the shingle – and every few minutes the fog signal sounding from the lighthouse – an eerie mechanical intonation.

Tim crunched slowly through the pebbles, allowing Carrie to get further ahead. He picked up a stick, and then a rusted metal bucket that he found half buried in a shelf of larger stones. The tide had left a spine of flotsam along the shoreline, and Tim sifted through it with the stick. He collected some of the more interesting stones and shells, pieces of driftwood and stripped bone, smoothed by the sea and dried by the salty blasts of wind. There were flaps of unteased netting, cork floats, slices of treadless rubber tyring, thick umbilical trails of rotting rope and cordage. He found a glove, a shoe, and even a cigar in an aluminium tube. Everything ended up in the sea, thought Tim. All kinds of shit, all kinds of waste. He found a dead dogfish. It had been perfectly preserved, coiled and desiccated by the wind. He poked at it with the stick and then picked it up in his hands. He was pleased, because it had hardened like a fossil, and didn't lose its shape when he put it into the bucket.

By the time they reached the first of the boats, Tim's bucket was nearly full. In between the windowless little black huts there were broken sections of rail track – the sort the boats must use for launching, thought Tim. There were winches, and scattered components of decaying, dismantled machinery. He found the remains of a shed door lying flat on the shingle. He could see it was a door, but most of it had disintegrated, leaving only a skeleton of rusted hinges and dried wooden splinters with flakes of bleached paint clinging to them. He put down the stick and the bucket and photographed the remains of the door. Not a skeleton, he thought, but a ghost of itself. The whole place was like the scene of some terrible disaster.

Tim looked up, and saw that Carrie was waiting for him. She was leaning against a blue boat named *Arlita*, and was holding a white plastic bag. He put his bucket down beside her.

'So what have you got, then?'

She held up the plastic bag. 'Oh, a bit of all sorts. How about you?'

'Well, look at this beauty.' Carefully, Tim took the dogfish from the bucket and held it out to Carrie. 'A photo opportunity, I think.'

'Oh Tim, no! Don't.'

'Oh, come on now. Don't be so squeamish. You won't feel a thing.'

He handed her the dogfish and lined up the shot. He hesitated as he looked through the viewfinder. Carrie held the fish out in front of her, looking past him. He waited, sensing her discomfort. He took the photograph, and then held out the bucket so that she could put the dogfish back. She didn't look at him as she dropped it into the bucket. He could see that she was trying not to cry. How sad, thought Tim, that it had come to this. He sat down and started to take off his shoes.

Carrie buried her hands in her pockets, looked over her shoulder as if she were thinking of walking back to the car, and then looked down at him. 'What are you doing, Tim?'

'I'm going for a swim.' He pushed his socks into his shoes and started to remove his coat.

'What? You must be mad! It'll be freezing. And look at the waves. Not to mention there's a nuclear power station over there. You'll come out glowing! Please don't.'

Tim laughed, unbuckled his belt and pulled off his trousers, and then, in one swift movement, his jumper and shirt. 'It'll be fine. Don't worry. I'll be fine.' He hobbled across the pebbles to where the waves were breaking. He felt the wind on his bare skin – not as cold as he'd expected – and a prickling sensation from the tiny particles of grit and sand swept up from the bone-dry shingle. As the sea gripped his ankles it took his breath away, but he was determined not to turn back. He began by edging out a step at a time, leaning into the powerful, surging water. As it reached his knees he stopped, and with his legs braced apart, he waited. It was too misty to be able to see the horizon now. The sea and the sky seemed to be one and the same. He watched as a gull arced across the darkening sky above him, and then he pressed on, struggling to keep his footing as the shingle shifted beneath his feet. The water was bitterly cold, and the breaking waves were reaching his midriff now. He knew that he would be swept over soon, unless he began to swim. He wondered if Carrie was watching, but he didn't want to turn back and look.

He felt himself losing his footing again as the shingle gave way to sand and silt. Another wave hit him, and as it did he raised his arms, held his breath and threw himself forward. His body registered the shock of being beneath the freezing water. But as quickly as he had gone down, so he came back up, struggling to control his breathing, taking in air in great spasms, unable to breathe out. He swallowed several mouthfuls of the salty water, coughing and spluttering as he lifted his head and tried to regain control of his limbs. After a few moments, he began to breath more easily, and he started to swim out. He pushed beyond the point where the water began to crest into the roiling waves, and on to where he could feel the greater depth beneath him. He turned, treading water, and felt himself lifting and falling with the swell. He looked back to the shore. Carrie was sitting on the beach, looking out at him. He half expected her to wave, but she didn't. He wondered if she was crying yet. He hoped so.

Tim remembered how his mother used to wait for him, ready with a towel, when he was little. The sea probably hadn't been full of shit then. He thought about Vera and her sister, who hadn't survived Auschwitz, and wondered whether they had felt each other's pain. And he thought of Mengele, who'd evaded capture and drowned in Brazil after suffering a stroke while swimming. He thought too about the stone with a hole through the middle.

As he turned and began to swim further out, he wondered whether it would have been a boy or a girl but, most of all, he wondered what his other presents would be.

Eat

In the beginning was the word – and that's when everything went wrong. Dad wrote it down on a piece of paper and killed my mum. I didn't know it for a long time, but now I think it's killing me too, and I'm not sure if I can stop it. I'm ill you see. I've been ill for a long time, and it all started with that word; it was the word that made me ill. I'm in hospital now, and they won't let me out because they think I'm going to die. They keep telling me that I have to eat, but they don't understand. They don't understand that I can't eat. Even now, when I feel so hungry, even now, when I know I have to eat, I can't.

It's my birthday today. I'm twenty-one years old, and I weigh four stone. I know it's bad, but I'm just too heavy. There's too much of me, and I shouldn't be here. If I press my hand down on my stomach I think I can feel my backbone. My hair's falling out in big clumps, and I can't see properly any more. I'm so weak I can hardly get out of bed, but I can't sleep either, because I won't eat. Theresa, one of the nurses, told me that you need so many calories just to be able to sleep. Sometimes I manage to drift off for an hour or two, when it's getting light, and the nurses are coming round with cups of tea. This morning I had a dream.

I dreamt that all the words in the world disappeared. It was night, and the moon was full, and there were blank sheets of white paper floating down from the sky, like angels, and I was one of them. At first it was wonderful, but then I could see, down below, a lake – an inky black lake. I knew that was where all the words had gone, and that I was falling, falling into it. I could see that word, the one Dad wrote, written on me, and it made me heavy. It made me fall faster and faster, and I knew I was going to end up in the lake, that the word was going to make me sink to the bottom where all the other words were. I tried to cry out. I tried to shout for Mum to rescue me, but my voice was gone.

Now I'm awake. I'm awake, and I'm holding Dad's pen, and I'm going to have to write. It feels so heavy, but I'm going to have to find my voice and write it all down or I'll never be able to eat anything ever again, and I'll die.

*

I grew up in a little village far away from anywhere, in the north of England. There was a pub, a shop, and a post office – and there was the church. St Lawrence's was a small, ancient church, where my father was the vicar. We lived in the vicarage, which stood at the far end of the overgrown churchyard. My bedroom was at the back of the house and I could see the church tower from my window. There was a little path that led to the church, through the long grass and the gravestones. Bats liked to nest in the tower, and when I lay in bed on summer evenings, listening to the church bells chime every quarter, I could see them swooping around the house.

Dad was a big man, with wiry white hair and a white beard. He had blue eyes, like a Sunday school Jesus, but his eyebrows were black, like the hair on the backs of his hands and his fingers. Sometimes, when we walked to church on a Sunday morning, I wanted to reach out and take Dad's hand, but I was always afraid he wouldn't let me. Dad spent a lot of time in his study, often with the door closed, or at the church, or visiting. I remember once seeing him in his study writing a sermon. He was sitting at his desk, writing with his pen - this pen - and I remember thinking how tiny it looked in his hand. He looked up from his writing. He looked at me for a few moments and then he got up. He walked over to the door, and without saying anything, closed it.

I don't think Mum was suited to being a vicar's wife and to all that came with it. She didn't enjoy company, and avoided visitors whenever possible. We didn't go into the village very often either. I used to play in my room, or in the garden in the summer, or sometimes I'd help Mum with the housework. Dad liked the house to be clean and tidy, and Mum was always telling me not to make a mess, and not to make too much noise, especially if Dad was working in his study. Sometimes he'd get angry and shout, or sometimes he'd just shut himself in and not come out, even at mealtimes. Once he shouted at Mum in the kitchen. I was listening at the top of the stairs. I don't know what Mum had done, but Dad told her she had no idea. He kept shouting that she 'had no idea about evil.' I heard what sounded like the noise of a chair leg scraping across the kitchen floor, and then I heard something smash. I found out later that it was the fruit bowl. I ate one of the apples that had been in the bowl. It was all bruised and brown inside.

*

Everything went wrong when I was twelve. That was the year I was confirmed in church. Dad was spending even more time than usual in his study. Sometimes whole days passed without me seeing him. Mum would knock gently at the door and call his name, but he'd ignore her. She'd sometimes write little notes to him and slot them under the door. He stopped eating with us, and Mum started to leave sandwiches for him on the table in the hall, outside his study. He often left these, so she'd take them and throw them into the compost bin in the kitchen. He kept up to his parish duties, though, paying his pastoral visits three or four afternoons a week, attending meetings in the evenings and holding the Sunday services, of course. I'd see him striding across the back garden towards the church, wearing his big black cloak.

Because I was being confirmed, I had to start attending weekly classes with some of the other children from the village. We were going to be confirmed at a special evensong service on Easter Sunday. The first class was strange, because it was in Dad's study and it felt like I shouldn't be there. The room had a tall bay window which overlooked the front garden, and a gravelled forecourt and driveway. But there was a large beech tree to the right, which meant it was always much darker than any of the other rooms in the house. Dad's desk was by the window, and there were books on shelves all round the walls. There was a leather sofa, and above the fireplace a picture of Jesus on a Galilean hillside, surrounded by little children. There was a standard lamp in the corner which was always on. We sat on wooden chairs from the church, in a semicircle round the desk. On one side of the desk there was a lamp, and on the other a neat pile of books. In the centre, there was a blank sheet of paper with Dad's pen on it. Dad talked about how God showed himself to us through Jesus, and how Jesus had come to rescue us, and how by making our confirmation promises and taking the sacrament we'd be saved and become part of the body of Christ forever.

At the last class, Dad opened a copy of a children's Bible, and showed us a picture of the virgin Mary, and asked everyone if they thought she looked like me. One or two of the other children nodded awkwardly, but none of them said anything. Dad picked up his pen and unscrewed the lid, as if he was about to write something on the sheet of paper, but he didn't. He brought the class to a close, saying that we were very fortunate to be confirmed at such a special time of the year. He looked at me as he spoke, 'Now the queen of seasons, bright with the day of splendour, with the royal feast of feasts, comes its joy to render.'

*

The Thursday before my confirmation was Maundy Thursday, the day when Jesus and the disciples ate their last supper together. Mum said that we'd be remembering it by having a special supper of our own, and that Dad would be joining us. She'd bought me a white dress, and some beautiful white satin slippers with ribbon bows on them. When I tried on the dress, she said I looked like an angel. I wanted to wear my new clothes for our special supper, but Mum said they were only for my confirmation. In the end she said I could wear the slippers if I wanted, since it was a special occasion. They pinched my toes, but I didn't care because they were so beautiful. When Dad came into the dining room, I tried to make sure that he could see the new slippers, but he didn't notice them, or if he did he didn't say so.

Dad had brought a bowl of water and a hand towel with him, and he put these on the sideboard. We all sat down together, and he read from the Bible about how Jesus had washed the disciples' feet. Then he got up and took the bowl of water and the towel from the sideboard. He put them down beside me, then knelt down and removed my new satin slippers. He dipped the corner of the towel into the water and started to wash my feet gently. The water was warm. He washed them one at a time, and then he dried them with the dry part of the towel. It felt nice, but I could see that Mum was uncomfortable. She sat watching us stiffly, her hands laced together, waiting.

When he'd finished, Dad picked up the bowl of water and looked at Mum. I thought he was going to wash her feet too, but she folded her legs under her chair. Dad stood up and put the bowl and the towel back on the sideboard, and then he sat down. He said a prayer, broke the bread and poured some wine for himself and Mum. Mum had grilled some fish, which we had with potatoes and some broad beans that she'd grown in the garden the previous summer and frozen. Nobody spoke, but my knife and fork kept making scraping noises on the plate. I didn't enjoy the food. I couldn't seem to swallow properly. I kept looking down at my naked feet and thinking I should put my slippers back on.

*

We went to church on Easter morning. Dad's sermon was about Jesus spending forty days and nights in the wilderness, being tempted by the devil. He told us about Jesus having nothing to eat, and how hungry He must have been when the devil tempted Him to turn the stones into bread. He said that Jesus was stronger than the devil, and that even though we were all weak and sinful, we should remember Jesus's words – 'Man shall not live by bread alone' – and take strength from them when the devil tempted us. He talked about the confirmation service that was going to happen that evening. He said that confirmation would help to make us stronger, and that if we let Jesus into our hearts, God would send His angels to protect us. And then we sang.

Glorious angels downward thronging
Hail the Lord of all the skies;
Heaven, with joy and holy longing
For the Word Incarnate, cries,
"Sun and stars and earth rejoice!
Christ is risen again!
All creation find a voice;
He o'er all shall reign."

At the end of the service everyone was fussing, and Mrs Herbert said I was a lucky girl. 'I think it's lovely, your own father giving you your first communion. You're not a little girl any more, my dear. And such a fine man.' Mrs Herbert was very old, and there was something wrong with one of her eyes, which always seemed swollen, and was almost completely closed. She kissed me on the cheek. She had a moustache, and I could smell the thick white face powder she wore. 'I hope you've got a nice new frock. Oh yes, you'll be all grown up now.'

When we got home, Mum gave me a big chocolate Easter egg. We put it on a shelf in the kitchen, and she said I could have some of it after the confirmation service. In the afternoon I went back to the church with her, to help her arrange some special little bouquets of flowers for all the children being confirmed. I put out the service books and trimmed the flower stalks, and then Mum told me to go out and enjoy the sunshine while she finished.

It was a hot day, so I sat on the bench outside the vestry door for a bit and then I walked through the graveyard and looked at the names on the old gravestones. I kept to the dusty little path that led back to the vicarage, because Mum said the long grass wasn't safe. We'd seen an adder a couple of weeks before, slithering through the orchid grass, and Dad had come out and killed it with a spade. After a while I went back into the church. Mum was having a rest in one of the pews. She said she liked to sit quietly when no one was around, because it was peaceful. She held my hand in hers, and we both looked towards the altar at the front of the church. She said that sometimes, when she sat there in the evenings, the bats from the tower would come out, and fly about, high up in the chancel and the nave. She asked me if I was looking forward to the service, and I said I was. She said that she was glad, and that I'd look beautiful in my new dress. She said everything would be all right. As we left, she showed me one of the pew ends in the north aisle. It was decorated with a carving of a bull with a man's head.

After tea Mum did my hair for me and helped me into my new dress, and then we went over to the church. As we walked through the churchyard, the bells started to ring out, and mum smiled at me and said that it was a joyful sound for a joyful occasion. I had to stand at the front of the church with the other children and answer the questions that Dad asked us. 'Are you ready with your own mouth and from your own heart to affirm your faith in Jesus Christ?' We replied together that we were, just as we'd rehearsed it. Then Dad asked us if we rejected the devil and renounced evil, and if we repented of our sins and accepted Jesus as our Lord. He laid his hands on each of us in turn. And as I knelt at the altar, Dad put the wafer into my mouth and pressed it down onto my tongue. It stuck there, and at first I couldn't work it loose. It tasted sort of mouldy, and made me think of our compost bin. It started to dissolve into a hard pellet, but when I tried to swallow it, it got stuck in my throat. I thought I was going to be sick. Then Dad lifted the big cup of wine to my lips so I could take a sip. It washed what was left of the wafer down, but I didn't like the taste of the wine either because it was sour, like vinegar. It made me feel strange, eating the bread and drinking the wine, eating the body and drinking the blood of Jesus. As if He was inside of me now and would know everything about me. As if He would see everything I ever did, and hear every thought.

*

A few days after the confirmation service, we went on holiday. We stayed in a little village in Yorkshire, just outside Whitby. One day we went into Whitby and visited the old abbey and St Mary's church. We had to climb lots of steps to get to the abbey, and at the top there was a wonderful view of the town and the harbour below. We went to the museum, where there were glass cases filled with fossils of ancient sea creatures, jewellery made from local jet, dolls, toys and model ships. Mum showed me the Hand of Glory, the mummified hand of an executed criminal, which was kept in a wooden case. She said that it was a kind of lantern, and that the fingertips used to be lit like candles. It was supposed to have special powers, and was said to be used by burglars to stop householders from waking.

Our cottage had a lovely garden from which we could see the sea. We went for long walks along the beach, and after tea, if it wasn't too cold, we'd sit out and watch the sun go down and the tide going out. One evening, we saw the moon, pale and full and high in the cloudless sky above the bay. Later, when it was dark, I looked out of my bedroom window and saw that it had sunk right down to the cliff tops. It was so big and bright, and it made me think of the communion wafer. Beneath it, a great ribbon of moonlight stretched across the water.

We got home the day before I had to go back to school. I didn't feel well. I had stomach pains. Dad said I needed to have a bath and go to bed early because it was a school day tomorrow. Mum said she was going to make us some boiled eggs and toast for tea. I went upstairs to run a bath. I locked the bathroom door, took off my clothes and got into the water. I washed my hair, and then I took the sponge and a bar of soap and started to wash my body. Then I slid down into the water. I felt tired, bloated and heavy. When I looked at myself in the water, I sensed that something wasn't right with my body. I got out of the bath and stood in front of the mirror. My body looked all wrong, and as I stared at it I felt frightened, because it just didn't look like me standing there.

That night, when I was lying in bed, I heard Dad shouting at Mum downstairs. After a while they came up to bed, and I could hear them talking in their room. I crept out onto the landing. I could see Dad lying on the bed, cradled in Mum's arms like a baby. He was crying, and Mum was holding him and stroking his head. She was rocking him in her arms and staring up at the ceiling.

*

The next day I still didn't feel very well, but I didn't say anything about it to Mum. She made me some toast for breakfast, but I said I couldn't eat anything. I walked through the village to the bus stop and waited with some of the other children for the school bus to come. It was windy, but not cold, and the tall poplar trees opposite the bus stop were bending and thrashing, making a sound like a rough sea. My stomach pains got worse as the morning went on. In English we were set a writing exercise. English was my favourite lesson. I wrote about the day we'd spent in Whitby on our holiday. When I told my teacher, Mrs Curtis, what I was writing about, she asked me if I'd ever read the book *Dracula*, but I hadn't. She said that the author, Bram Stoker, had been inspired by a visit to Whitby, and by the story of a local shipwreck. The ship was called the *Dimitry of Narva*, and in the book it brings Dracula to Whitby from his home in Transylvania. I told Mrs Curtis I wasn't feeling well, and she said that I should come back and see her after lunch if my stomach ache hadn't gone.

At lunchtime I didn't feel any better. I went into the field at the back of the school playground. It was common land, and there were always three or four horses tethered there. There was a wooden bench, and I liked to sit there and watch the horses, and be on my own. It was still windy, and the sky was heavy with clouds, as if it might rain. I walked across to the bench and sat down. One of the horses was straining at its tether as if it wanted to get free and find shelter. As I sat there I felt a wetness in my pants, and when I looked there was a brown stain. I went back into school, and Mrs Curtis helped me. She said that she'd give Mum a call and that I could go home if I wanted, but I said it didn't matter and that I'd carry on with my lessons.

*

When I got home later that afternoon the back door was open, but Mum wasn't in the kitchen and the house was quiet. I looked around to see if she was in the living room or the dining room, but she wasn't. I noticed that Dad's study door was ajar, and so I crept across the hall and looked inside. The standard lamp and the desk lamp were switched on, but Dad wasn't there. I turned and listened for voices upstairs, but everything was still and silent. I pushed gently at the door, half expecting it to creak, but it didn't, and I stepped inside. The study looked just as it had when we were taking our confirmation classes. As I edged into the room, I ran my finger along one of the shelves of books. There were so many of them. I wondered how anyone could have managed to read so many books. I tiptoed across the room to the mantelpiece, in the centre of which was a small crucifix. There was also a Bible, and a copy of the *Book of Common Prayer*. I looked up at the picture of Jesus with the children. They all seemed to look ill, with pale faces and dark rings under their eyes, but maybe it was just the light in the room.

I went over to Dad's desk. I wanted to sit in his chair, but I was too afraid to. It was a wooden chair, with a leather studded seat and solid wooden arms, and it spun round. I stood beside it and held onto one of the arms. I looked down, and there on the desk was another piece of paper, with Dad's pen on top of it like a paperweight. Except that the piece of paper wasn't blank this time. There was one word written in big capital letters at the top of the page: EAT. It had been written by Dad, with his ink pen. I looked at the word, and the more I looked, the stranger it seemed to be, until I didn't recognise it any more, or know what it meant. I couldn't understand what it was doing there on its own, or why Dad had written it. As I stood there, I suddenly felt that someone was watching me, and when I looked up, Dad was standing by the door. I gasped and jumped back from the desk. He stepped into the room and slowly came towards me. He moved round the desk, touched my hand, and sat down. He picked up his pen, took off the lid and turned to look at me. He pointed to the word with the nib of his pen and said that he'd been thinking about it for some time. He asked me what I thought that word might mean, what it made me think of. It made me think of the communion, and Jesus's words to his disciples, 'Take, eat: this is my body, which is broken for you: do this in remembrance of me.' But I couldn't speak. I just stood there, waiting.

*

It's later. It's dark outside, and something is wrong. Mum picks up the car keys from the table in the hall and opens the front door. She holds my hand tightly as we crunch quickly across the gravel and get into the car. I can see the moon tangled up in the branches of the beech tree. I don't understand why, but Mum is holding Dad's pen in her other hand. I don't know where we're going, but I can tell that Mum is upset. Something is very wrong. Mum is crying, and I think she must be angry with me. It must be me. I must have done something wrong. We don't speak. Mum starts the engine and grinds the car into gear. The wheels spin and spit gravel as we drive through the gateway and out onto the lane. We pass through the village. The headlamps light up the road, and Mum's driving fast – too fast. Soon we're out of the village and into the countryside, and I can see the road twisting and turning in front of us. I can see the moon over the black fells. Mum looks directly ahead, occasionally checking the rear-view mirror. She doesn't look at me, or say anything. I can feel that I'm gripping the car seat. I'm tense all over, and I have a pain in my stomach, and I want to be able to say something, or do something, that will stop this.

We're going really fast now. I can hear the drumming sound of the tyres on the road and the noise of the engine. Mum's gripping the steering wheel, and her hands are white in the moonlight. She's still holding Dad's pen, wedging it between her right hand and the wheel. The numbers on the speed dial are glowing, and the needle is at seventy. Suddenly, Mum turns the wheel, and the tyres start to screech, and there are more headlamps. And there's a van. It's coming straight towards us. Its headlights fill the windscreen. There's more screeching, then a horn, then the crash of metal on metal, scraping, sparks and shattering glass. Mum's not holding the wheel any more. Her hands are up to her face, and she's not holding Dad's pen any more, either. The car is smashing through a fence, hurtling upwards. The windscreen is full of stars. The world is turning. The car is in the air. It's flying. No, falling. Falling into something darker than the night. It's falling into a black lake glittering with darkness, and it's swallowed whole. Everything is black. Everything is cold. The car is twisting, slowly sinking. Up is down and down is up, and I'm struggling, but then floating, weightless. My feet kick against the open car door and I feel something touch my face. I grab it and hold on. It's Dad's pen, and the freezing water is churning in my ears and pouring into my mouth, and everything's black. I'm coming up, but I don't know where Mum is.

*

Every time I look in the mirror I remember, and I wish I could step into it and stop being me. I think about Mum. I see her in the lake, in the blackness at the bottom of the lake where no one can find her, and I wish no one could find me either, that I could disappear. I think of Dad, too. He comes to visit me sometimes, but it makes me anxious when he's here. He's not well either. He

74

had to retire due to poor health and now lives in a respite home for clergy. I think he knows what I'm thinking about – about that word, and how it got written on each of us, got inside us all.

Theresa will be here soon with the wheelchair. She takes me to be weighed every day. They say I can't lose any more weight because my body has eaten itself up, and the only thing left is my heart. They think my body's going to eat its own heart. I try and drink lots of water just before she comes, but I'm too weak to do even that now. She's nice, Theresa. I know she means well, and I'd like to be able to please her. She bought me one of those silvery plastic keys for my birthday. 'Key to the door', she said, and a Creme Egg. They're on my bedside cabinet. Anyway, I'm glad I've written this all down. It's made me feel better. I'm going to stop now and put this pen down, because it's heavy and I think this is the end. I don't know what's going to happen next, but I hope that one day I'll be able to eat, and that I'll be well again.

Xanadu

Raymond woke early and pulled back the covers. He stepped into his slippers, put on his dressing gown and lit a menthol cigarette, before opening the curtains and looking out across the lake. There were already signs of activity out on the water and down by the slipway: a barge mounted with a yellow jib crane about a hundred metres from the shore, circling dinghies, Land Rovers, and a small group of people unloading equipment and gesticulating towards the barge. Raymond flicked on the battered stainless-steel kettle that stood on the table by the window and tore open a sachet of coffee, pouring the grains into a china mug. The kettle boiled, and he poured the hot water into the mug. Then he sat down on the chair beside the window, and waited for Penny.

By the time Penny's bicycle turned into the driveway, Raymond had had time to smoke a second cigarette and finish his coffee. Penny looked up at the window, rang her bell and waved, the bike wobbling slightly as she did so. Raymond waved back, and smiled to himself as he noticed that she was wearing the tasselled suede coat he'd bought her for her birthday. He'd got the idea after she'd started line dancing classes at the local school. As she disappeared from view, he slipped across the hallway and into the bathroom to take his morning shower.

*

Raymond had moved into Xanadu not long after his mother had died, in early 1998. Penny had been his first visitor. She'd knocked on the door one morning, introduced herself and explained that her mother and father had once owned the house, and that she and her brother had grown up there.

Raymond had invited her in for a cup of tea and they'd chatted for an hour or so, hitting it off straight away. Penny had talked about life in the village and what the house had been like when she was small, and then Raymond had taken her on a guided tour. When they returned to the kitchen, Penny told Raymond that she had a fifteen-year old daughter, Hannah, but said that they were on their own now – that Hannah's father hadn't been around for a long time. And then Penny had cried, apologising and explaining that seeing the house after so long had brought back lots of memories.

Raymond told her about his plans to open the house as a bed and breakfast, and by the time Penny left, they'd come to an agreement that she would be part-time housekeeper; help with breakfasts and cleaning, and that sort of thing. She'd said that it would be nice to spend time in the old place again, and that the extra cash would come in handy.

It was Penny who'd given the house its name, Xanadu. 'From *Kubla Khan* – the pleasure dome? It'll give the place a touch of class,' she'd said.

*

Raymond pressed the power button on the portable CD player and stepped into the shower. He liked to listen to music when he was showering. Loud, rousing music. Last Night of the Proms sort of music, Penny called it. He smiled to himself as Elgar's 'Pomp and Circumstance' suddenly burst into life, and dipped his head under the powerful jet of hot water. The water felt good, penetrating his itchy scalp and irrigating his parched skin. He washed his hair, soaped and scrubbed himself, and wondered if Penny would remember their arrangement to go down to the lakeside.

'The whole business is gruesome,' he'd argued. 'A media circus. I mean, why do people want to see that kind of thing? It's totally beyond me.'

Penny replied that it was curiosity, and that people couldn't help themselves. Hannah said she wanted to see it because, after all, it was, 'Well, sort of history.'

Raymond shaved and dressed, smoked another cigarette and arranged his blue silk cravat carefully. He looked in the mirror and straightened his waistcoat before taking one final look out of the window and across the lake. He noticed that people were gathering by the slipway, many of them with cameras and binoculars, and that some had positioned themselves on the jetty that stretched out into the lake. If they did have to go down there, he thought, he'd make sure they were well away from that lot. 'Slime,' he whispered to himself, as he turned and left the room.

*

Raymond passed through the swing doors into the kitchen, and there was Penny, spooning coffee into the filter machine. 'Morning, sweetie.' As he collapsed into the armchair beside the Aga, she passed the morning newspaper to him and carried on buzzing round the kitchen, humming to the sound of the radio. After she'd finished making the coffee, she opened the fridge and slid out two large trays of sausages and bacon rashers. She poured oil over them and crashed them down onto the hotplates. Next were the milk and orange juice, which she poured into glass table jugs from huge plastic containers. Raymond didn't move as Penny continued to prepare the breakfasts. Occasionally he shouted out the odd headline from the newspaper over the noise of the cooking and the burble of the radio, until the sound of eggs hitting hot fat signalled that it was time for him to move.

'C'mon. Front of house, please. Get yourself out there. Knock 'em dead.'

Raymond grunted, slipped the newspaper under the cushion of the chair, picked up his notebook from beside the telephone and headed through to the morning room.

*

The morning room was dominated by a large slate fireplace. There were dried flowers in it, and above it was a framed photograph of Princess Diana. Penny kept telling Raymond that he should take it down, but he told her it was a family heirloom. In the corner of the room was a grandfather clock, which Raymond had bought at an auction but which had never worked properly. Opposite the clock stood a huge sideboard which Penny called 'the coffin', on account of its size and shape, and Raymond's having stained it black. Arranged along the top of the sideboard were small boxes of cereals, jugs of milk, yoghurts, and assorted condiments,

'Morning campers!'

This was one of the greetings from Raymond's morning repertoire. There was a snigger from Miss Armstrong, who was in her usual seat over by the window. Raymond smiled at her. Miss Armstrong was a regular, and came to Xanadu two or three times a year without fail. She'd been a nun, and had spent many years living in a Carmelite convent somewhere in Scotland. Now she seemed to spend most of her time travelling and indulging her passion for climbing mountains. She usually stayed for a week and, whatever the weather, and despite being in her eighties, would always tackle the Old Man. She was an eccentric and Raymond liked her. He always served her breakfast first. 'You look a little grey this morning, Raymond, a little like the weather,' she whispered, as he closed the window behind her. 'You should come and walk with me, you should. You look like you could do with some fresh mountain air, and some spiritual nourishment too.' She rested a fingertip on his arm and leant closer. 'Like Abraham, Moses and Jesus himself. It's where we find God, alone in the high places.'

'And what about the low places, Miss Armstrong?'

'Ah yes, well there are times when we find him there, too'.

Raymond smiled and squeezed her arm. 'Is it the usual, Miss Armstrong?'

'Milk and honey, Raymond. Milk and honey.'

Raymond nodded and moved on, weaving between the tables, clutching his note pad as he traded pleasantries with the other guests and took their orders for tea or coffee, English or continental. He made his way back towards the kitchen, noting as he did a deep ticking sound coming from the grandfather clock, which seemed to have started working again sometime since the previous morning. He also noticed, out of the corner of his eye, someone entering the morning room from the hallway behind him. He turned, and there was Evans, who nodded and sat down at the table by the kitchen door.

*

Evans had arrived late the evening before, wanting a room for just one night. He'd introduced himself and apologised for his late arrival, explaining that he'd driven up from London. He was wearing a leather jacket and a denim shirt, jeans and, much to Raymond's amusement, cowboy boots. Raymond showed him to one of the empty rooms, explained where everything was, told him what time breakfast was served and gave him a key. Evans asked Raymond if it might be possible to get a sandwich, and Raymond replied that he'd rustle something up. Evans went out to collect his things from his car, and when he returned Raymond noticed that he had a leather holdall thrown over his shoulder and was also carrying a large camera case. It was then that Raymond realised why he'd come. 'Photographer?'

Evans put down his bags and closed the front door behind him. 'Yes, that's right. Tomorrow. Down at the lake. I imagine there'll be a lot of interest?'

Raymond wedged open the fire door that led upstairs. 'Yes, of course.'

'People from abroad too, I expect?' Evans picked up one of the newspapers from the table beside the door. 'OK to take this?'

Raymond nodded. 'Of course. Yes, everyone's in quite a state about it.'

Evans slotted the newspaper under his arm and picked up his bags. 'Well, I couldn't miss this one. I used to live here, nearby. Long time ago now, of course. First time back really.'

Raymond observed that Evans, while not generally heavy built, had a paunch that meant he should have known better than to try and carry off a tight denim shirt. 'Ah, family still in the area?'

'No, not really.' Evans smiled, thanked Raymond and set off up the stairs to his room.

*

Once the breakfast rush was over, Penny sat down at the kitchen table with a magazine while Raymond cleared the tables in the morning room and loaded up the dishwasher. They made themselves fresh coffee and shared one of Raymond's menthol cigarettes. Raymond watched Penny silently turning the glossy pages of the magazine. Penny finished her coffee, put down the magazine and looked at her watch. 'So, we'd better crack on, I suppose, if we want to get down there and see it.'

Penny had remembered, of course. She stood up, emptied their coffee dregs into the sink and went over to the cleaning cupboard. She took out a large carrier box of cleaning equipment. Raymond followed her upstairs, took clean sheets from the airing cupboard and began stacking them outside each of the four guest rooms. He took the ring of master keys from the cupboard and opened the first door, where Evans had spent the night. He picked up the sheets and walked in, followed by Penny, carrying her box of cleaning equipment. The curtains were still closed, and the room was heavy with the smell of stale sweat and fresh deodorant. Penny went to clean the bathroom while Raymond swished open the curtains and pulled up the sash window to let in some fresh air. He tossed the duvet off the bed, stripped away the sheets and pillowcases, and replaced them with fresh ones before changing the duvet cover. When he'd finished, he sat on the bed and listened to Penny swilling water round the bath and flushing the toilet. He opened the drawer in the bedside cabinet, which was empty apart from the Gideon Bible, and closed it again.

'It's going to be busy down there.' Penny stepped out of the bathroom, holding the newspaper Raymond had given to Evans the evening before and pointing to the headline, 'Bluebird Back from the Deep.'

*

Penny had arranged for Hannah to call at the house at ten o'clock so that they could set off down to the lake together. They completed the rooms in record time, finishing in Raymond's favourite, which had a view of the lake almost as good as his own. 'Then reached the caverns measureless to man,' he read from the framed copy of Coleridge's poem that hung on the wall by the window. He lit another cigarette and looked down to the lake again.

The operation had been underway for several days now. A salvage platform had been erected above the site where *Bluebird* had been located. The remains of the craft had already been raised to within a couple of metres of the surface, and carefully towed inshore by the barge. Today was to be the final stage, when *Bluebird* would see the light of day again, after nearly forty years at the bottom of the lake. Activity had been steadily increasing since Raymond had first looked out of his bedroom window that morning. There were now people moving around on the barge, divers bobbing up and down in the water, struggling with yellow air hoses and fluorescent orange lift bags that had been used to help pull Bluebird up out of the mud. More people had gathered at the water's edge and the jetty was lined with photographers unpacking equipment, erecting tripods, and training their lenses on the activity out on the barge. Raymond opened the window and extinguished his cigarette on the stone sill. As he did, he noticed Hannah arriving. She was dressed in black from head to foot, just as she'd warned she would be when he'd complained that the whole business was morbid.

He smiled to himself and called out to Penny, 'A damsel, without a dulcimer. The Abyssinian maid's here.'

Penny turned off the shower so that she could hear. 'What's that?'

'The Abyssinian maid ... singing of Mount Abora.'

'Who is?'

'The Abyssinian maid is. She's here.'

*

'Morning, Dulcie.' Raymond kissed Hannah on the cheek.

'Who?' Hannah sat down in Raymond's chair, a half-eaten rasher of bacon gripped like a rose between her teeth.

82

'Oh never mind.' Raymond put on his coat and his boots while Penny boiled the kettle for a thermos of coffee.

'So, like the outfit?' Hannah lowered the rasher of bacon into her mouth, wiped her hands on a tea towel and spun round for Raymond.

'Oh yes. Yes, very grave I'm sure.'

Penny pulled on her coat and put the flask in a canvas bag. 'Right, shall we go.'

They walked down to the lake, where a crowd of fifty or sixty people had gathered to watch the salvage operation. They found a spot away from the slipway and the jetty where most of the people had congregated, and sat down on the bank. Penny took the flask of coffee from the canvas bag, along with three polystyrene cups and a Tupperware container of home-made biscuits. She unscrewed the lid of the flask and poured the coffee carefully. She handed Raymond and Hannah a cup each, then peeled the lid from the container and passed it to Raymond.

He snorted, 'Anything else in there, for goodness' sake?' and took one of the biscuits. He held out the container for Hannah, who shook her head and carried on looking out towards the barge and the divers. 'You know what we're like, don't you?' Raymond continued. 'We're like those medieval peasants who used to go and watch executions for fun. Or, no, no! We're like those paparazzi people – those gutter press photographers.'

Penny and Hannah ignored Raymond's outburst. He dipped his biscuit into his coffee and turned his attention to the crowd of onlookers who were watching the small figures moving round on the barge. He recognised one or two of the locals, but there were a lot of strangers too, mostly TV and radio people, he suspected. He noticed Evans skulking about on the bank with a camera round his neck, speaking into his mobile phone. He wondered why he wasn't on the jetty where all the other photojournalists seemed to be. Somewhere near the front, right by the water, a spotlight was being hoisted, and a small gaggle of people were gathering to listen to somebody being interviewed.

Penny rummaged in the canvas bag and pulled out a small black leather case, from which she took a pair of binoculars. Raymond laughed, and nudged Hannah, rolling his eyes. Penny looked through the binoculars, first out at the lake, and then into the crowd. 'Someone said his wife or his widow or whatever is here.

Wonder if she saw it happen?' She turned back to look across the lake at the masked divers in the water who were busily signalling to each other.

'I imagine so.' Raymond lit another cigarette and began to watch the divers. 'Hell of a job, isn't it – what they do?'

'Who?' Penny turned to look at Raymond, took the cigarette out of his fingers and drew on it deeply.

He retrieved the cigarette as Penny blew the smoke into the sharp morning air. 'Those divers out there. Down there in all that blackness and God knows what else. More than just a few bits of old *Bluebird*, I should think.'

'I suppose.' Penny adjusted the focus wheel on the bridge of the binoculars and continued to scan the water.

'Yes, I prefer the surface myself. Smooth, clear, undisturbed. I don't want to see to the bottom, thank you very bloody much.'

Hannah had picked up a handful of stones and was lobbing them into the shallow water. 'I wonder if he'll be inside it – what's-his-name?' She turned to Raymond and waited for an answer.

'Campbell. Donald Campbell.'

'Yeah. I wonder if he'll still be inside the boat, or whatever it is.'

Raymond smiled. 'A hydroplane is what it is, or was – uses the water for lift, not buoyancy.' He imagined *Bluebird's* carcass being dragged to the edge of the lake, covered in silt and weed. There'd be a sharp hiss of stale air as the cockpit was opened, and then gasps of amazement, or perhaps horror, as the hood was lifted to reveal Campbell, peering up at the crowd, his hands shielding his eyes from the sunlight, still clutching his lucky mascot, Whoppit the teddy bear, and unharmed – looking just as he had done thirty-four years before.

'So, do you remember it happening?' Hannah lobbed one last stone into the water and tucked her arm through Raymond's. Penny said she could remember it being on the news, but Raymond didn't answer. Not that he couldn't remember, of course. After all, spending a whole day with his dad was something that hadn't happened very often when he was a child.

*

The whole *Bluebird* business had made Raymond think about his childhood, and about his mum and dad. They'd lived in a semi-detached house in Salford, and Raymond's dad had been the manager of a car dealership in Manchester. He was always immaculately turned out, in beautifully tailored suits, crisp white shirts, usually a silk tie, or occasionally a cravat, and always Italian shoes. He was obsessed with cars, and speed, and rarely a month passed without a shiny new model appearing in the driveway.

'A fast car, Ray. The most exciting thing in the world. On your own, with the world speeding by like you're not part of it, like you're leaving all the ... like you're leaving it all behind. Bloody marvellous.'

Raymond's dad wasn't his real dad; he knew nothing about his biological father, who'd never been around. Whereas this dad had always been there. Or at least he'd often, rather than always, been there. Sometimes he'd be absent for just a day or two, sometimes longer. Raymond didn't think about it much, because it had always been so. He only noticed it was strange when he grew old enough to realise that this wasn't how things were in his friends' households. He missed his dad when he was gone, but nothing was ever said. He didn't ask any questions, and his mum didn't offer any explanations, and when his dad returned home, he'd simply behave as if he'd never been away. 'Hi, little man. Chips and egg?'

Sometimes, after these absences, Raymond's dad would bring him a present, and once he'd even let him take a day off school. They'd gone to the cinema to see a film called *Fantastic Voyage*, about a submarine crew who are shrunk to microscopic size and sent into someone's body to try and heal them of a brain disorder. After the film, they'd gone to Lightoaks Park and sat by the pond, watching the ducks.

Raymond's mum worked part-time in a solicitor's office. She was beautiful, and effortlessly so. Raymond never saw her adjust her hair, or apply make-up, or take anything more than a passing interest in how she looked. Yet, it was his mum whom Raymond thought of as sophisticated and stylish, not his dad, despite all his efforts. After school they'd walk to the shops, or sometimes they'd bake biscuits. They'd sit and draw together too. Raymond's mum was particularly good at portraits, and while he was busily drawing and labelling futuristic cars with retractable wings and concealed weaponry, she'd be quietly sketching him. 'It's your mouth I can never quite get, Raymond.' She'd said that time and time again.

When his dad wasn't at home, Raymond's mum would be more withdrawn than normal. Sometimes when he came downstairs at night, unable to sleep, there'd be a bottle of whiskey on the sideboard and a glass in her hand, clinking with ice cubes. But the house was always tidy, and there was always food on the table.

*

'You'd have thought it would have just disintegrated at that speed, wouldn't you? That there'd be nothing left.' Hannah stood up and took the binoculars from Penny, who was pouring herself another cup of coffee. Raymond was watching the activity on the lake. The lift bags had been deflated and the barge seemed to be moving, repositioning itself rather than heading for the shore. He wondered how long it would all take. The operation had already been underway for several hours when they'd arrived, and there was a growing sense that something would be happening soon. 'What are they going to do with it? That's what I'd like to know. Whatever's left, where are they going to put it?'

Hannah handed the binoculars back to her mother. 'Well, I suppose they'll put it in a museum or something.'

Raymond laughed, and threw a hand up to his forehead. 'A museum? He was killed in the bloody thing! Are they going to shove him in the sodding museum as well?'

'C'mon, let's walk for a bit.' Penny put the thermos, cups and container back into the bag and they set off towards the slipway. The cloud was thickening and sinking down over the fell tops, and Raymond could feel the dampness in the air and see it forming a thin mist on his coat. He didn't want to make straight for the crowd, so he led them up through the trees and towards the road, thinking they'd be able to drop down again once they'd got to the other side of the slipway. They passed a small group of latecomers who were laughing noisily as they approached, and Raymond heard one of them say something about a bluebird being no match for a duck.

Penny now led, followed by Raymond and then Hannah. Raymond watched Penny as she walked in front of him. He was so glad that they were friends, that they'd become a refuge for each other. There had barely been a day in the past three years when they'd not been together, looking after Xanadu. Guests would often mistake them for a married couple, and Raymond sometimes joked that it was about time he made an honest woman of her.

Hannah tapped Raymond on the shoulder. 'So, do you remember it happening?'

Raymond turned and stopped, as Penny walked on ahead. 'Well, you won't believe this, Hannah, but I was here.' He pointed through the trees and down to the lake. 'We saw the whole thing. Me and my dad.'

*

It was his tenth birthday, and his dad had driven them all the way to Coniston Water to see Donald Campbell attempt to beat his own water speed record in *Bluebird*. It was just after New Year, and Raymond was still on holiday from school. They'd set off the day before, as Campbell was due to take to the water shortly after dawn. Raymond's dad had booked them into a guest house. The drive had taken several hours, and it had been bitterly cold. Raymond recalled the strangeness of the motorway and the landscape, shrouded in freezing mist. They'd stopped at a service station for petrol and something to eat, and Raymond's dad had bought him sweets and comics. Back on the road, Raymond had sat and gazed out of the window, wondering about the people in the cars they passed. His dad pointed out a Bentley, and laughed as he put his foot down on the accelerator and sped past it. The driver glanced across at them as they swept by.

'See there, Ray? Look at that. Eighty. Eighty bloody miles per hour!' He tapped at the glass-fronted speedometer with his finger, pipped the horn in celebration at having successfully overtaken the Bentley and then gripped the steering wheel with both hands again. 'Stuck up bugger. Lovely car though – no question.' Eventually they left the motorway and made slower progress along winding country roads flanked by fields of sheep, until the dark Westmoreland fells began to appear and then the first, sudden expanse of water. Windermere. 'Mountains, eh, Ray? Fancy being at the top of one of them. What a view!'

There was snow on top of the Langdale Pikes, and Raymond tried to imagine what it would be like up there. How cold and still and quiet it would be, and how far he'd be able to see – maybe even as far as Salford. And he thought about how wonderful it would be to fly over the valley beneath, to glide over the snow-topped peaks and through the clouds. He'd circle effortlessly, high above the water, and then dive, skimming over the lake's perfect reflection of sky and fell and himself.

*

Penny cut down the bank towards the lake, Raymond and Hannah following 'That's pretty weird, don't you think, Ray?' said Hannah. 'You'll have experienced the whole thing, the whole cycle. All that time, with everything that's happened to you in between, *Bluebird* will have been sitting at the bottom of the lake, in the dark.'

Raymond nodded. 'Yes, I suppose so.'

When they reached the shore, they stood twenty or thirty metres away from the main body of the crowd. The air seemed colder and damper at this side of the slipway, thought Raymond, as if it was coming straight off the lake. He could feel it chilling his hands and his face, and the dampness making his hair lank. They watched as the operation on the lake continued. Penny took out her binoculars again to get a closer look. 'I think they must be pretty close now, don't you? They've been at it for hours.' The barge hadn't moved, but as they watched, two of the orange lift bags blossomed slowly back up to the surface, quickly followed by two more opposite them. There was the sound of cheering from the deck of the barge, and the people onboard gathered round where the lift bags were, looking into the water and pointing. One of them, a man in a bright blue diving suit and a blue hat, stepped off the barge onto something solid just beneath the surface of the water.

'Looks like progress, Ray?' Hannah nudged Raymond with her elbow.

'Do you think so?' Raymond ran his fingers through his damp hair and folded his arms. 'I'm not so sure. They should have just let it be. Left it where it was.'

Penny was still looking through her binoculars. 'Yes, I think that's it. I think I can see part of it sticking out of the water.'

Raymond noticed a dinghy set off from the slipway. A man in a yellow hard hat was operating the outboard motor, steering the vessel towards the barge – carrying a single passenger, a woman in dark glasses.

'Can I have a look?' Hannah put her hand on her mother's shoulder and Penny handed her the binoculars. Hannah looked out at the barge. 'Yes, it looks like it could be the tail fin, doesn't it? Maybe that's all that's left.'

They watched as the dinghy reached the barge and the man in the hard hat and the woman disembarked. The woman was approached by the man in the blue diving suit and led over to where the others were still looking down into the water, at whatever it was they'd raised from the lakebed. Raymond sat down and lit a cigarette. He pulled the collar of his coat up and lay back on the pebbles with his knees in the air. 'Oh God, can't they get on with it? Tell me when it's all over.'

*

Raymond and his dad had set out early the next morning, to find a good spot on the shore of the lake. Lots of other people were there already with their binoculars and cameras, and there was a real sense of anticipation and excitement. They watched as *Bluebird* sped across the vast emptiness of the lake, almost flying over it – a long comet's tail of white spray funnelling out in its wake. 'See, it's a hydroplane, Ray. Uses the water for lift, not buoyancy. So it's hardly in the water at all – it's skimming over the top of it. And all that spray's being forced up by the jet engine.'

Despite its name, Raymond hadn't expected *Bluebird* to be so blue. It was like a precious jewel on the dark water. He hadn't expected it to make so much noise either. The roar of its engine filled the frozen air and echoed all round the hills. When his dad told him that it was moving at over three hundred miles per hour, Raymond wondered what it would feel like to be inside the gleaming cockpit, seeing the world at that speed. How difficult it would be to see anything other than a blur of water and sky, and the hills too, closing in like waves, converging overhead and then crashing down.

As *Bluebird's* first run came to an end, Raymond's dad took a hip flask from his jacket pocket and drank from it. He passed Raymond the binoculars he'd brought, and told him to take a look. They were heavy, and it took Raymond a few moments to get a good grip, to adjust the little focus wheel and hold them steady. At first, he could see only a disc of water surrounded by blackness, but so wonderfully magnified that he could make out each tiny movement on its surface. The lake seemed close enough to reach out and touch. And then, *Bluebird* filled his vision momentarily: its snub nose, its domed cockpit, its two sponsons like a lobster's claws, each bearing a white roundel with a looping symbol that Raymond later discovered represented infinity, and the craft's K7 rating registration.

'Look, Ray! He's going again. Straight back.' As *Bluebird* turned to take its second run, Raymond handed the binoculars back

89

to his dad and watched the craft accelerating through the water, heading back into its own wash. It seemed to be moving through the water less easily, and Raymond wondered if it would stop. But it didn't. It picked up speed, moving faster and faster, so that it was difficult to see properly, and the noise of the engines grew louder, until, suddenly, it began to buck and then tilt slowly upwards. The nose lifted gracefully out of the water until *Bluebird* was almost vertical, and then it somersaulted, cartwheeling over the surface, and smashed into the lake - disappearing in a great explosion of water. It was gone.

Neither of them said a word. Raymond looked up at his dad, who scanned the lake, squinting, his hip flask poised, before exchanging stunned glances with the other onlookers. They waited as the water grew still, waited for Campbell to suddenly bob to the surface waving his arms. They waited, but they knew it was impossible. Raymond suddenly became aware of his dad gripping his hand. That had never happened before. Not once, as far as Raymond could recall. His dad had never held his hand, not until that day beside the lake.

*

As Raymond lay smoking his cigarette, he closed his eyes and found himself thinking of that moment, all those years ago, when *Bluebird* had first been lifted up out of the water. By what? - lost engine thrust, or fuel starvation, or airstream disturbance, by the minutest structural failure - by accident? It had seemed quite impossible, watching the craft rise like that, nose first into the frozen air, defying gravity - like a levitation trick. But then disappearing into the blackness. Gone. Raymond remembered his dad gripping his hand, and the look on his face, and the look on the faces of everyone who'd gathered there to watch. And waiting to be told that this wasn't a disaster, that it was perfectly normal, but knowing and feeling, as he looked around for reassurance, that it wasn't.

Raymond had recently read a piece about *Bluebird* in one of the newspapers. It had talked about Campbell's father, Malcolm, who'd been a great record-breaker himself, setting the world land and water speed records multiple times. He was lionised by the press and feted as a national hero, but was a rather distant father. Donald had worshipped him, so the article said. 'Do you think the old man would be proud?' friends often quoted him as saying. And then there were Campbell's last words from that fateful run. 'Full nose up ... pitching a bit down here ... coming through our own wash.' Raymond felt sorry for him - he'd never managed to step out of his father's shadow, continuing to seek his approval, even after his father was dead. 'Getting straightened up now, on track .... I can't see much and the water's very bad indeed.' Raymond wondered if Campbell knew - knew that it would kill him in the end. 'I'm galloping over the top ... I can't see anything ... I've got the bows out ... I'm going ...'

The article had mentioned some family dispute about whether *Bluebird* should be salvaged, and what should happen to Campbell's remains, if they were found. 'Skipper and boat stay together,' Campbell was always reputed to have said.

Yes, thought Raymond, as he opened his eyes and stared up into the blankness of the sky, skipper and boat should stay together. Let it be.

*

'Here we go Ray. It's happening.' Hannah looked down at him and pointed towards the barge. She held out her other hand to him, which he took and slowly pulled himself up. The barge had moved closer to the shore, and there was a cable stretching out towards it from a Land Rover that had been positioned at the bottom of the slipway.

'Looks like they're going to winch it in.' Penny was looking through the binoculars again, although the barge was close enough to see what was happening quite easily with the naked eye.

The barge was stationary now and the lift bags were gone. It looked to Raymond as though *Bluebird* must have been mounted on a trailer beneath the water, and the winch was being used to haul it in. The man in the blue diving suit and hat seemed to be standing on the trailer, which was moving slowly towards the slipway, the water up to his chest. Another diver was face down, monitoring what was happening beneath the surface. As they moved closer to the slipway, the tail fin that Penny and Hannah had seen earlier emerged again from the water.

'Good heavens! Look at that. The Union Jack. You can see it on the tail, clear as anything.' Penny handed the binoculars to Hannah.

'So you can. And it's still blue. After all this time, it's still blue.'

Raymond watched as the rest of *Bluebird* followed. The front end of the craft, where the sponsons and the cockpit would have been, was gone. It had been completely destroyed, leaving only a dark knot of twisted metal. The hull was battered and smeared with black mud, but still clearly recognisable – and still clearly blue. The tail fin appeared undamaged, and it looked as if a small area had been scrubbed clean to reveal the Union Jack. As the whole of *Bluebird*'s remains, and the trailer carrying it, became visible, the man in the blue diving suit smiled and waved, and the people watching clapped and cheered.

Raymond imagined how Campbell might have smiled and waved, and how they might all have clapped and cheered him, if things had worked out differently on that cold January morning. 'It looks like some great sea creature that's been hunted down, doesn't it? Poor thing.'

*

That night, Raymond and his dad had gone to a local pub and sat in a corner of the bar. His dad had drunk pints of beer and glasses of whiskey. Raymond had Coca-Cola and crisps, and read one of his comics, at the same time listening to the people at the bar talk about the accident. It was the first time Raymond had ever been in a bar, and although he was shy and embarrassed at being amongst so many grown-ups, he liked the warmth of the huge coal fire, the cosiness of the velvety flock wallpaper and the dazzling array of bottles and mirrors behind the bar. It reminded him of a church, with the aromatic cigarette smoke hanging in the air, the hushed tones of the other drinkers and the bar itself, like an altar or a grotto. Raymond's dad didn't talk much at first. He still looked shocked by the events down by the lake. 'I suppose it only takes the slightest little miscalculation for everything to go wrong. Everything looks good, and then, well, you don't notice it at first, but then suddenly it isn't. I mean, the way that thing lifted up out of the water. It was beautiful. Until it wasn't.'

When they got back to the guest house they listened to the radio and ate biscuits before settling down for the night. It seemed strange to Raymond, sharing a room with his dad, but he liked it. His dad snored and kept him awake, and as he lay there, Raymond wished that his mum could be with them. He thought about the accident, and wondered how it was possible for someone to be alive one instant, and gone the next. He imagined wading into the lake and sinking through the water right down to the bottom, where the smashed bits of *Bluebird* lay. And he imagined finding the cockpit, still intact, with Campbell inside, wearing his helmet and his life jacket and clutching Whoppit, the teddy bear that his dad had told him about. He imagined pulling at the domed cockpit until it opened, and Campbell opening his eyes, smiling and holding out his hand for him to take.

*

'That's her! I bet that's her – his wife.' Penny pointed to a woman being led gently away from the slipway. She was holding a handkerchief to her face and looked upset. 'She was a singer, it said in the paper. Married him three weeks after they met. True love.' Hannah lifted the binoculars again, and Raymond watched as people moved out of the woman's way, all except for one man, who was walking backwards ahead of her, taking her photograph. Evans.

'Would you look at that? No bloody respect.' Raymond tutted and shook his head. 'They've got to get their picture, haven't they? That's what this is all about.'

He thought about running over, pulling the camera out of Evans' hands and throwing it in the lake. Eventually, though, Evans stopped photographing the woman and turned his attention back to the remains of *Bluebird*. Raymond stood silently looking out across the lake. He thought about Evans, and about how much he disliked him, with his tight leather jacket, his denims and his idiotic cowboy boots, his air of entitlement and disregard for people's feelings.

'What a nasty piece of work. I've had about enough of this. Let's head back.' He thrust his hands into his coat pockets and started to move back to the road, Hannah handed the binoculars to Penny and followed. When they reached the bank of trees he turned round, and it was then that he noticed Penny still standing on the shore, her binoculars directed, not out towards the barge, or *Bluebird* on the slipway, but straight into the crowd. He called her, but she didn't answer, so he walked back down towards her, leaving Hannah leaning against one of the trees. 'C'mon, Pen. We're off.' He touched her arm and she lowered the binoculars but continued to look into the crowd. Raymond followed her gaze, which appeared to be locked onto Evans, who was moving slowly in their direction, speaking to someone on his mobile phone again, and laughing.

*

It was about a month after the trip to Coniston that Raymond's dad had finally left for good. At first, Raymond had thought it was just one of the usual periodic absences. His mum hadn't said anything to make him think otherwise, and it happened often enough for it not to be unusual.

One day after school, while his mum was downstairs, Raymond crept into their bedroom and opened the wardrobe where his dad kept his suits and shirts. They all seemed to be there still, which Raymond took to mean that he'd be back, as he usually was. But a few days later, while they were sitting at the kitchen table, eating breakfast and listening to the radio, Raymond found himself asking his mum where his dad was. He hadn't meant to ask the question so suddenly, bit it just came out. His mum didn't seem surprised. She looked across the table at him and shook her head. 'He's gone, Raymond. He's not going to be around. He's not going to be here any more.' And then she wept. She sobbed, and shook, and buried her face in her hands. Raymond had never seen his mum cry before, and it frightened him. He felt that same unease he'd felt after *Bluebird* crashed, at the suddenness with which someone could simply disappear. As he sat there, watching his mum cry and wondering what to do, he felt as if she was far away, out of his reach, and that he was completely alone. He stood up, and thought about putting his arm round her. 'It'll be all right, Mum. I'll look after you.' After a few minutes she stopped crying. She wiped her face and blew her nose. Then she turned to Raymond and smiled, as if nothing had happened.

'So, what shall we have for tea? Fish fingers? And some peas?'

A few weeks later Raymond checked his dad's wardrobe again, and this time all his suits and shirts were gone.

*

The day Lady Diana Spencer married Prince Charles, Raymond and his mum had decorated their living room with Union Jack bunting and hung a framed photograph of Diana over the fireplace. Raymond's mum had bought sparkling wine for them, and made little triangular sandwiches which they ate as they sat together and watched the ceremony on the television.

Raymond was now in his twenties. He'd graduated, and was working for the Council, in a department overseeing the demolition of factory sites which were being replaced with grass, and occasionally trees. He was doing well, earning enough money to have his own place but still living with his mum.

'This is irony, isn't it, Mum?'

She smiled, and took a gulp from her champagne flute, 'Don't be cynical, Raymond. Look how beautiful she is.'

'Yes, but it's a shame about him, isn't it?'

And Diana was beautiful, though Raymond would never have admitted this to his mum. She was the most beautiful woman he'd ever seen, and the whole occasion affected him in a way he could never have imagined. The two of them sat there together, watching silently as the event unfolded: Lady Diana's slow emergence from the glass coach, in her ivory taffeta and lace, the briefest glimpse of her silk slippers, the bridesmaids unfurling her vast train, the tumbling bouquet of gardenias, the trumpet fanfare as she entered the magnificent interior of St Paul's Cathedral, the solemnity of the vows, the joyful music, and the bells and cheering crowds afterwards.

Raymond's mum refilled her flute and munched on a cheese spread sandwich. 'Well, I hope they live happily ever after. That's how it's meant to be, isn't it? In the fairy tales?'

'Yes, I suppose so. Not real life though, is it?' His mum didn't respond, and Raymond wished he'd kept his mouth shut. He watched as Princess Diana and Prince Charles exited the cathedral, walking down the long stretch of carpeted steps to their open-topped carriage. He realised that his mum's affection for Diana, and her hope that she'd enjoy a fairy-tale future, was completely genuine and, to his surprise, he felt it too.

*

When they got back to Xanadu, Raymond and Penny sat in the morning room while Hannah made more coffee. Raymond was looking out of the window, conscious that Penny didn't seem herself. She hadn't taken off her coat, and she was still wearing the binoculars round her neck There were spots of rain on the window, but shafts of sunlight were beginning to break through the clouds, and Raymond watched as a rainbow suddenly swept across the sky.

'God's unbroken covenant to man, Raymond!' Miss Armstrong had come in from the hallway on her way out. She was dressed in her full walking regalia and was clutching a gnarled walking stick.

'Good heavens, Miss Armstrong! You look like you're about to tackle Everest.' Raymond smiled, glad of the interruption.

'Shouldn't that be Mount Ararat, Raymond, with that rainbow and all?' Miss Armstrong laughed, and smiled over at Penny, who'd remained silent during the exchange. She was now gazing at the grandfather clock, which had stopped again.

'No, it's the Old Man today, Raymond, as usual. Wrestling with the Old Man again.'

She looked from Raymond to Penny, smiled broadly again and turned to go, 'So, I'll be seeing you later, all being well.'

'Yes, you be careful now.'

Miss Armstrong closed the door behind her, and Raymond watched her striding down the driveway, swinging her walking stick as she went.

Raymond turned back to Penny, and sat down beside her. Penny sighed, looked away and then straight back at him. Then she went to get a cigarette from his coat pocket. She lit the cigarette and sat back down. Raymond put a hand on her shoulder and took her free hand. 'Are you all right?'

Penny nodded, smiled and squeezed his hand. 'I'm fine, Ray. It's just that sometimes ... well, you know. The past resurfaces when you don't expect it – pardon the pun.'

They sat in silence, holding hands and sharing the cigarette. Raymond looked up at the photograph of Princess Diana, and he remembered the day he'd heard about her death, about her car speeding through the Paris night and into the Pont de l'Alma tunnel, about her being pursued by paparazzi and smuggled like a fairy-tale princess into the underworld, never to return. And then he remembered the funeral. The pitiful sight of those two young boys walking in the funeral procession, their mother's coffin mounted on a gun carriage, draped in the Union Jack and bearing a wreath, not of gardenias this time, but of white lilies. He remembered the hearse making its way slowly through the applauding crowds, the road ahead of it strewn with flowers.

Penny put out the cigarette and finally removed the binoculars. 'It's too late, Ray, isn't it? That's the problem. It's always too late.'

*

That night as he lay in bed, Raymond thought about Campbell, and wondered if his remains would ever be found. He thought about his dad and wondered where he was, whether he was alive or dead, and he thought about his biological father too. He thought about his mum, who'd died only a few months after Princess Diana.

He still missed her terribly. And again he felt that unease. He hoped that Campbell's body wouldn't be found.

Miss Armstrong had once told Raymond that she believed in a bodily resurrection. 'Christ was lifted up on the cross and raised from the dead, so that we might be also. Death isn't nothingness.' She'd held up one of her hands in front of her face. 'Think of my hand, Raymond.' She'd slowly moved it from left to right, tracing its journey from the corner of one eye to the corner of the other. 'If I move my hand across my field of vision, I see it until it reaches a point at which I can no longer see it. But it hasn't passed into nothingness, into blackness, only to a place where I no longer see it.'

As Raymond felt himself drifting into sleep, he recalled his dad's binoculars and the rim of blackness surrounding the magnified image of *Bluebird* and the lake. He thought about the black depths of the lake too. He imagined Campbell, still in his blue racing suit, and Princess Diana, and Whoppit, together, smiling and happy, all of them wreathed in drifting swathes of ivory taffeta and lace. And he wondered why Penny had been so upset, and what she'd meant when she said it was too late.

Blue Spanish Eyes

Jude sat at the Formica breakfast bar and gazed vacantly at the blank sheet of paper in front of him. The occasional spot of rain found its way through the small amber skylight that was clipped open to stop the caravan from steaming up with condensation. He felt one land on his cheek, and saw another forming a tiny dark stain on the sheet of paper. He picked up the postcard that was leaning against the coffee jar and looked at it. He would have recognised Danny's handwriting anywhere – those loose rows of carefully spaced words, slanting neither left or right, and the large, rounded letters. Almost childlike. He turned the card over and looked at the picture on the front: a bear standing, poised, in a river, its great jaws open before a leaping salmon. The card was addressed to a mutual friend who had forwarded it together with a short letter to Jude, saying he might want to know that Danny was back.

Jude stood the card back up against the jar of coffee and looked down at the sheet of paper. He rolled his pen between his fingers, paused, and wrote, *Dear Danny.* He paused again, put down the pen and stood up. He sat down on the orange banquette seating by the window and looked out across the field. Mrs Ogden's pony, Tara, was standing in front of Bethesda, her head bowed and her back end to the driving rain. She had free rein of the field, but only ever seemed to walk in a circle round Bethesda, where the grass no longer grew.

*

Bethesda was a large, dilapidated old farmhouse with tiles missing from the roof, a disintegrating latticed porch, rotting window frames and grey net curtains. It belonged to Mrs Ogden, as did the caravan, which Jude had moved into not long after his mother's death. He had cared for his mother during the last few months of her life, and had taken to walking, often many miles, to get out of the house and clear his head. He had passed Bethesda one day and, seeing the caravan, had found himself knocking on the door of the house. Mrs Ogden had answered, peering at him through a crack in the door. 'Hello. Sorry to bother you. I just wondered if the caravan belonged to you? I need somewhere. Somewhere to stay.'

She stared silently at him and then, after a few moments, took off the security chain and opened the door. She was frail, with pale, almost translucent skin, delicate features and eyes of bright, startling blue. Her hair was fine and pure white, but was mostly hidden beneath a tartan beret. She wore a matching scarf.

Jude took his hands out of his pockets, 'I have money. I can pay.'

Mrs Ogden smiled, and pointed to a framed photograph on a table inside the hallway. 'My husband. Larry. We used to take the caravan up to the borders. Happy times. You pay what you can, dear. Post something through. When you can.'

Jude looked over at the photograph and nodded. He thanked her, and said that if there was anything he could do to help, any errands, or work he could do round the place, to let him know. As she closed the door, he caught a sharp tang of something in his nostrils, carried on a draft of air escaping from somewhere deep inside the house.

Jude had found himself thinking of his Aunt Judith that day, as he walked away from Bethesda and past his new home, and how there was something about Mrs Ogden that reminded him of her. Maybe those startling blue eyes. Blue Spanish eyes.

*

Aunt Judith had had no family of her own. This was how Jude's mother had explained why she always accompanied them on their summer holidays. Jude and Danny had often visited her when they were growing up, and would spend the night at her house when their mother and father went out for the evening. She would sit and watch television with them, while her two Siamese cats curled up together in a ball in front of the fire. She was an amateur painter, and her pictures hung on the walls of her house: bowls of fruit, arrangements of flowers, and her cats. She had married young, an older man who had owned a pyjama factory. But he had died when Jude was only a baby. They had not had any children.

'Hello there, Jude. Did I wake you? I'm keeping watch for the fox'. It was one of their sleepovers and, having woken up in the middle of the night, Jude had not been able to get back to sleep. He had gone to the toilet, and seeing a light on downstairs, had decided to go and investigate. Aunt Judith was sitting in the dining room. She was wearing her dressing gown and slippers, and was sitting by the French windows, which were ajar. She was smoking a cigarette, and the cool night air carried the smell of the smoke towards Jude, now standing by the door that led into the hallway. 'He's very determined. I don't know how he manages to get in, but he does. And when he does, well, he does a lot of damage. The poor chickens don't stand a chance.'

Aunt Judith kept chickens at the bottom of her garden, in a large wooden coop. It was a ramshackle old thing that stood on stilts, with a small rectangular door that could be slid open and shut and a ramp that the chickens used to go in and out. Several of the chickens had been taken by the fox. Aunt Judith gestured for Jude to sit down on the chair opposite her.

'It's a nuisance, but I suppose he's just doing what he has to. To survive. They live in little families, you know. They're called skulks. A skulk of foxes. He's providing for his family.' She talked about the chickens, and told Jude that when they were children, she and his mother had kept a chicken in their back yard. She said that his mother had found the chicken out in the street, and that it was skin and bone, with a deformed foot which made it hard for it to walk. She described how his mother had nursed the chicken back to health, hand feeding it scraps from the kitchen.

They must have sat there for over an hour. Aunt Judith did most of the talking. They spent some of the time sitting quietly too, looking out into the darkness and waiting for any sign of the fox approaching, any disturbance down at the coop. Eventually, Aunt Judith said that they should go back to bed. 'We don't want your mother thinking you've been up half the night.'

She emptied her ashtray into a plant pot outside, closed the French windows and locked them with a little gold key. As they left the dining room, she asked Jude about his mother. 'Is your mother happy, Jude? I mean, do you think she's happy? Does she laugh, sometimes?' Jude nodded and said that yes, she laughed. 'That's good.' Aunt Judith paused as they climbed the stairs. 'You must be good for her. It will make her happy if you're good.'

*

Jude gave up on his letter. He put on his waterproof jacket, opened the door and stepped out into the warm rain. It felt good to be outside in the fresh air after being shut up in the caravan all morning. He skirted round the seaside windbreaker that was pitched in front of the caravan to hide his rubbish bags, and set off across the field. He made the same journey most days, to Ben's garage, where he bought bread and milk, and sometimes eggs. He collected his mail from the garage too. Ben let him use it as a care of address, since Jude didn't want to impose on Mrs Ogden any further.

There was something bleak but beautiful in the flatness of the landscape, the great patchwork of open fields, the unnaturalness of the concrete cooling towers, and the motorway slicing through it all. Jude watched the cars in the distance, and listened to the drone and hiss of the traffic on the wet surface of the road. He noticed how much taller the grass had grown, without the cattle there to graze it, and the thick sprays of buttercups and daisies that now stretched down towards the road. The cows had been culled following a recent outbreak of foot-and-mouth at Tranby's farm. Jude recalled watching one of the pyres burn, and the dense columns of acrid black smoke rise into the pale evening sky. 'Biblical. Like a bloody plague! I've half a mind to paint a cross on the door.' This was how Ben had described it.

Jude wondered how the garage survived. There were just two pumps on the forecourt, and the small cabin which stocked motor oil, screenwash, bread, milk and sweets. Ben lived in the bungalow next door, and kept two sheep in a paddock behind it. He called them Lost and Found.

'Morning, Jude. How you doing?'

'Morning, Ben. Good. How about you?' Jude removed his hood and unzipped his jacket.

'So-so. Tired. Not been sleeping the last couple of nights.' Ben scratched at his stubbly chin. 'The smoke started it. All that bloody smoke.'

Jude picked up a loaf of bread and a carton of milk. He took out his wallet and started to dig in the purse section for change. 'Yeah, it's been bad, hasn't it?' He counted out the right change and handed it to Ben.

'Too right. And they're still here. The MAFF, or whoever the hell they are. Snooping about. It's the sheep I'm worried about now.' A bleating sound came from the paddock.

Jude took the shopping from the counter and pulled his hood back up. 'Yeah, it's bad. Really bad, Ben. Any post today?'

Ben dropped Jude's coins into the till. 'Nothing today, Jude.'

Jude nodded, and moved towards the door. 'Thanks, Ben. See you soon.'

'Take care, Jude.'

When he got back to the caravan, Jude hung up his jacket, dried his hair with a towel and then sat back down at the breakfast bar and stared blankly at the two words he had written. It was nearly five years since Danny had left for America. They had exchanged a few letters at first, but then one of Jude's had been returned with the words *Gone Away* scrawled across the envelope.

He scrunched the sheet of paper into a ball and threw it into the sink, took a fresh sheet and began to write.

'Danny, I hear you're back. I don't know if you want to be in touch, but in case you do, here's a c/o address where you can contact me. Jude.'

He added Ben's address and folded the paper. He placed it in an envelope and copied Danny's address from the postcard. Then he sat and looked at the sealed envelope. He felt a swell of mild panic as he imagined slotting it into the darkness of the letterbox. He left it on the breakfast bar and went over to the window. The rain was easing. Tara was disappearing behind the house.

The following day he walked into the village and posted the envelope.

*

It was the first time they had flown on an aeroplane or been abroad. Jude was twelve, Danny fourteen and their destination, Palma de Mallorca. They had stayed near the marina, which was surrounded by dazzling white hotels, pavement cafés and restaurants. Jude had barely recognised Aunt Judith as she appeared in the hotel lobby on that first morning wearing a floral tea dress, Polaroid sunglasses and a wide-brimmed raffia sun hat. His father was also transformed, in an open-necked, short-sleeved check shirt, cream cotton trousers and tan leather sandals. Only his mother had seemed ill at ease. She wore the same woollen cardigan she often did at home, and even a pair of tights as they ventured out into the heat. His father had teased her all morning, until eventually she had slipped into the bathroom in a café and removed them. 'Good God, Monica! You need to get some sun on them now, those legs of yours. Like a pair of milk bottles!'

They hired a car, and set off early each day, to 'see the sites' as Jude's father put it, while it was still cool. They explored the old town, wandering through its narrow streets, and climbed the steps up to the Royal Palace of La Almudaina. They visited the Castell de Bellver, where Jude, Danny and their mother sat in the cool of the gardens and looked out over the Bay of Palma while their father and Aunt Judith looked round the museum inside. It was there that they saw snakeskins hanging from the pine trees, and a gardener told them that the island was full of horseshoe snakes that had come with the olive trees brought from the mainland.

In the afternoons, they would sit by the pool at the hotel, and swim. Their father bought a beach ball which he and Aunt Judith would throw to each other from opposite ends of the pool, with Jude and Danny in between trying to intercept it. Sometimes they would take a trip to one of the local beaches. Their favourite was the Calo Des Moro. It was a hidden cove, with warm white sands and crystal turquoise water, reached by a long, rugged pathway down from the cliff tops. There were rocky outcrops in the water that Jude and Danny swam out to, and they explored the dark caves where the cliffs reached the waterline.

On the last day of the holiday, they went to the huge sandstone Cathedral of Santa Maria. It was one of the most beautiful buildings that Jude had ever seen. Above the altar, the morning sun poured in through the great rose window, illuminating the nave and the slender stone columns, ringed with candelabra, which soared up to the vaulted ceiling above. Jude wondered how it didn't collapse, and Aunt Judith told him about the flying buttresses outside that helped to hold it in place. Jude's mother sat in one of the carved wooden pews, crossed herself and gazed up at the rose window and the massive wrought-iron crown of thorns that hung beneath it.

They had seafood stew for lunch at a little café overlooking the Parc de la Mar, before setting off to the Baleares Cloiseu bullring.

*

It was a clear, bright day, about a month after Jude had sent the letter to Danny. He decided to take a walk, setting off across the field with two carrots to give to Tara, who had been standing, staring at the caravan all morning. She watched him as he approached, rooting in his pocket for the carrots. Jude felt sorry for Tara. Mrs Ogden said she had been mistreated by her previous owner, and she still bore deep scars round her charcoal neck where she had once been permanently tethered. As he approached, Tara began nodding her head and flicking her tail. Jude scratched her rough, grey forehead and offered up one of the carrots. She rolled it between her soft lips and then plucked it carefully from Jude's open palm, momentarily revealing a set of long yellow teeth. Jude laughed, and patted her side. As he gave Tara the second carrot, he looked over to Bethesda and noticed that Mrs Ogden was at the window, beckoning to him. He raised his hand to acknowledge her, gave Tara another pat, and set off towards the house.

Mrs Ogden opened the front door and called out to him. 'I didn't think you'd seen me, dear.' She was holding a red Bovril mug in her hand. 'It's my kitchen, I'm afraid. A flood. Well, a pool, I suppose. Coming up out of the ground, through the floor. It seems to be getting bigger by the hour!'

'Ah, right. Shall I take a look for you?'

'Well, I don't want to trouble you.'

'It's no trouble. Just out for a walk.' Jude followed Mrs Ogden into the house. They entered the hallway that Jude had seen briefly when he had first met Mrs Ogden. It was so gloomy that it took several moments for his eyes to adjust. He noticed the framed photograph which she had pointed out to him previously, and which she now touched lightly and unconsciously as she passed it. The hallway was bigger than Jude had expected it would be. A series of prints hung unevenly on the wall, rustic scenes, one of which showed a prize bull towering over its handler who was holding it by a rope attached to a metal nose ring. Cobwebs stretched between the banister rails, and to the right of the stairway were two doors, one of which Jude assumed must be Mrs Ogden's sitting room where he often saw her at the window.

They passed into a large, bright kitchen. To the left stood a wooden table, entirely clear apart from one tin of meatballs and another of new potatoes. Opposite the table there was an old-fashioned range and, above this, a creel draped with tea towels. By the window that overlooked the field to the rear of the house was a stoneware sink, and it was in front of this, at the centre of the uneven, flagstoned floor, that a pool of murky water had formed.

'It's happened before, but it doesn't usually get this big.' Mrs Ogden bent down and tried to scoop up some of the water with the Bovril mug.

Jude examined the pool. 'Maybe there's a blocked drain, or a broken pipe or something.'

'There's supposed to be a spring somewhere deep under the house – it's built on top of it. A stagnant pond, if this stuff's anything to go by. That's why it's called Bethesda. Pilgrims used to come. There were miracles, so they say.'

'I see.' Jude touched the surface of the water with his finger. 'You could always open up as a shrine, I suppose.'

Mrs Ogden laughed and put the mug into the sink. 'Maybe I should ask Mr Tranby. He'll get one of his lads to look at it. Though he does have a lot on at the moment. I'll give him a ring.'

Jude nodded. 'Maybe you should put some towels down in the meantime, to mop it up – so you don't slip?'

'Yes, I'll do that.'

'I'm afraid I'm not much good with DIY, but I'll check your drain outside and make sure there's nothing obvious blocking it.'

Mrs Ogden shuffled past Jude and into the hallway. He followed, and at the first of the two rooms she stopped, turned the handle and pushed the door open. She called to Jude from inside. 'Come through a moment.'

*

Jude's father had insisted they see a bullfight, though his mother had only been persuaded with a promise that it would be a mock fight, and that no bulls would be killed. It was late afternoon when they arrived and entered the plaza surrounding the bullring. It was a great circular amphitheatre of imposing arches and monumental towers topped with ornamental balustrades. There was a festival atmosphere as the crowds gathered, with loud voices calling out and singing, and trumpets playing. The smell of cigarette smoke, sweat and perfume was thick in the air.

Inside, steep tiers of stone seating overlooked a perfect golden circle of sand. A red wooden barrier divided the seats from the arena, and a narrow partition provided the matadors and peons with protection from the bulls. They sat close enough to the ring itself to see the faces of the president, the matadors and their teams as they processed across the sand. The first bull was released to a fanfare of trumpets and cheers, and to a waving of handkerchiefs from the crowd.

'Isn't it wonderful? This is the real Spain,' his father called out to them above the cheers of the crowd, visibly exhilarated by the spectacle. 'Life and death and everything in between is down there!' He lit a cigarette and remained standing while everyone else sat down, until Aunt Judith gently tugged at his shirt and he sat beside her. At first, they clapped and cheered as the peons drew the bull with their large purple capes. But then the two picadors entered on horseback. They swept across the ring, and the first of the lances was plunged into the bull's great neck. They continued to watch as more lances pierced the bull's neck and shoulders. Blood was streaming down the animal's flanks, and when Jude looked up at his mother he saw that she was staring down at the wounded bull with a look of stunned incomprehension on her face.

'No, this isn't right. This is terrible,' she called across to his father, who was sitting next to Aunt Judith. 'What is this, Malcolm? It's meant to be an exhibition, isn't it? No killing?'

His father shrugged, with an air of irritation. 'I'm sorry, Monica. I didn't realise. There's not a lot of difference. Let's just enjoy it now we're here. It's a good experience for the boys.'

'There's a difference for the poor bull! No, I'm sorry. We can't stay and watch this. It's barbaric. We need to go. Now!' She stood up, taking Jude's hand so that he had no choice but to rise with her. She looked at his father and Aunt Judith, waiting for them to get to their feet. People behind began whistling, and calling for them to sit down.

'Go if you must, Monica. We'll see you outside. There's no point in us all leaving.' Jude's father frowned, edged forward in his seat and put his hands on his knees, preventing Danny from leaving. Aunt Judith remained seated, watching intently as the picadors exited the ring and the matador joined the peons for the next stage of the fight.

Jude's mother gestured to him to move down the aisle towards the exit. 'It's cruelty, plain and simple. Utterly cruel.' She had tears in her eyes.

*

Jude followed Mrs Ogden into the room, which was in darkness. She flicked on a lamp which stood on a large desk by the window. On top of the desk there was also an old-fashioned telephone and an empty wooden tray, and behind it, the wall was lined with solid oak bookshelves. There were paintings and animal skins hanging on the other walls, and glass-fronted cabinets crammed with ornaments and elaborately decorated pots, carved wooden and ivory figures and strange seedpods. In the corner by the door, there was a battered elephant's foot umbrella stand.

'They used to make those from whale's penises as well, you know.' Mrs Ogden sat at the desk and opened one of the drawers. 'Or was that golf bags?' She looked back at Jude as she rummaged through the open drawer. 'Mostly from Africa, all this.' She gestured round the room with her free hand. 'This is Larry's room.' She eventually found what she was looking for and closed the desk drawer. 'He was a collector.' She held out a small packet of photographs. 'These were taken when we got married. You can borrow them. Bring them back when you've had a look.'

'Yes, lovely. I'll do that. I've always liked old photographs.' Jude followed her back into the hallway.

At the door she thanked him, adjusted her tartan scarf and again looked towards the photograph on the table. 'We couldn't have children, you know.' She smiled. Jude wondered if he should say something, but he just smiled back at her and stepped outside. Mrs Ogden turned and went into the house, and Jude set off across the field, glad to be back outside in the fresh air again, and looking forward to his walk.

*

The crowd continued to cheer as Jude and his mother exited the bullring. They descended a long flight of stone steps and walked quickly across the deserted plaza, which was surrounded by a low stone wall studded with posts and cream metal fencing. They passed through a gate on which someone had daubed *Toros Si, toreros No!* in black paint. They continued down a narrow street with tall buildings on either side of it, eventually stopping at a little café, where they sat down at one of the street-side tables. Jude's mother told him to wait while she went inside, and a few minutes later she returned, followed by a waiter carrying a cup of coffee and a bottle of fizzy orange juice.

She didn't mention what had happened at the bullring, and they sat opposite each other in silence. Jude watched as an elderly woman passed by on the other side of the street. She was dressed from head to foot in black, a silk mantilla covering her head and shoulders. She stooped as she walked, and each stiff, tiny step looked difficult and painful. Occasionally she would stop, and lift her head slowly to look around, as if to see how far she had come, or how much further she had to go. Jude's mother turned her head to follow his gaze. Then she lifted her coffee cup, drank slowly and placed the cup carefully back onto its saucer.

'She dresses like that because she's in mourning, Jude.' She turned back and faced him. 'Sometimes, when a woman's husband dies, she'll dress like that for years, even for the rest of her life. As if life has stopped for her. I suppose it's changing now, for the younger generation.'

Jude nodded and took a sip from his orange juice. 'She looks very sad.'

'She does, doesn't she? What a shame. To be sad for so long.'

They sat at the café table and finished their drinks quietly. Jude watched the other customers and the passers-by, and wondered what would happen when the bullfight was over and they met up with his father, Aunt Judith and Danny again. When they had finished their drinks, his mother paid, and they made their way slowly back towards the bullring. They stood by the iron fence and watched as the crowds spilled out onto the plaza. It was Jude who saw them first, near the gate with the graffiti painted on it. His father saw him too, and took Danny's elbow to steer him in the right direction. Aunt Judith followed behind them. When they met, nobody spoke.

They walked through the narrow streets that occasionally opened onto little squares filled with people eating and drinking. They passed through a busy market where there was a stall selling leather goods. A man sat at a small bench, working the leather into cowboy hats, belts and bags that were displayed on tables either side of him, and hung on panels above them. Beside the man there was a pile of dry, hard strips of leather and an array of knives, punches, stamps and other tools. There was a stand of leather wrist straps and necklaces, and Jude's father bought him one of the necklaces with a bronze-coloured lion's head pendant. Later that night, Danny showed Jude the gift that their father had bought him. It was a flick knife. The handle was covered in goat's skin, and it had a little metal button on the top, which activated the blade. Jude had not seen his father buy the knife, and wondered if his mother knew about it. Danny held it in his open palm, as if he feared he might accidentally press the button and release the blade. He looked embarrassed by the gift, not sure why he had been given it, or what to do with it.

*

Jude had walked for two or three hours that morning, making the most of the fine weather. The warmth of the sun on his face, the sweet smell of honeysuckle in the hedgerows and the sound of the blackbirds and wood pigeons had left him feeling more content than he had been in a long time.

As he arrived back home, he noticed that Tranby's van was parked outside Bethesda, and that the front door of the house was open. Tara was staring suspiciously at the van. Jude was tired but quickened his pace, not wanting to be drawn into further discussion about the pool of water in Mrs Ogden's kitchen. When he reached the caravan he opened the door, which he had left unlocked, took off his boots and stepped inside. And there, sitting by the window, smoking a cigarette, was Danny. 'Howdy, pardner.'

Danny was wearing jeans and a dark blue hoodie. His hair was shorter, and he looked tanned and fit, more muscular than Jude remembered. He stood up, extinguishing his cigarette in the saucer he was using as an ashtray. 'Door was open so I came on in. The farmer gave me a lift up, showed me where to find you.'

Jude stared, unsure what to do or say. 'I didn't expect you. I mean I didn't expect you to come. Here. A letter or something, but this is ...'

'What, a letter? That would have been a bit impersonal, wouldn't it? A bit rude, after all this time?' Danny held out his hand for Jude to shake.

'Sure.' Jude laughed nervously and shook Danny's offered hand. 'I mean, it's good to see you. It's strange, but yes, it's good.'

'This is quite a place you've got here. But I thought you were the sensible one, the one who'd have the proper career and the nice place to live and all that. What happened?'

When Danny had left for America, Jude had a good job, with prospects. He had studied hard and gone into quantity surveying, was earning a decent wage and looking at buying a place of his own. But he had quickly become bored of his job, and had not formed any lasting relationship that might have made him take his career more seriously. When Aunt Judith had died, she had left both brothers money in her will. It was this that funded Danny's trip to America and enabled Jude finally to leave his job. The following summer, Jude had started doing agricultural work. It paid poorly, but he enjoyed it and Aunt Judith's money, along with his savings, meant he was able to live as comfortably as he wanted to.

'Just didn't work out. But I get by.' Jude put the kettle on the small gas hob and Danny tossed him the matches. 'So, what about you? Where are you living, and what are you doing with yourself?'

'Well, until just recently I've been in Alaska, working in a national park, a kind of nature reserve. It's called Denali.'

'Alaska! Right, that makes sense. The postcard.' Jude gestured towards the card on the breakfast bar, with the picture of the bear and the salmon. 'Is that even in America? How did you end up there?'

'I met a guy in Seattle. He worked there, so I went with him. It's a beautiful place. But cold as hell.'

'I thought you'd be back before now, to be honest. I didn't think you'd stay away.' Jude made coffee and nodded towards the door. 'Outside?'

'Sure.' Danny followed Jude. 'Well I did. I guess it was touch-and-go at first. It was a bit crazy for a while. But then everything sort of fell into place when I started working at Denali. But now ... Well, now I'm home.'

Jude was glad to be back out in the open air. He had two old deckchairs behind the windbreaker. He pulled them out and set them up to face Bethesda. Danny sat down, and Jude handed him his mug of coffee before easing himself into his own chair.

'Still, this is a nice spot, Jude, I have to say. Very nice indeed. Rural.'

Jude looked towards the house, from where Tranby and Mrs Ogden were emerging. As Tranby got into his van and drove away, Mrs Ogden noticed Jude and Danny, and waved. Jude waved back as she turned and went inside.

*

There was a pond where Jude and Danny used to fish when they were children, just a couple of miles from where they lived. It was owned by the police, presumably for the use of off-duty officers and those who had retired from the service. But Jude and Danny still fished there. They were regularly chased off, so they kept a close eye out for anyone coming across the fields or out of the woods. There was a fence round the pond, and a gate at the main entrance. A police sign on the gate announced that trespassers would be prosecuted, and that fishing was prohibited to those without a licence. Through trial and error they discovered that the evening, an hour or two before sunset, was the time they would be most likely to find the pond deserted.

It was late that same summer, the summer they had been to Mallorca. It had been a warm day, but the light was fading and there was a chill in the air, so they had agreed to cast one final time and throw in the last of their groundbait before calling it a day and heading home. As they sat on the dusty, sunbaked ground, watching the luminous tips of their floats drifting in the darkening water, Jude suddenly noticed a movement amongst the trees on the far side of the pond.

'Did you see that?' He stood up, holding his rod in one hand and pointing to the trees with the other. 'Danny,' he hissed. 'Did you see that?'

'What?' Danny got up.

'Over there, in the trees. Something moved.'

'Maybe it was a deer. I've seen them here before. They come down to drink sometimes.'

'Watch.' Jude gestured for Danny to be quiet.

As they watched, they saw a dark shape moving through the trees. It disappeared again, but then a moment later a man emerged. He had thick, black hair and a closely shaved beard, and was wearing a donkey jacket, dark trousers and heavy boots. He was moving quickly, and diagonally, away from the trees and towards the edge of the water. He had clearly seen them, and looked as though he was intending to skirt round the pond and intercept them before they had a chance to pack up and run for the gate. Jude had just enough time to register that the man was carrying something – which he took to be a truncheon – before tossing the remaining wriggling maggots into the pond and thrusting the bait tub into his rucksack. Frantically, he reeled in his line and could see, out of the corner of his eye, that Danny was doing the same. The man was moving quickly, but he had not yet broken into a run. As he got closer to them, he called out. 'You there! Stop right there, you young buggers! Don't you make me run, do you hear?'

Jude continued reeling in his line, but he knew that he would have to run soon to stand any chance of escape. In one swift action he lifted his rod and bent down to fling his rucksack over the other shoulder. As he did, he heard Danny's voice, 'Run! Move it! Now!' He realised that Danny had already moved away from the bank and was running in the direction of the gate, having calculated that he could get there before the man. Although Danny was only a matter of seconds ahead, Jude knew it was too late to follow him. He ran in the opposite direction, towards a part of the fence that was overgrown with dense rhododendron bushes, and on the other side of which was a field of wheat. He threw his rod and rucksack over the bushes and into the field. As he did so, he saw Danny leaping over the gate and into the woods, a few metres ahead of the man.

The man seemed to ignore Danny, and instead ran straight towards Jude, shouting, 'You wait there, sonny! You move and it'll be the worse for you!' For a moment, the idea of giving himself up and waiting for the man to reach him crossed Jude's mind, but almost as quickly as it had entered his head, he found himself scrambling on his belly through a narrow gap in the dense bushes, and between the fence rails to the field beyond. He could hear the man approaching, breathing heavily, his voice much closer than before as he shouted 'I'll have you, you little sod! You're not getting away from me!' Jude could feel the strike of the man's boots travelling through the hard earth, up into his thighs and the palms of his hands as he dragged himself to safety.

In those few seconds, Jude half-expected to feel the man's hand seize him by the ankle, but it didn't, and suddenly he was up on his feet. As he stooped to pick up his rod and his rucksack, he glanced down and saw the man's hand reaching through the bushes, searching for him, grasping at air. He noticed a gold ring on one of the man's fingers, and the thought of stamping on the hand flashed into his mind. But he was already moving, running as fast as he could through the wheat. He was confident that if he reached the other side of the field he would be safe. There was a ditch and a concrete drainage culvert that passed under the driveway of a nearby school and looped back to emerge at the edge of the woods. Jude and Danny had often walked through the culvert. As he ran, he kept turning his head to look back, expecting to see the man chasing him, but he didn't appear. His lungs burned and his leg muscles began to stiffen as he turned one final time before leaping down into the ditch and ducking into the darkness of the culvert.

*

'Morning, Ben. OK?'

'Mornin', Jude.' Ben held up his newspaper. 'Look at this! They're calling in the army now. They can't keep up with it. Too many beasts to kill. It's shocking. Take years to recover.'

'Yeah. Awful. Let's hope Tranby can get back on his feet. This is my brother Ben – Danny. He's been over in the US for a while, but he's back now. He's visiting. Staying with me for a few days.'

Danny held out his hand. 'Good to meet you, Ben.'

'Likewise, I'm sure.' Ben smiled, folded his paper and shook Danny's hand. 'America? Nice. Whereabouts?'

'Did some travelling, then stayed a while in Seattle, and then Alaska for the last couple of years.'

'Alaska! Out in the wilderness. Beautiful, I imagine? Cold, but beautiful.'

'For sure.'

Jude picked up bread, milk and eggs and placed them on the counter. Ben checked the price of each item and punched at the buttons of his battered old till. 'Always fancied a bit of wilderness. A cabin in the woods. You know, Davy Crockett kind of thing. King of the wild frontier and all that. Still, this is pretty close!' Ben looked round the cabin and laughed.

Danny asked Ben for cigarettes and insisted on paying for the shopping.

They headed back to the caravan, dropping down from the field behind the garage onto a dust track that led up to Tranby's farm. They crossed the track and jumped a wooden gate into another field where the cows would normally have grazed. They sat down, leaning against an old stone water trough, and looked out across the empty field. Danny smoked a cigarette, and when he had finished, dropped it over his shoulder into the trough where it was extinguished with a sharp hiss. 'Do you remember that time when we went to Spain and Dad took us to the bullfight?'

'Yes. Poor Mum. She was really upset, wasn't she?'

'It was horrific, you know. I never told you, but it was. We sat there and watched one bull after another come out to be tormented and slaughtered. And the crowd were all shouting and cheering. One of the bulls, when it died, it collapsed onto its knees, and the blood just poured out of its nostrils. You wouldn't have believed how much blood could come out of an animal. It left this trail of blood in the sand as they dragged it out. I remember Aunt Judith saying that it was their culture. Jesus. At the end they threw pesetas up into the crowd. I caught one, and she said it was good luck.'

'Do you think Dad made a mistake? Mum thought it was going to be one of those mock fights.'

'Of course he didn't. He knew what he was doing. He had no intention of going to a mock bullfight.'

Jude remembered the flick knife his father had bought Danny. He wondered if Danny still had it and, if he did, how he had managed to smuggle it through the security checks at the airports.

'You know what was going on there, don't you?' Danny turned and looked at Jude directly.

'What? What do you mean?'

'Dad and Aunt Judith. Jesus, don't tell me you never realised! When we were sitting there in that bull ring, he kept putting his arm round her and leaning in, saying things to her. It was obvious, but it was like I wasn't there. I suppose they just thought I wouldn't understand what was happening.'

Jude could feel that he was blushing. What Danny was saying had never occurred to him. 'But you never said anything?'

Danny reached into his jacket pocket, took out another cigarette, and lit it. 'Well that's how it was, wasn't it? Nobody said anything about anything. Mum, Dad, Judith ... you, and me. Don't say anything. It'll go away. And I guess it did, didn't it, in the end? Fizzled out, without anything being said. And you know what's worst of all, and kind of sad?' Danny added. 'I don't think I remember Dad ever looking as happy as he did that afternoon. I hated him, you know. I was frightened of him, but I really hated him too.'

He drew on his cigarette, shaped his mouth into an exaggerated O and eased a large smoke ring out into the still air. It drifted upwards, grew, and then began to break and fade. 'But you know what? Now I'm really not sure. I'm not sure that Dad chose to be a shit, or that anyone does. We're not free agents. We're just acted on by forces that we can't begin to understand or do anything about. Nature and nurture, and chance. People do, for good or bad, what they're capable of. Which makes you wonder why we all feel so fucking guilty all the time! So anyway, I'm trying to forgive him, if I can.'

After a few moments, Jude felt himself beginning to speak. As the words came, he heard them as if they were being spoken by somebody else. He felt their uselessness and wished he could recall them. 'I'm sorry, Danny.'

*

As he entered the culvert, Jude saw that there was a channel of dirty water clogged with leaves and twigs stretching out in front of him. He felt the dampness seeping into his shoes, and quickly adopted a wide gait to keep his feet on the dry concrete at either side of the stagnant water. He felt his rucksack scraping along the top of the culvert and so quickly removed it and clutched it close to his chest. He was still holding his fishing rod in his other hand, and he cursed it as its tip caught in the decomposing leaves and scraped along the sides of the culvert, slowing his progress.

At the midpoint between the wheat field and the woods, Jude found himself in almost complete darkness. He remembered the first time he and Danny had walked through the culvert, and how it was here that one had to hold one's nerve and press forward, until daylight became visible again. He recalled too how they had tucked their trousers into their socks, after Danny had joked that there were rats that would run up your trouser leg, given the opportunity. Eventually, a small circle of light became visible at the far end of the culvert and Jude moved quickly towards it. As he did, the fear of the man pursuing him through the darkness faded, and was replaced by the fear of him lying in wait at the exit. Jude's back, neck and shoulders ached from the unnatural stooping posture that the narrowness of the culvert necessitated. As he reached the final few metres, one of his feet slipped into the cold, filthy water and he felt it fill his shoe, splash up his legs and onto his face as he staggered towards daylight.

The light blinded Jude momentarily as he swung round to check that there was no sign of the man. Once he was sure that he was alone, he dropped the rucksack and fishing rod, stretched his arms towards the canopy of leaves above, and breathed deeply. To his left, the woods stretched back towards the pond, and he knew that Danny would have run through them when making his escape, perhaps even straight past where he was now standing. To his right, the trees thinned and were replaced by long grass and the decaying remains of a camp that had been used to house those bombed out of their homes during the war. All that was left now were the cracked concrete foundations of hastily erected huts, sections of crumbling brick wall and the odd sheet of corrugated iron, all overgrown with course grass, weeds and wild flowers. Jude picked up his rucksack and fishing rod again and headed into the camp, taking the route that he expected Danny to have taken. He moved quickly and cautiously, still aware that the man could have backtracked and followed Danny into the woods. The sun was beginning to drop down below the trees, and the sky was growing darker.

*

The day after Danny had told him about his father and Aunt Judith at the bull ring, Jude was hanging some washing out on the windbreaker when he saw Mrs Ogden waving at him from her window again. As he made his way across the field towards Bethesda, Mrs Ogden appeared at the front door, one arm shielding her eyes from the bright sunshine, the other waving weakly to Jude.

'Yoo-hoo! Yoo-hoo!' She moved forward, sidestepping a pile of logs that were stacked against the wall. Jude noticed she was still wearing her slippers.

'Morning, Mrs O! Is everything OK? How's the flood?'

'Oh yes. The waters are subsiding a little.' Mrs Ogden adjusted her tartan scarf and dabbed at her nose with a tissue. 'I just wanted to catch you to see if you'd like to come over for a cup of coffee later. You and your brother? Mr Tranby tells me your brother is visiting you. From America? How nice. Larry was American, you know. Please do come.'

Jude smiled, and replied that they would love to. Mrs Ogden nodded approvingly. 'Shall we say eleven, then?'

'Eleven it is. Elevenses!' Jude laughed and looked across the field towards the caravan. 'I'm sure Danny'd like to meet you.'

'Good. That's settled then.' Mrs Ogden raised her arm in a wave, then turned and went back inside. Jude walked back across the field to the caravan. He remembered the packet of photographs she had given him. He stopped, and felt inside his breast pocket. They were still there.

'So, this Larry, some kind of big game hunter? Kenya or somewhere like that, by the looks of it.' Danny looked at each of the photographs and then passed them to Jude. They had obviously been taken decades ago. They were black and white, smooth and papery to the touch, and curling at the edges. Most of the pictures were of a man whom Jude guessed to be Mrs Ogden's husband,

Larry. He was slight, dark and handsome, and in several of the photographs was dressed in a crisp safari outfit. In one, he was standing with a woman whom Jude could clearly see was a very young Mrs Ogden. Jude was struck by how beautiful she was, and how much younger she looked than her husband. She was smiling and looking up at Larry, who had one arm wrapped tightly round her shoulder, and in the other was cradling a rifle. Behind them lay the huge figure of a dead African elephant.

'Jesus, hard to believe this kind of thing really went on!' Danny tossed the last few photographs over to Jude.

It explained the room at Bethesda, Jude thought, as he looked through the photographs: the animal skins, the pots and the carved figures. He wondered how, and when, Mr Ogden had died.

'She has this room in the house. Like a shrine.' He pulled himself up out of the deckchair and watched as Tara appeared from behind the house. 'It's full of his stuff.' He paused, looking again at the photograph with the elephant. 'She was beautiful, wasn't she?'

Danny didn't seem to have heard Jude. 'That's one crazy little horse. Round and round and round she goes, all day long.'

Jude stepped into the caravan and took a couple of carrots from the cupboard. They could give Tara a snack on the way.

*

Mrs Ogden showed them into the sitting room. It was brighter than Jude had expected, with a surprising amount of light penetrating through the net curtains. The wallpaper looked to him like something from the 1970s, a striking, abstract design of exotic foliage that made the net curtains look as if they might be for keeping mosquitoes at bay. Beside the window was a large cage, with a white parrot sitting on a perch inside it; Jude recalled the smell that he hadn't been able to identify the first time he had met Mrs Ogden. There was an ancient leather sofa, with a matching armchair pulled in close to it. To the right of the door was a small table with cups and saucers on it, and a plate of sliced fruit cake and biscuits. Mrs Ogden gestured towards the sofa, and Danny and Jude sat down.

'Does he talk?' Danny sat forward and stared at the parrot, which seemed to Jude to be sleeping.

'Oh, he talks all right, when he feels like it. He takes everything in. He has a wonderful memory. He comes out with things from years ago that Larry taught him, and then he goes on and on and on, saying the same thing over and over again. Larry bought me a record once. 'Spanish Eyes'.'

Danny sank back into the sofa. 'Al Martino! Remember that one, Jude? Dad used to play it. Had this thing about old crooners.'

'That's it! Yes! "Blue Spanish eyes", he says, and "Adios, adios".' Mrs Ogden poked her finger in between the bars of the cage and pursed her lips into a kiss. 'Yes, you're a clever boy, aren't you?' The parrot leant forward and screeched. 'Anyway, I'll go and fetch the coffee.'

As she went off to the kitchen, Danny smiled at Jude and shook his head. Mrs Ogden returned a few minutes later with a coffee pot and a jug of milk. She placed them on the table beside the fruit cake and biscuits and invited Jude and Danny to help themselves. 'You don't mind, do you? I'm not so good on my feet these days.' She shuffled over to the armchair and fell back into it with a heavy sigh. 'You could pour one for me too, if you don't mind. Milk, no sugar.'

Danny poured coffee for everyone, and filled a plate with cake and biscuits before sitting back down. 'So, Jude was saying you had a flood.' He offered the plate to Mrs Ogden, who smiled and shook her head.

'Oh yes. A small one in the kitchen. I'll show you later. Perhaps your brother told you that it has healing properties?' She sipped noisily at her coffee.

'Erm, no, he didn't mention it.'

Jude took the packet of photographs from his coat pocket and placed them on the arm of the sofa. 'We enjoyed your pictures of Africa, Mrs Ogden. Beautiful.'

'Oh good. Yes. Larry and I were so happy there. He loved it. I was very young, you know, and it was all so exciting. He was from Massachusetts.' She leant forward and addressed Danny.

'And you've been in America, I understand?'

'Yes, that's right. Alaska, for the last couple of years.'

'Oh, my word! Alaska! Very cold, I imagine. Did you live in the wilderness? It must have been rather lonely, mustn't it? But then you can be lonely anywhere, can't you?' Mrs Ogden sank back into her chair again and sipped at her tea. 'Are you married?'

'No.' Danny looked across to Jude. 'I'm young, free and single at the moment.'

Mrs Ogden eased herself forward and put her cup down purposefully. 'Well, I recommend marriage. Life alone is a poor state. To be avoided at all costs, in my opinion. Still, you have time enough. Both of you.'

She heaved herself from her chair, and Jude stood up and took her elbow. 'Are you all right?'

'Fine. Don't fuss, dear.' She steadied herself and walked over to a cupboard in the corner of the room. 'It'll be in here somewhere. I'm sure it will. I'll put it on, shall I?'

Jude and Danny glanced at each other, and then watched Mrs Ogden as she opened the cupboard, lowered herself stiffly onto her knees and began to look along one of the shelves inside it. After a few moments she found what she was looking for. 'Yes, here it is. I knew it would be here.' She pulled out a record and lifted the lid of the cupboard, beneath which was concealed an old-fashioned gramophone player. She removed the vinyl disc from its sleeve, placed it carefully onto the turntable and flicked a switch. There was a crackling sound as the stylus landed heavily on the record, followed by an orchestral arrangement which Jude recognised instantly. He could recall the tune, but not the lyrics. Mrs Ogden swayed unsteadily, and Danny picked up the record cover while Jude listened to the words of the song. It made him think of their holiday in Mallorca, and of his father. Jude recalled him whistling the tune every morning as they descended the cool marble stairs of the hotel, and calling out, 'Adios, not goodbye', when he and Aunt Judith went to the bar for a cigarette after dinner. 'Adios, not goodbye.'

*

There was only one small building left standing in the camp. It had always been known as 'the hut'. It was a square, red brick structure, with an empty doorway and window to the front, and to the back two slots in the brickwork, like loopholes in a pillbox. Jude and Danny had occasionally sheltered from the rain there but it was far from inviting. It was dark and damp inside, and over the years the floor had become covered in a layer of debris. There were discarded cigarette packets, crushed beer cans, and the remains of pornographic magazines. Graffiti had been scratched into the brickwork with sharp stones and sometimes marker pens, and the word 'Help!' was scrawled in large black letters on the ceiling.

Jude approached the hut, continuing to watch and listen carefully for any sign that the man, or Danny, had followed him out of the woods. He stooped again, and moved slowly as he drew closer to the rear of the hut, lifting his feet over the tops of the long dry grass that had grown up against its walls. He held his breath and peered in through one of the loopholes. Inside, he could see Danny, crouched on his heels in the darkness towards the rear of the hut, his rod beside him. He was facing the door, his T-shirt pulled up, held in place by his chin, exposing his chest and stomach. In his right hand Danny was holding the goatskin flick knife that their father had bought him in the Spanish market. Jude could see that the knife was open, and he could see, too, the sharp, bright finger of the blade in the gloom. Danny was carefully moving its point across his chest and stomach, as if he were writing something there. Jude watched, not daring to move in case Danny became aware of him. Danny seemed entirely absorbed in what he was doing, looking down at himself with cold detachment as the knife did its work. Slowly, Jude moved his head back from the loophole and began to edge away from the hut. Then he turned and began to run again, away from the camp, away from the woods, towards home.

*

'Well, it was nice of you both to come. I don't often have company.' Mrs Ogden, Jude and Danny all stood looking at the pool of water in the middle of the kitchen floor. The gramophone in the sitting room was still playing 'Spanish Eyes' quietly on repeat, and the parrot was screeching 'Adios!'

'It was very kind of you to invite us.' Danny knelt down and touched the surface of the water.

'Yes. Thanks, Mrs Ogden.' Jude fastened his jacket. 'You shouldn't have gone to so much trouble.' He pointed down at the water. 'Good to see this shrinking a little too.'

Mrs Ogden reached for one of the wooden chairs, dragged it across the flagstones and sat down. 'After all that waiting, he didn't need to go down into the pool, did he?'

Jude frowned and Danny looked up, the palm of his hand now resting on the surface of the water. 'Sorry Mrs O?'

'You know. Bethesda. The paralysed chappie. He waited all that time to be lifted into the water, but he didn't need to, did he? He just needed to want to be well, and to have faith that he could walk. That he could be well.' She folded her arms and sighed. 'But then I suppose he was lucky, bumping into Jesus like that. Doesn't happen to us all, does it? Most of us have to make do with a pool, don't we? We sit at the edge of the pool waiting for someone to help us into the water. Sometimes someone comes along, and sometimes they don't. Larry used to rent a house sometimes when we visited his people. That had a pool.'

*

That night, with Danny lying next to him in the caravan, Jude could not get to sleep. He was thinking about his father again, about how little he knew of who he really was. He kept thinking about what Danny had said - that he had never seen him so happy as he had been that afternoon at the bullring, with Aunt Judith. He felt sorry for him, and for his mother, too. Danny began to snore, and Jude decided to get up. He eased himself down the bed, and clambered round the breakfast bar towards the caravan door. Seeing Danny's cigarettes and lighter, he picked them up before quietly opening the door and stepping out into the chilly night air.

He took one of the cigarettes out of the packet, lit it and looked across the moonlit field towards Bethesda. Tara was standing in front of the house. As he inhaled the smoke and felt his head grow light, he remembered another moonlit night, at the hotel in Mallorca, when he had looked down from their balcony to the swimming pool. Aunt Judith and Danny had been in the pool on their own, swimming, talking and laughing, and Jude remembered feeling jealous - terribly jealous. He had watched them for a few moments and then gone back into the apartment to sit with his mother. He remembered wondering where his father was.

When Danny and Aunt Judith had come back upstairs, Jude had ignored them and stepped back out onto the balcony. He remembered hearing the sound of voices and laughter somewhere below, and the wailing of a cat. And watching as the bats swung out of the darkness in front of him, disappearing as quickly as they came.

The Laughing Captain

'We need to get out. As soon as we can.' Mrs Clay is wearing a pair of bright yellow rubber gloves. She darts round the kitchen, clearing away bowls and plates. The radio is playing 'Jolene' by Dolly Parton. Jack yawns and smiles at Rachel, who is slumped in the chair opposite him.

'Hey, Sis! It's Dolly!' He cups his hands beneath his chest and readjusts a pair of imaginary breasts. Rachel tuts and looks away, nibbling at the corner of a piece of toast.

'C'mon, Rachel. Eat. You've hardly touched a thing. You're pale, do you know that? I don't want to be stopping anywhere on the way.'

'I'll be fine, Mum. I'm not hungry.'

Jack spreads jam on a slice of bread and looks out of the window. Tom is playing football in the garden. He's wearing his best tartan trousers and a jumper with a ship on the front - his favourite jumper. It's early, just gone eight o'clock. It's still hazy outside, and there's a thick, silvery dew on the grass. Tom dribbles the football towards the house. It leaves a dark trail through the damp grass behind him.

'He's going to get filthy out there.' Jack is pointing out of the window with his piece of bread and jam.

'Oh, for heaven's sake!' Mrs Clay pulls open the window and shouts to Tom to come inside.

Jack sniggers when Tom comes into the kitchen. His shoes and the bottoms of his trousers are caked in mud. 'Look at you, Tom. You idiot. You're filthy.'

Rachel gets up and puts her half-eaten toast in the bin. 'Why don't you shut up and leave him alone? It's ok, Mum. C'mon, Tom. Take off your shoes. I'll sort them out for you.' She leads Tom out into the porch and helps him to take off his shoes.

Jack can hear Tom telling her about the raspberry patch at the bottom of the garden. 'All the raspberry canes have fallen down. The birds are eating them – the raspberries. They're on the ground, in the mud. Big fat ones. All soft and squelchy.'

Jack remembers watching his father from his bedroom window, putting manure round the canes in spring, watering them through the summer, and cutting them back in autumn.

Rachel leads Tom back through the kitchen. His socks have slipped down to his ankles and are dangling from the end of his feet. She takes him upstairs to change his dirty trousers.

'Football mad! He's ruined the garden.' Mrs Clay finishes clearing up and turns off the radio. 'Five minutes, then we're off.' Jack remains seated and finishes his bread and jam. Mrs Clay closes the window and moves across the kitchen towards the hallway. 'It's like old times, isn't it, Jack? Going off to the seaside?'

Jack gets up and puts his plate in the sink. 'Yeah. Old times.'

As he makes his way upstairs, he hears Rachel singing in Tom's room. She has a sweet voice. He knows the song from somewhere, but he can't place it. In his own room he opens the wardrobe and takes out a cotton dressing gown and a mask. The dressing gown is dark blue, with a sort of paisley pattern. It belonged to his father. He got the mask from a jumble sale. It's made of rubber and fits over his face snugly, with holes for his eyes, nostrils and mouth. It's a dark brown colour, and it has shoulder-length black hair. It looks like something between an old man and a monkey, Jack thinks. He puts the dressing gown and the mask into his rucksack and picks up his cine camera from the bedside table. He hopes that the sea will be rough. That would be perfect for his film, he thinks.

*

Rachel and Tom are waiting in the hallway. Tom is wearing a clean pair of trousers. Rachel is carrying a small shoulder bag with a heart woven onto it. After a few moments she calls out to Mrs Clay, who is opening the curtains and straightening cushions on the sofa in the living room. 'Right, we're ready, Mum.'

'Right, we'd better get off, then.' Mrs Clay looks around as if they're forgetting something.

'Right, let's go then.' Jack brushes past Rachel, opens the front door and exits the house. He has his rucksack on his back, and is also carrying his cine camera and a beach bag that Mrs Clay has handed to him. Rachel and Tom follow. Mrs Clay picks up her handbag from the telephone table, locks the door and walks up the driveway to the garage. It's very quiet, except for the birds singing. The air is cold and the sky is blue, but already growing hazy. Jack hopes it won't get too dark and wet for filming.

They used to go to the seaside regularly – almost every weekend in the summer – and nearly always to Whitby. Jack and Rachel were small then, and Tom wasn't even born. Jack remembers the last time. His mother was pregnant with Tom. She sat in a deckchair on the beach and laughed as his father lifted her smock and rubbed sun cream onto her huge belly. He was wearing a straw Stetson and had a cigarette in his mouth, Jack remembers.

Mrs Clay reverses the car down the driveway. The exhaust spews out thick grey clouds of smoke, and Rachel and Tom cough. She never drove then, Jack thinks, as she stops the car beside them and turns off the engine. Mum never drove. It was always Dad. He feels a sudden sense of irritation with her, as she roots through her handbag looking for something.

*

Jack opens the car door and puts his cine camera in the glove compartment. He puts his rucksack and the beach bag in the boot as Rachel and Tom climb into the back of the car. Then he closes the boot and gets into the passenger seat beside his mother. He can see Rachel and Tom in the rear-view mirror. Tom is snuggling up to Rachel and she has her arm round him. Mrs Clay starts up the car again and reverses out onto the road. They drive through the estate and pull in at the parade of shops on the corner. A girl comes out of the newsagent carrying a loaf of bread. Jack knows her from school – Donna. He asked her out once, but she said no. His friends say she's never been out with a boy. She has an older brother, Rob. Jack has seen Rob and Rachel hanging around together on the estate. Once, he saw them coming out of The Anchor. He didn't say anything to Rachel, or to Mum. Jack doesn't mind Rob. Rob bought cider from the off-licence for him one time and they got talking about horror films. Rob told him that he was going to be leaving home soon, to join the navy.

'Just nip out and get me a paper will you, Jack? And some sweets?' Mrs Clay hands him some change from her purse.

'Can I go too, Mum? Can I go with Jack?' Tom grabs onto the back of Jack's seat.

'No, Tom. You stay here with us. He'll only be a minute.'

Jack goes into the shop. It's empty. The man behind the counter is drinking a mug of coffee and watching a small television. There's a children's programme on, and the man laughs to himself as Jack holds up a *Daily Mirror* and a large bag of Fruit Pastilles. When Jack gets back to the car Mrs Clay takes the sweets and hands them to Tom. 'Just one or two mind, Tom. Make sure he doesn't eat the whole bag, Rachel.' She starts the car up again and pulls out. 'Right. Now we really are off.'

Jack takes his cine camera from the glove compartment and unzips the cover. He takes the camera out and removes the lens cap. Holding the viewfinder up to his eye, he studies his mother. He zooms in on her face. He pans round and adjusts the zoom as they pass Donna cutting across the common, back towards the estate. He sees her face clearly for a just a second or two, and then blue sky. Blue sky followed by blackness as he replaces the lens cap. He wishes he hadn't asked Donna out now. It was definitely a mistake.

*

I had the dream again last night. The dream about Dad. That I was in this place, this totally dark place, and I couldn't work out where it was at first, but I knew that he was near, really close, and that I was with him. The darkness was close too, all around me, and I was curled up like a baby in a womb. I could feel these walls of blackness all around me, and I could hear the sea. I could hear the sea heaving and crashing outside. And that's when I knew I was inside him. Inside Dad. But I couldn't hear his heartbeat. All I could hear was the sea, and I knew that he wasn't alive, that we were out in the middle of the ocean, and that I was never going to get out, because he was dead. Because he was dead, and far out to sea. That's where it came from. The idea for the story. For the film. The horror film, with a creature that comes out of the sea. My horror film.

First, there'll be blue sky. That's how it'll start. The first shot. Blue sky, a shaft of blinding sunlight, and then the sea, and the beach. And Mum and Rachel and Tom, having a picnic. No one else around. Just them, on their own, by the cliffs. They'll be a long way off to begin with. Just three tiny specks on the beach, below the cliffs. But then I'll move closer. Closer, and closer again, quickly, until they fill the frame. I'll circle them, stalk them as they smile and laugh and put food into their mouths, happy and carefree. Then, back to the sea and, wading in towards the shore, out of the depths, the creature. The monster. Coming nearer and nearer. Me. I'll be the monster, born of the sea. I'll be wearing Dad's dressing gown, and the rubber mask. There'll be seaweed trailing from its hair, and from my shoulders. And from my arms and my hands. Rachel will have to work the camera for that bit.

The monster will come right up to her. I'll come right up to her, till I fill the frame, and then I'll cut back to the picnic. To Rachel's face, her eyes wide in horror, a sausage roll raised towards her gaping mouth, held frozen in mid-air. She'll point, and scream, and Mum and Tom will see it too. The monster. And they'll all get up and start running. They'll run, but the monster will follow, gaining ground. Gaining ground on Rachel, who will keep looking back, who won't watch where she's going, who will trip, lose a shoe, and fall. And then blackness.

Blue sky again. The beach, the sea, the beach again. The wrecked picnic. And a trail of torn, bloody clothing. And Rachel's severed hand. And then her eyes. One of her dead, staring eyes, before ... blue sky again.

*

'It's a stupid idea, Jack. It'll look ridiculous.' Rachel still has her arm round Tom. 'I mean, what kind of storyline is that? There's no plot or anything. And what kind of monster is it going to be? That mask just makes you look like an old chimp. A chimp coming out of the sea in a dressing gown? Terrifying!'

Tom laughs. Rachel wipes his nose with a tissue and then looks out of the window. She sees a field of bright yellow rape. 'Look, Tom. Look at that field – how yellow it is. And anyway, all those films you watch are stupid, Jack. There's nothing clever about blood and gore.'

Jack eyes Rachel in the mirror. 'What do you know, Mary bloody Poppins? You don't know anything.' Rachel doesn't respond. She looks out of the window again. They're passing an area of dense woodland now. The trees are only two or three metres from the edge of the road and are packed tightly together. They must have been deliberately planted that way, Rachel thinks, so that they can be harvested for timber, perhaps. The woods look dark and inviting. Rachel imagines that somewhere, on the other side of the trees, there's a river. A clear, bright river. She imagines floating down it on a summer afternoon, lying in a little boat with Rob beside her.

Mrs Clay gears down and then brakes sharply as they approach a bend in the road. 'I hope you two aren't going to argue all day. Otherwise we might just as well turn round and go home now.' She glances at Jack, who is gripping the edge of his seat. He says nothing. 'Well then?' The engine strains as she accelerates again.

'Anyway, we're going for a picnic, not to make some silly horror film.'

Rachel watches Tom. He's looking out of the window too. 'I feel sick. The trees. They're making me dizzy,' he says.

'Well don't look at them, then.' Rachel twists his head round and pinches his nose. He smiles at her. She registers the smallness of his hands, his mouth, his nose and his deep brown eyes. The same colour eyes they all have. 'How about I spy, Tom? C'mon, Jack. You play too.'

'Yes, go on. Let's play I spy, Jack.' Tom pushes away Rachel's arm, which is still wrapped round him, leans forward and pulls at the sleeve of Jack's jacket.

'OK, OK.' Jack rubs his thighs with the palms of his hands. 'Right then. So, I spy with my little eye, something beginning with ... S.'

Tom sits back and looks round for a few moments. 'Sky?'

'Nope.'

'Sign.' Rachel whispers the word to Tom.

Tom repeats after her. 'Sign?'

'Sign?' Jack smirks.

Tom turns and looks at Rachel. 'Sign?'

'You know. Road sign.' Rachel points as they approach a sign at the side of the road. 'Slippery surface sign, in fact!' She laughs at the alliteration.

'No, not sign. Or even slippery surface sign,' Jack replies.

Rachel and Tom pause. They look out of the window and then round the interior of the car. 'Steering wheel?' Rachel rummages in her bag.

Jack shakes his head. 'No. Not steering wheel.'

'Is it sea?' Tom looks up at Rachel and smiles.

'Oh, and where's that then, Tom? Can you see the sea already? So, c'mon, do you give up?'

'Sea!' Tom shouts. Rachel follows quickly with 'Seaweed!' And then Tom again, with 'Stromboli!' They burst into laughter.

'Yes, we give up. You're probably cheating anyway.'

'Sun! It was sun. So, I wasn't cheating. And what's stromboli?'

'Go on, Tom. Tell him.' Rachel nudges Tom.

'Pinocchio! Stromboli's the bad puppet man in Pinocchio. He buys Pinocchio from Honest John and won't let him go home. He has a scary laugh, doesn't he, Rachel?'

'Yes, he does. And what does Honest John sing, Tom?'

Tom turns to Rachel and they sing together. 'Hi-diddle-dee-dee, an actor's life for me!'

Rachel sits back and hums the song softly to herself. She remembers the music that her father used to play in the car. Old-fashioned country music. He loved John Denver. She remembers driving home from Whitby, with the sun setting behind them. A huge, burning sunset. The light fading and darkness leaking across the sky in front of them. The first pale stars. The moon, too. She remembers Jack asleep beside her and her father driving, her mother in the passenger seat, unwrapping sweets for him, putting them in his mouth as he hummed along to 'Darcy Farrow'. She remembers wishing she could sit in the front and give him sweets.

Darcy Farrow, with her sweet voice and her bright eyes and her lover, Vandy, who gave her silver rings and lacy things? They were going to marry before the first snowfall of the year, but they didn't because she fell off her pony and died. Vandy couldn't bear it, and killed himself, and they were buried side by side as the snow began to fall. Yes, a little silly, she thinks now, but she remembers listening to it in the back of the car, feeling cold and faraway, and imagining herself as Darcy Farrow, wandering through the forests and the streams with her lover, Vandy.

*

We walked across the common together, early one evening. The horses watched us. One tried to walk over to us but had to stop when it reached the full length of the rope tethering it. The sky suddenly turned dark, and you could taste the coming storm in the air. Rob said he knew where we could find shelter. As we walked across the fields, we talked. He said he liked the common, because you could walk from one end to the other without ever coming across another person. He said that sometimes he walked across it at night, and that it was the best place to see shooting stars if you lay down on the grass on a clear night. He said he sometimes pitched a tent on the common and camped out overnight. He said we should camp out together one night. On the common.

I like him a lot, but I'm not sure he feels the same way. I'm not sure he understands. I think about him all the time. I imagine what he's doing when I'm not with him. I always want to be with him. No one knows, though. I think Jack has his suspicions, but Mum doesn't know. I don't think Mum would like me seeing an older boy. Part of me wants everyone to know we're together, but I like that it's a secret, too. Rob says it's good to keep it a secret for the time being. He says it's good to have secrets. Sometimes I talk to Dad about things. I write things in my diary too. Like letters. I write letters to him. I tell him how much I miss him. I've told him about Rob, and I tell him how I'm looking after Tom for him. I can't talk to Mum. I don't want to upset her. And I can't talk to Jack. So I talk to Dad.

It started to rain. It started to rain, so we ran. We ran, and we laughed as we got wet, and then we reached an old wooden shelter. It had a sloping roof and a large doorway, but no door. It was there for the horses I suppose, but there were no horses inside. There was nothing inside. Just some dry hay on the ground. We sat with our backs against the wall looking out of the doorway. As the rain started to come down more heavily, we listened to it hammering on the roof and watched as it bounced off the backs of the horses standing out in the field. Rob said a barn owl had nested in the hut last summer. He said that owls don't build their own nests, that they'll nest anywhere that gives them shelter from the wind and the rain. Anywhere they feel safe.

Rob lit a cigarette and blew smoke rings. Then we lay down on the hay together and he kissed me.

*

'I'm hungry.' Tom has taken his seatbelt off and is leaning forward between the two front seats, one hand on Jack's shoulder and the other on his mother's.

'Tom, no! Don't ever take your seatbelt off. It's very dangerous!' Rachel pulls him back into his seat and refastens his seatbelt.

'Don't ever do that again, Tom. Do you hear?' Mrs Clay looks at him in the rear-view mirror. 'You'll go straight through that windscreen. Now you sit back.'

They're driving across open moorland. Too early for the heather, thinks Mrs Clay. 'Anyway, we're nearly there. Only a few miles now, and then you can have some food.' Tom sinks back into his seat and screws up his face with a whine, as if he's going to cry. Mrs Clay watches him in the mirror. 'Don't be a baby, Tom. *And* you've eaten all those sweets.'

'Ooh, is Tommy-wommy's little tummy-wummy all empty?' Jack turns in his seat and pokes at Tom with the newspaper.

'Don't be pathetic, Jack.' Rachel snatches the paper out of his hand.

Eventually the moorland gives way to fields and they pass houses, a shop and a caravan park. 'See if you can spot the sea now, Tom. See if you can see it first.' Mrs Clay flicks on the wipers and washes the windscreen, which is flecked and spattered with squashed insects. She knows that soon they'll see the coast, the cliffs, the abbey and a triangle of pewter-coloured sea in the distance. She thinks of how happy that view has always made her.

Tom sits up and looks out of the window. 'Can't see it. Can't see the sea.'

'Keep looking. You will.' How quickly he's grown, thinks Mrs Clay. How quickly they've all grown. On days like today, it makes her feel old. Old and tired.

'I see the sea! Look Mum, I see!' Tom points. 'Can you see it, Jack? The sea?'

'Yeah. I see it.'

'And look, Jack. The abbey, too.' Mrs Clay slows the car down so that they can take in the view. 'Do you remember the abbey? We used to go up there sometimes. All those steps.' The abbey is perched high on the cliff top above the sea and the town, a gothic ruin, a skeletal black silhouette against the empty sky.

'What's an abbey, Mum?' Tom leans forward again.

'Well, it's a bit like a church, but one where people used to live hundreds and hundreds of years ago. Monks.'

'I remember.' Rachel stretches. 'I remember the photos. That one of you, Jack, lying in that funny-shaped grave with the round bit for your head. And there was that gravestone with a skull and crossbones on it. In the churchyard next door. The one Dad showed us.'

'Oh yes. Something to do with Dracula.' Mrs Clay remembers him telling them that the skull and crossbones were used to mark the graves of those who'd taken their own lives.

'Who's Dracula, Mum?' Tom asks.

'Dracula's a story, Tom. A kind of story.'

'It's a horror story, Tom, and Dracula's a monster.' Jack turns and bares his teeth at Tom. 'He's a monster that won't die, that can't be killed – well, not easily anyway, because he's already dead. He lives in a coffin, in the dark, and he only comes out at night-time. Sometimes he's a wolf, sometimes a bat. He has lots of disguises. And do you know what he does, Tom? He drinks people's blood. He drains the life out of them so that they become sort of dead, even though they're still alive. He was probably normal once, like everyone else, but somehow he turned into this monster. It got inside him, and now he can't stop it – drinking blood.'

'All right, Jack. That's quite enough, thank you. It's just a story, Tom. Just a silly story. There are no monsters. They're only make-believe.'

It seems strange to be back in a place so familiar, after so long, thinks Mrs Clay. They'll not go up to the abbey today. They'll look around the town and walk on the beach. 'We'll park up on the west cliff, near the whalebone arch and the Captain Cook statue.'

'Who's Captain Cook, Mum?' Tom is kicking his legs against her seat.

'He was an explorer, Tom. Don't kick, there's a good boy.'

Jack turns. 'He was eaten by cannibals, Tom.'

Mrs Clay tuts. 'No he was not, Jack.'

They're silent for the last part of the journey, as they approach the outskirts of the town and pass along the streets of tall town houses towards the seafront. Mrs Clay looks at Rachel and Tom in the mirror, whispering to each other, and at Jack reading the newspaper. She worries that they'll be strangers to her one day, as they grow older.

She parks the car in a space facing out to sea. Jack, Rachel and Tom get out. Rachel holds Tom's hand. Jack takes his rucksack and the beach bag out of the boot, and then passes the bag to Rachel while he ties his shoelace. Mrs Clay sits back and closes her eyes. When she opens them again, she notices that the tide is in and the sea is rough. She can hear it, and smell it. Thick cloud is gathering and darkening overhead. She thought it might be a fine day, but it looks like rain now. She looks at herself in the mirror, takes the key from the ignition and gets out of the car. She can taste the moisture in the air, and she can feel the wind buffeting her. It's bending the tall grass flat. It won't be so bad down in the town, she thinks. There's no shelter up here. Tom and Rachel are running on ahead, towards the whalebone arch. Mrs Clay remembers the view from there, across the town and the harbour, beyond the east cliff and the abbey and out to sea. She watches the waves roll and crash, breaking along the harbour wall, pure white, and she wonders when she'll feel less tired

*

It was as if the whole world was white. White, like a blank piece of paper, so white it hurt my eyes. Outside, through the window, the hospital buildings, the surrounding fields, the roads, everything. All white. Even the sky was white. Heavy with more thick, white snow ready to fall. There was just the odd tree, with bare black branches, that stood out against all that whiteness. And inside too, of course. Inside the hospital. So much white, so much light. The crisp white sheets and gowns, the white linoleum floor, the white walls and ceiling. It felt good to be somewhere so white, so full of light. So clean and pure and safe, with Tom asleep in his little cot beside me.

I didn't want to spoil it. I didn't want to stain that beautiful white place with something so sad. So when she asked, that young nurse, I made up a story. She asked if he would be coming. She smiled, and touched my hand, and asked if he'd be coming. I told her that he was away from home, far away, but that he'd be back soon. I didn't want her to know the truth, for it to stain her. Nobody else asked, none of those who knew better. She was so kind, so beautiful, and I loved her for asking, for not knowing better, for her naivety. And later, when she'd gone, I cried into the white sheets for her, because she asked, because she didn't know that such dark things happen. I cried for her, and for Rachel and Jack. And for Tom. I cried, and I tried to remember ... the smell of cigarette smoke.

When you lose something, when you lose someone, you make up stories all the time. It never stops. But the thing that stops is telling the truth. You stop telling the truth. To protect people, to protect yourself, to cope, to not cry out. And sometimes what you've lost becomes something else, changes into something else. Something terrible. You don't tell the truth about it. You tell stories. But before you know it, the truth is hunting you down in every story you tell. Without meaning to, you cry out from some faraway place, in every story you tell. You become a victim. The truth feeds on you. It drags you under and makes everything dark.

I often wonder about that nurse. There was something about her. Her smile. Her attentiveness. The way she asked if he would be coming. And maybe it wasn't because she didn't know better,

133

*because she was naive. Maybe she wasn't afraid to invite the truth.
To sit with it, listen to it. To not run away from it.*

*

'What are these, Rachel?' Tom points to the whalebone arch overlooking the sea and the town below.

'They're whale bones, Tom. Jaw bones, I think. Ships used to sail out of Whitby to hunt whales in the arctic.'

Tom looks up at the apex of the archway where the two huge bones meet. 'Like Monstro in *Pinocchio*?'

'That's right.'

They all walk through the arch together. Tom notices a seagull standing on Captain Cook's head, looking down towards the town. It's bigger than he would have imagined a seagull to be. It looks as if it's struggling to balance, stretching out one wing and then the other. Tom notices it has a red spot on its bill and that its eyes are the same colour as the white plumage on its chest, but with a small black bead at the centre. The statue is covered in seagull droppings. 'Can I have a piggyback, Jack? My legs are tired.' Tom lets his arms hang loose at his sides, and scrapes his feet along the ground.

'Don't do that, Tom.' Mrs Clay taps him on the top of his head. 'You'll fall, and you'll ruin your shoes.' They approach a steep flight of concrete steps leading down to the town and the west pier.

'Just walk properly, you idiot. Walk like a normal person, can't you?' Jack pushes Tom towards the edge of the steps.

Rachel turns and punches Jack's shoulder. 'Don't be stupid. You nearly pushed him down the steps, Jack. What's the matter with you?' She thrusts the beach bag back into Jack's arms.

'Please!' Mrs Clay stops in her tracks. 'Please! Can we not argue?'

Rachel bends down in front of Tom. 'C'mon, Tom. Jump up. I'll give you a piggy.'

'Not on these steps, Rachel! It's dangerous. He's too heavy to carry round like that.' Mrs Clay takes Rachel's arm.

'I'll be fine, Mum. Don't worry.' Tom jumps onto Rachel's back, and she makes her way carefully down the steps. Tom watches as Jack passes them, descending quickly, two steps at a time. He rests his head on Rachel's neck and closes his eyes, glad not to have to walk any further. But he wishes that Jack had given him a piggyback.

The gulls swoop and cry overhead as they make their way down the steps, and the noise from the town below grows louder. As they reach the last flight of steps, Tom lifts his head. He looks down at the narrow entrance to the harbour. He sees the two great stone limbs of the east and west piers, the old lighthouse, and the rolling sea beyond it.

'What's that out there?' He's pointing to something in the distance, beyond the harbour walls. 'Is it a boat?'

Rachel stops to rest. She hoists Tom up, readjusts his position and follows the direction of his outstretched hand. 'Not a boat, I don't think. Maybe a buoy.'

'A boy?' Tom looks puzzled, and Mrs Clay smiles.

'Not a real boy, like you.' She spells out the word for him. 'B.U.O.Y. - a buoy. It's a thing that floats in the water and sometimes rings a bell. To keep boats away from the rocks.'

Rachel looks towards the buoy. 'Jack reckons there's a legend here that when a ship is lost, bells can be heard out at sea. It's in the book, *Dracula*, apparently.'

'What's a legend, Rachel?' Tom rests his head back on her shoulder.

'It's a story, Tom. Sort of. A story that isn't really true, but might be. Nobody's sure.'

'Is it a lie, then? If it's a lie, Jack's nose will grow.'

Rachel laughs. 'It's not a lie. It's just not exactly true.'

They set off again, down the last few steps. Tom is listening. He listens for the sound of a bell, but there's too much noise coming from the crowds of people and the amusement arcades below. He closes his eyes, and imagines that Rachel's movements as she carries him down the steps are the movements of a boat out at sea.

'Made it! Gosh, you are heavy, Tom!' Rachel lets him down and leans against the wall at the bottom of the steps, breathing heavily.

Jack joins them. 'You took your time.'

'Ha ha, Jack. Very funny. Manage with that heavy bag, did you?'

They all squat, their backs against the wall. Tom is hungry. He leans over to Jack and peers into the beach bag. 'Can we have the picnic now, Mum?'

Mrs Clay takes the bag from Jack and rests it on her lap. 'Soon, Tom. We'll go over and have a look at the harbour and the fishing boats first. Then we'll go down to the beach and find a nice spot for our picnic. We can come back up into the town later, and maybe have a look in some of the shops and get an ice cream. At least it's not so windy down here.'

Tom jumps up. 'C'mon then. Let's go and see the boats.' They all get up, and Mrs Clay leads the way. A narrow road runs the full length of the harbour. They cross at the corner, where it turns sharply up and away from the seafront. They pass a red brick building, with a stone balcony that has letters and a date carved into it. There are two large open doors to the front of the building, and Tom can see that inside there's a blue and white boat on a trailer.

'Why isn't that boat in the water, Rachel?'

'It's an old lifeboat, Tom. That's the lifeboat museum. The lifeboat goes out when people are in trouble at sea. If a boat's sinking.'

Tom watches the people sitting along the harbour wall. Some are eating fish and chips from polystyrene trays, others doughnuts or ice creams. On the opposite side of the road are the amusement arcades and the snack bars. Above the shrieking of the gulls, the gabble of conversation and the music coming from the arcades, Tom can hear a cackling, mechanical laugh. He looks around and realises that the laughter is coming from a puppet sea captain in a glass case, standing outside the entrance to one of the arcades. He thinks of Stromboli laughing at Pinocchio. The sea captain is wearing a blue and white peaked cap with a badge on the front of it, and a jacket with bright silver buttons. There's the sound of a bell, too, but he doesn't think it's coming from the buoy.

They continue along the busy pavement, weaving through groups of people walking in the opposite direction. They pass wooden shacks selling crabs, cockles and mussels, and come eventually to a sheltered part of the harbour where the fishing boats are moored. A man is calling out, inviting people to join a half-hour sea trip on a pleasure cruiser. Finding a space amid the crowds, they lean against the iron rail at the harbour's edge. Tom looks down at the fishing boats, across to the swing bridge that connects the east and west halves of the town, and up to St Mary's church, high on the east cliff. 'Can we go across the bridge later?' he asks.

'I don't see why not. I'm not sure I want to walk up all those steps to the abbey, though.'

'That's the church where the gravestone with the skull and crossbones is, Tom.' Jack takes his sunglasses from his jacket pocket and puts them on. 'I remember it now. All the gravestones are disintegrating.'

'Yes. Must be the wind and the rain, and the salt in the air, I suppose.' A sudden gust of wind whips Mrs Clay's hair across her face. She brushes it back and tries to hold it in place. Tom is remembering what Rachel said about the skull and crossbones on the gravestone, and the monster, Dracula. He wonders if Dracula is a sort of pirate. He looks over at the church again. Perhaps that's where the sound of the bell came from. The church looks like it shouldn't be there, he thinks. It looks like a haunted house, not a church.

'C'mon, let's go and have this picnic before Tom wastes away.' Mrs Clay guides him back into the flow of passers-by, her hand on his shoulder. 'Watch where you're going, Tom.'

Rachel and Jack follow. They walk back in the direction from which they came, but now they're on the other side of the road, where the amusement arcades are. The air is full of the smell of chips and frying onions. When they reach the puppet sea captain in the glass case, Tom stops and looks at him. The puppet is still and silent, leaning awkwardly to one side as if he's falling over. His face is crudely painted and he has cracked red cheeks. His eyes and his mouth are wide open, and he looks as if he should be laughing, but he isn't. Tom notices that one of his hands is missing.

As they near the lifeboat museum and the pier beyond it, Tom becomes aware of a noise overhead. It's a strange thumping sound. At first it's distant, but quickly it comes closer, and gets louder, until it seems to fill the sky. Tom feels it inside of him. They all come to a stop on the corner, by the museum, and look up. A large yellow helicopter is rising up over the cliffs. It hovers, dips slightly, moves forwards and backwards, forwards and backwards. And now the thumping noise alternates with a kind of chopping sound. After a few moments the helicopter begins to descend slowly towards the beach.

'It must be the coastguard. I wonder what's happening.' Rachel holds Tom close to her.

'It's probably just a training exercise or something,' replies Mrs Clay.

Jack has unzipped his camera from its case, and is starting to film the helicopter. 'This is great! I can use this in my film.'

'What are they doing, Rachel? Has a boat sunk?' Tom doesn't like the noise of the helicopter. People all round them have stopped, and are looking up. Tom notices that there's also a crowd of people lining the left side of the pier ahead of them, watching something that's happening down on the beach, or in the sea.

'I don't know, Tom. I'm sure it's nothing.'

'Yes, it's probably just an exercise.' Mrs Clay gestures for them to move on. 'It'll be nothing. It'll soon go. We'll go down anyway and have our picnic.'

The helicopter drops out of sight, behind the cliffs and onto the beach, but the thumping, chopping sound continues. They cross the road and walk on, towards the pier and the concrete slope that leads onto the beach. As they get closer, Tom can see the sea, and the white waves racing in from far out, crashing onto the beach. There are some people standing at the top of the slope, talking to a man. Tom sees that the man is wearing a cap like the puppet sea captain's, a bright orange life jacket and yellow rubber boots. He's talking to a couple who have a dog with them. The dog is soaked. It must have been playing in the sea, Tom thinks. Its dark coat is clinging to its body, and its legs seem unusually long and thin. It's pacing from side to side – alert. It looks towards the beach, sniffs the air, the ground, the man's yellow boots. The man holds up his hand as more people approach the slope.

'He's not letting anyone onto the beach. He's stopping people from going onto the beach,' Jack says. He stops, lifts his camera to his eye and begins to film again.

As they reach the slope, the man calls to everyone to move back. He says he's sorry, but the beach is closed. Jack hears the word 'incident'. He thinks the man looks anxious and upset. He can see the helicopter on the beach now. Its blades have slowed but are still spinning round, and the thumping, chopping sound has eased to a high-pitched wheeze.

There's a small group of people not far from the helicopter, and a large orange dinghy is beached on the sand. Suddenly there's a lot of activity, and someone runs to the helicopter and then back to the group. Rachel thinks she can see someone lying on the sand, a young man perhaps. The couple with the dog move away from the slope. The dog approaches Mrs Clay and sniffs at her feet. She bends down, lets it sniff the back of her hand and then pats its head. She smiles at the woman holding the dog's lead. The woman smiles back. 'There's been an accident. Two youngsters have been pulled out of the water.'

'Oh, how awful!' Mrs Clay looks over the woman's shoulder and down towards the beach. She feels a sudden knot in her stomach, as if she might somehow have a connection with these youngsters. 'Are they all right?'

'I don't know. Someone said they were only in the shallows, but they got caught in a rip current. One of them got to the ladder on the pier wall there, but then he swam back to try and help the other one and got into difficulty.'

'Oh, how awful! I do hope they're all right. The sea is so dangerous when it's like this.' Mrs Clay is gripping her coat lapels. Tom thinks she looks frightened. He looks round for Jack, and sees that he's moved towards the pier and is filming the scene on the beach. Rachel is watching a police car approach, its lights flashing and its siren drowning out the noise of the amusements and the helicopter and the wind. Tom wonders where they'll eat their picnic now.

*

Mum says there aren't any monsters. She says they're only make-believe. Stories. If there are any real monsters they must live in the sea. The sea is the best hiding place for monsters. Because it's so big and deep, and because it's hard to find things there. Like Monstro in Pinocchio. He sleeps at the bottom of the sea with Geppetto's little boat inside him. But Pinocchio does find him in the end. He searches for Geppetto and he finds Monstro.

I feel sorry for Monstro. He didn't do it on purpose. It was an accident. Poor Monstro. It wasn't nice to light a fire inside him. It filled him with black smoke that made him cough and sneeze. It must have burnt his insides. It made him angry, and that's why he chased them and smashed the raft into little pieces and killed Pinocchio. But it wasn't really Monstro's fault. He wasn't really a monster. He didn't mean to kill Pinocchio. And anyway, that's how Pinocchio got to be a real boy, in the end. After all the bad things that happened to him, he came back to life as a real boy, not a puppet, and everything was all right.

I wonder if that person lying on the beach is all right. Those other people were helping. The people who came in the helicopter, and the man who stopped us going down onto the beach for our picnic. The man with the hat like the laughing sea captain. If I made up a story about a monster, my monster would be the laughing captain. Maybe one day I'll be able to go out to sea. I could go far out to sea and look for my dad. I don't think Mum and Rachel and Jack would want to come. They don't talk about him. I'd have to go so far. I wouldn't be able to see the land. And I'd have to listen for the sound of the bells, because that's where I'd find him.

Fifteen to One

I won't be seeing Dad any more. It's over. Part of me feels sad, and I'll miss him, but I know it's better this way. I've decided to unplug the television and the telephone for a while, just in case, until my nerves are a little better, but it's just a precaution; he won't be back. It's not every day that you see your dead father on the television, or start getting telephone calls and strange visits from him in the middle of the night, but that's exactly what happened.

It began late one afternoon, about a month ago, when I was watching a television quiz programme called *Fifteen to One*. I wouldn't normally have been home at that time, but I'd been having this terrible trouble with my teeth and had left work early for a dental appointment. Fifteen contestants are asked general knowledge questions by the host of the show. Each contestant has three lives, which show up as neon stripes on the front of the lecterns they stand behind. When they get a question wrong, they lose a life and one of the illuminated stripes goes out. When they've lost all three lives, they're eliminated from the quiz. The three contestants who remain at the end of the game then compete in a final round, the last surviving contestant being the winner.

I made a cup of tea and sat down, and it must have been about halfway through the first round when I noticed him.

> Host: Number four. Cathy, diamonds are a form of which chemical element?
> Cathy: Carbon.
> Host: Carbon is right. Question or nominate, Cathy?
> Cathy: I'll nominate ... number nine, please.
> Host: Number nine. Geoff. At nearly eleven thousand metres, the Mariana Trench is the deepest point in any of the world's oceans. In which ocean is it found?
> Geoff: Erm, the Pacific?
> Host: Correct. Well done, Geoff. Question or nominate?
> Geoff: Nominate three.
> Host: Number three. Ronald. Egyptian mythology. The name, please, of the dog-headed god who ushers the souls of the dead into the afterlife?

And there he was! Dad. Number three was Dad, standing behind his lectern with only one neon life left. I moved closer to the television, but there was no doubt about it. He was even wearing his white rubber apron with the matching rubber gloves. I could see from his blank expression that he didn't know the answer to the question. A loud buzzer sounded to show that time was up, and Dad's last life was gone. The spotlight that had been on him went out, and he stepped back into the darkness.

Dad had always loved quizzes and sometimes, when we were just sitting around watching television or walking down to the shops, he'd fire questions at me. 'Which country's the Grand Canyon in?' he'd ask, or 'What's the longest river in the world?' They were usually geography questions, because the *National Geographic* was his favourite magazine. He used to read it in the evenings after work, and he'd tell me about all the strange, faraway countries in it, and show me the pictures.

The last time I saw Dad was nearly forty years ago – the last time I saw the *real* Dad, that is, before this other Dad started appearing on the television. I was twelve years old, and I remember it clearly because it was an unusual day. It was the day that Prince Charles married Lady Diana Spencer, and I was upstairs, stealing a packet of cigarettes from Dad's sock draw, which is where he used to keep them. He called goodbye to me up the stairs, but by the time I'd crept back to my bedroom with the packet of Benson and Hedges and run downstairs, he was gone. His work was only next door, but he never left the house without saying goodbye. I ran into the front room and looked out of the window. There were two men outside, hanging up flags and ribbons from the lamp posts, and Dad was saying something to one of them who was standing on a step ladder. It was a 'driving' day. I could tell, because Dad was wearing his black tailcoat, and his top hat with the black scarf.

*

It was a family business. My grandad had been the original Undercliffe of Undercliffe's Funeral Services, which Dad and my Uncle Terry had taken on in their twenties, eventually assisted by Uncle Eddie and my older cousin, Paul. Two of them looked after the front office and 'the garage', as Eddie always called it, and two drove the hearse. From outside, the front office looked like a normal house, except for the window, where there was a set of velvet curtains, a vase of plastic flowers, and two headstones, one blank and the other carved with the words *Undercliffe's Funeral Parlour*. The garage was at the back, and from our yard I could see the door. It was a huge green sliding door, like the ones you get on old railway trucks. It was usually shut, but sometimes Dad or Uncle Terry would pull it open to come out and collect a tray of tea from Mum, who'd hand it to them over the fence. Sometimes, when Mum wasn't watching, I used to climb onto the wash house roof and wait for Dad to come out. I only ever saw him a few times, though, and I remember thinking how odd he looked in that white rubber apron and those rubber gloves. But I knew why he wore them. I knew that there were dead people in the garage but I never said anything. I don't know when it was that I realised the dead people were kept there, but I think it must have been quite early on. I used to pester Dad, and try and persuade him to take me to work with him, because I wanted to see a dead body. I didn't tell him that, of course, but I remember lying in bed at night thinking of how I could get in the garage and see one of the bodies, and maybe take a photograph to show Michael and Christopher.

*

It was Michael and Christopher I'd arranged to meet with that morning. Michael was my cousin – Uncle Terry's son – and Christopher was a friend from school. Mum didn't really like me playing with Christopher. She said that he was a troublemaker, and that he was always up to no good. We used to go up to the embankment a lot in the summer. The railway line was long gone, and the embankment was overgrown with bracken, cow parsley and nettles. There were blackberries to pick there as well, and some good trees to climb if you went further out of town. The old line ran for miles, right out into the countryside. We used to pinch things from home (Christopher called them our supplies), which is why I'd taken the cigarettes from Dad's drawer. We usually tried to bring food too, preferably something we could cook easily on a fire.

On that particular morning, Michael had brought a huge jar of his Mum's home-made pickled onions, much to Christopher's disgust.

'So, what've you got?'

'I've got pickled onions.'

'Pickled onions? Bloody hell, Michael! Is that it? Is that the best you could manage?'

Michael didn't like stealing things. He once told me that he didn't steal at all. He used to ask his mum instead, and she'd give him things to bring.

'It's all I could get. They're home-made, they are!'

'Pickled shaggin' onions. What about you, Gordon? Whatya got?'

I was a few years younger than either of them, so Christopher was usually easier on me. 'Fags. Twenty, mind. Twenty B and H.' I looked up to Christopher, and always tried to bring something that I thought would impress him.

'Good man. Now we're talking.'

Michael pointed to the sack that Christopher had slung round his shoulder. 'And what about you. What you got?'

Christopher hung onto the sack, refusing to open it and show us what he had until we were clear of the streets and houses and had reached the embankment. He usually came up with something out of the ordinary, quite often something dangerous. When we reached the safety of the embankment, he put the sack down and opened it. Inside was a khaki jerrycan. 'There you go. I've got petrol.'

*

The day after I saw Dad on television, my toothache was worse and I decided to stay at home. The dentist had taken x-rays and said that one of my molars was the cause of the trouble. It would need to come out. I spent the day thinking about Dad and *Fifteen to One*, and wondering what would happen when the show came on again that afternoon. A few minutes before it was due to start, I switched on the television and sat down. When the theme tune came on I felt the hairs on the back of my neck stand up and my palms begin to sweat. I moved forward in my chair and turned up the sound.

The host of the show comes on first with his question cards and, after a short introduction, he hands over to a woman. You can't see the woman – you just hear her voice announcing the contestants, one by one. She says their names, what their jobs are and where they live. Dad wasn't one of the contestants this time, but he was there, in exactly the same spot he'd been in the day before. He was a silhouette, sitting just behind the others, out of the quiz before it had even begun.

As the programme went on, I didn't take much notice of the questions. I just waited, and watched very carefully when Dad came into the frame. Each time I expected him to be gone, but each time he was there. There was one question, though, that struck me as soon as I heard it. It was the one that Dad had been asked the day before. The question on Egyptian mythology. What was the name of the dog-headed god who ushers souls into the afterlife? This time the question was directed at Margaret, a laboratory technician from Weston-Super-Mare, who happened to be standing behind the lectern next to Dad. Only now Margaret was gone. It wasn't Margaret any more; it was Mum.

*

There were often arguments between Christopher and Michael but, because I was younger, they usually left me out of them. I'd never seen them actually fight, though – with their fists, I mean. I'd never seen anyone really fight, not in the way they fought that day. I knew Christopher had got into fights at school occasionally, but not Michael.

About three miles down the embankment there was a reservoir where we used to go swimming. There was a wood nearby, and a tree house we'd built the summer before. We'd all helped, but it was Michael who'd done most of the work. He'd spent just about every day of the holidays on it, making sure it was solid and waterproof. He'd persuaded Uncle Terry to give us a few sticks of furniture from his allotment shed, and even managed to get an old piece of carpet to put down. Back at school, he'd made a door, in Woodwork, and bought a padlock so that we could keep it locked when we weren't there, but he made sure to give Christopher and me a spare key each.

It was a hot day, so we settled down by the reservoir with our pickled onions, our cigarettes and Christopher's jerrycan of petrol, and we spent most of the day there. We went swimming, ate some of the onions – which Christopher said looked like eyeballs – smoked the cigarettes I'd pinched from Dad, and talked. It was later in the afternoon that all the trouble started. Christopher left Michael and me by the reservoir, saying he was going to check on the tree house and get a fire going. After a bit we decided to follow him, so we set off into the woods, but when we got to the tree house there was no sign of him.

Michael climbed up the rope ladder to check that the padlock on the door was still locked. 'Where's he got to, then?'

'Maybe he's collecting some wood for the fire.'

Michael hauled himself onto the main branch that supported the tree house, and tugged at the padlock. 'Locked. You got your key?'

'Yes.' I kept the key in one of my shoes if we were going to the woods. I took it out as Michael came back down the ladder.

'Well, you go on up and unlock it then. I'll see if I can find him.'

I climbed up, unlocked the padlock and went inside. There was a dead owl, right in the middle of the carpet. All that was left of its body was a heap of pale, downy feathers, but its head was intact. It must have found a way in but not been able to get out. I waited, but neither Christopher nor Michael turned up, so I climbed down and set off through the trees to find them.

*

Actually, it wasn't Mum. It couldn't have been Mum. Mum's been living in a care home for the last five years. She often doesn't recognise me, and easily gets confused and upset. The person on the television screen was another Mum, the Mum I knew when I was a child. She had an overcoat on, with a fur collar, and the beret that she always wore when she went shopping, and she had her handbag looped over her arm. She looked puzzled, as if she'd wandered into the programme by accident and didn't know where she was, and it was obvious that, like Dad, she didn't know the answer to the question. The buzzer sounded and she sat down beside him. I thought they might say something to each other, but they didn't. In fact, one didn't seem to know that the other was there at all.

I couldn't keep having days off work just so I could watch *Fifteen to One*, so I started to record it instead. In the next couple of shows, after the one Mum had appeared in, she and Dad were sat in the shadows. They still didn't seem to be aware of each other. In the third show they were gone. There was no sign of either of them, except for one thing: that question about the dog-headed god. It came up again, but this time the person who was asked the question was no one I knew. They didn't know the answer either.

*

I found Michael first. He was crouched down watching something, peering through a gap in the trees. As I moved towards him he spotted me, and motioned with his hand for me to keep quiet. I crept through the trees, trying to make sure I didn't stand on any twigs that might snap and frighten away whatever it was that he was watching. Maybe it's a deer, I thought. Michael didn't say anything. He didn't smile, or laugh, or point. He just crouched and watched, and I crouched and watched too. It was Christopher. He was lying on his back, eyes closed, with his trousers round his ankles and his hand jerking away at himself. I knew we shouldn't be watching, but it seemed riskier to move than to stay quiet and still. In any case, we weren't watching so that we could make fun of him. We didn't mean him any harm. But once he spotted us, it was always going to end badly. We were probably as shocked as Christopher when he turned his head towards us and opened his eyes. He jumped up quickly, turned away from us and struggled to pull his trousers back up. Michael lifted his hands and looked away apologetically, as if he wanted to say that it was all right, that there'd be nothing said, no mockery. But it was too late. When he saw the expression on Christopher's face he turned to run. I ran too, following him into the trees. We ran until we couldn't run any more, and then we lay down, breathless – listening for Christopher coming after us.

*

It must have been about a week after Mum appeared on the television that the telephone calls started. I was in the bathroom, dabbing my tooth and gums with some clove oil that the chemist had recommended, when the telephone rang. It was Mum. I was surprised because she doesn't normally call. She sounded far away and confused, and I couldn't make any sense of what she was saying. 'It's Ronald. It's your dad. Maybe he's collecting, wood for the fire?' She repeated it, over and over again. I kept telling her who I was, and asking her if she was all right. I said that she should speak to one of the care assistants if she was feeling upset, but in the end she put the telephone down. Just before she did, though, she said one other thing. She said, 'Cry if you want to. It's all right to cry.'

I thought about calling the care home but before I'd made up my mind the telephone rang again. This time there was nobody there, or at least nobody spoke. Something made me keep listening, though. It was a noise in the background, and I could only just hear it. It was the sound of a car passing, its engine straining and its tyres sizzling through the rain. It was almost like a recording; the sound of the same passing car being played over and over again. Then there was a voice, and I knew straight away that it was Dad's.

'Gordon? Gordon? Gordon?'

I tried to answer, although I knew it wouldn't do any good. I knew he couldn't hear me. 'Hello, Dad. Hello. Yes, it's Gordon. Can you hear me?'

'Gordon?'

'Yes, Dad. I'm here. It's Gordon.'

Eventually I gave up and just listened again. I could still hear the passing car, but I could hear something else as well. Dad's breathing. He seemed to be listening too. It was as if we were both listening to each other's breathing. For some reason it frightened me. I suddenly felt as if I was falling. I couldn't catch my breath, and I thought I was going to collapse. I put the telephone down, got myself a can of beer from the fridge and sat down. After a few minutes I dialled the call-return number, to see if I could find out where Dad had called from, but the number had been withheld.

There were three more telephone calls from Dad, each one the same. No words, just breathing, both of us listening and breathing. And each time, as I listened, I could still hear that passing car in the distance, with its straining engine and its tyres sizzling through the rain. But the last call was different, because this time there was another sound. It was like the sound a baby makes in its pram, gurgling and laughing and shrieking.

*

After a little while, we decided to make our way back to the tree house, but as it came into view we realised that something was wrong. We could see smoke, and then flames, and we could hear the cracking and splitting as the fire took hold. By the time we got there the tree house was an inferno, an enormous knot of flames and thick black smoke.

'It's burning! It's all burning!' Michael ran to the foot of the tree and picked up the rope ladder that had burnt through and dropped to the ground.

'Where is he? He's not in there, is he?' I pulled Michael away as burning pieces of the tree house started to crash down. At first I thought that Christopher might be inside, that he might have had an accident with the petrol. But he came from somewhere behind us, without any warning. We didn't see him, because we were both looking up for signs that he might be trapped inside the tree house, and we were also trying to dodge the falling wreckage. One second I was watching the flames sweeping up through the branches, the next Michael was doubling up and falling, holding his head, and Christopher was flinging the empty jerrycan down onto the ground beside him.

*

The night after the last telephone call, I wasn't sure if I wanted to watch my recording of *Fifteen to One*. I had a couple of beers to help dull my toothache, and finally I decided to put it on after all. When the contestants were introduced there was no sign of either Mum or Dad, and as the programme continued I sat back in my chair and began to relax. After about ten minutes I started to feel light-headed. There was a humming in my ears and my eyes couldn't focus properly. I held my hands up in front of my face, but I couldn't see them. Everything was a kaleidoscope of exploding lights and dark blotches. Eventually the television screen began to re-emerge, but it was as if everything else had disappeared. The room had gone, and everything was darkness. The humming in my ears began to die away as well, but it didn't go altogether. It began to turn into something else. The car, the sound of the passing car.

I could still hear the host's voice, but he wasn't forming words properly any more. He gurgled and giggled and shrieked out his questions, like a baby in its pram. The contestants didn't seem to notice. They answered their questions, made their nominations and carried on as usual. But there was something wrong with their voices, too; they seemed to be getting further and further away, smaller and smaller, weaker and weaker – as if I was listening to them on a poor telephone line. This went on for about five minutes, I think, until suddenly everything stopped. The humming, the sound of the car, the host's babbling baby noises, the contestants with their telephone voices – it all stopped. I stared at the screen as the host turned and looked straight at me and said, in his normal voice, 'Egyptian mythology. The name of the dog-headed god who ushers the souls of the dead into the afterlife?'

As I looked back at him, not knowing the answer, everything started to change again. The person looking at me from the television screen wasn't the host any more. In his place was a woman, a young woman holding a sleeping baby in her arms. She was pretty, and had long brown hair with a yellow butterfly clip in it. Behind her, little union jack flags were fluttering from the contestants' lecterns, and a shower of confetti was falling from above. And it was then that I noticed all the contestants had changed as well. There was Uncle Terry and Eddie, cousin Paul, and Christopher and Michael, and Mum – two mums in fact, one each from past and present – and there was Dad. And then I noticed that I was there too, but it was me as a boy. There was a policeman, and a woman in a headscarf carrying a shopping basket, and two boys I thought I recognised from somewhere. And there was Lady Diana in her wedding dress. They were all looking at me, just standing behind their lecterns looking at me. And just before it all faded, they spoke. They all called out to me together. They called, 'It's burning. It's all burning!' And somewhere, far away, there was the sound of a dog barking.

*

The fight must have lasted for about ten minutes. Christopher and Michael rolled about on the ground and punched and kicked, and then they got up and punched and kicked some more. Flaming pieces of the tree house were still coming down, and I was frightened that one of them might get hit by a piece of falling debris, but there was nothing I could do. I just watched and waited. I'd never seen Christopher so mad in my life; he just kept throwing himself at Michael, though hardly any of his punches landed. He whined and sobbed and wiped the tears out of his eyes, and then went at Michael again. Michael didn't want to fight, but he knew he had to. He didn't throw any punches, holding his fists up to defend himself, like a boxer, instead. He tried to trip Christopher up and pin him down, but Christopher broke free and carried on punching. Eventually, he wore himself out and stopped. He picked up the jerrycan and staggered off towards the reservoir, and home, I suppose. I didn't see him again that day, nor very much in the days and weeks that followed. Michael and I watched as the tree house burnt down to a charred skeleton and finally spilt out of the tree, disintegrating into a cataract of blackened fragments and sparks. And then it started to rain.

*

As the host, and Terry and Eddie, and cousin Paul, and all the others faded, I felt quite suddenly that I was dreaming, even though

I was sure I was awake. And in this waking dream, Lady Diana came into the living room. She was still wearing her wedding dress, and she took my hand and led me out into the street. I couldn't stop looking at her, she was so beautiful. It was the middle of the night, and we flew up into the black, starlit sky and soared over the town and away. When I looked down, I could see the embankment, and the wood and the reservoir, and then a moment later, I realised that we were falling – heading straight for the water. The next thing I knew, we hit the surface and began to sink, deeper and deeper into the blackness, and I wondered if I was dead. And then the sinking feeling stopped, and Lady Diana was gone. I wasn't in the reservoir any more. I was on *Fifteen to One*, not watching it, but a contestant on the programme.

I looked around and felt my clothes to see if they were wet, but they weren't. In all the confusion, it was a moment or two before I noticed who was beside me: on one side Mum, and on the other, Dad. We must have reached the final, because there were only the three of us, and we were standing further forward than the contestants in the first round. Mum, who was to my right, looked exactly as she had done when I'd seen her on the show before, wearing her fur-collared overcoat and her beret, with her handbag looped over her arm. Dad was to my left, wearing his rubber apron and his gloves, and there were fat beads of sweat on his forehead and his upper lip. Neither of them looked at me or seemed to know that I was there. I shook Mum's arm and then Dad's, but they just looked straight ahead at the host with his question cards. Suddenly the lights dimmed, and he was explaining the rules of the final round. Mum and Dad seemed to be taking it all very seriously, listening carefully to every word in case they missed something. When the host finished speaking there was a short pause, and then he took the first question card and read, 'Egyptian mythology. The name of the dog-headed god who ushers the souls of the dead into the afterlife, please?'

Out of the corner of my eye I saw Dad pressing the button on his lectern to signal that he knew the answer. The light would normally light up the lectern, accompanied by the ringing sound. There must have been something wrong with Dad's button, though, because instead of the ringing sound, each time he pushed it, there was the sound of a car horn, but a car horn sounding somewhere far off. The host didn't seem to notice, and turned towards Dad.

Only it wasn't the host any more. It was the young woman with the long brown hair, and the yellow butterfly clip, holding her baby in her arms. Dad gazed at her as she looked at the answer on the card she was holding in her hand.

'Erm ... it's ... it's ... pickled onions.' Dad looked puzzled. He seemed to know that what he had said made no sense.

The buzzer sounded, to indicate that the answer was wrong, and one of Dad's three neon lives disappeared. The woman carried on with the next question. 'A cartographer would make what?'

This time it was Mum who was pressing at the button on her lectern. Like Dad's, though, it seemed to be broken, and each time she pushed there was a screeching sound, like the screeching of tyres. Mum looked as confused as Dad, as if she hadn't meant to push the button at all. 'It's ... petrol.' The buzzer sounded again, as one of Mum's lives disappeared. I looked at her and she was starting to cry. She rummaged in her handbag for a handkerchief, and dabbed at her eyes and her nose.

When I looked back, the woman had disappeared and the host was holding the question cards again. But the baby was still there. The host was holding the woman's baby in his arms, and when he spoke it was with her voice. 'Which of the Romantic poets was married to the author of *Frankenstein*, Mary Shelley?'

Dad had totally lost control of his hand and was jabbing at his button without seeming to know why. The same distant car horn noise sounded each time. 'The reservoir.' Again, the buzzer sounded and another of Dad's lives disappeared.

By this time Mum was sobbing uncontrollably. I took hold of her arm, but she just kept on crying. Nobody seemed to know I was there. The questions continued 'In the Bible, who was the father of Shem, Ham and Japheth?'

I felt a growing sense of panic, and a need to stop everything. I wanted to run out of the studio, but something held me there. I found myself pressing the button on my lectern, even though I didn't know the answer, and as the host turned to me for an answer to the question, I felt a word form in my mouth and spill out. 'Noah! ... It's Noah.'

'Noah is correct. Question or nominate?' The voice had drifted back into that of the young woman. Again, the words just seemed to come, without my wanting them to.

'Nominate, please. I nominate Dad.'

Mum was sobbing so loudly by this time that I could only just hear the next question. I looked at Dad as the host read from the question card. Dad had changed now as well. He wasn't wearing his rubber apron and his gloves any more. Instead he had his black tailcoat and his top hat with the black scarf on. 'Egyptian mythology. The name of the dog-headed god who ushers the souls of the dead into the afterlife, please?'

The host wasn't holding the woman's baby any more. It was gone, but he was still speaking in her voice. Sweat was pouring down Dad's face by this time, and he was leaning on the lectern as if he might collapse. And then everything stopped again, and I could hear the baby crying, and the sound of the car, the straining of its engine and the sizzling of its tyres through the rain, the blast of its horn and then the tyres, not sizzling any more but screeching. And then I heard the sound of the dog barking again, and the crackling of flames, getting louder and louder, and there was suddenly a ring of fire all around us, and we were trapped. I wanted to run again, to try and break through the flames, but I didn't want to leave Mum or Dad. In any case, the flames were too fierce. And then I saw someone coming through the ring of fire, someone passing through the flames, untouched by them. Above the noise I heard Dad shouting, 'Lady Diana! It's Lady Diana!'

*

Michael and I didn't speak on the way home. When we got to the top of our road I could hear people singing and shouting at one of the street parties, but I didn't feel like joining in. Mum wasn't at home, so I checked for the door key under one of the plant pots where she sometimes hid it. It was there, so I unlocked the door and went in. I felt bad about what had happened with Christopher, and I didn't want to be on my own. I kept looking out of the window, waiting for mum to come back from the shops, and wishing that she'd hurry up.

I watched television for a bit and then heard Mum's key in the front door. I went to the window, and I saw that she was with a policeman. There were two women with her as well, one wearing a headscarf. The one wearing the headscarf was holding Mum by the elbow, as if she thought she might be about to fall over. It was Mrs Gill, one of our neighbours, who lived a few doors down the street. Her two children were standing at their gate, watching. The women talked on the doorstep for a minute, and then the policeman and

Mrs Gill and the other woman went off, and Mum came in. She came into the living room, took off her coat and her beret and said there was something she needed to tell me. She said it was better that we went upstairs.

I followed her upstairs and we went into my bedroom. She pointed for me to sit on the bed and then she sat down beside me. She was trying not to cry when she spoke. 'It's your dad. There's been an accident. A terrible accident. He won't be coming home. I'm sorry, Gordon, but he's dead. You can cry if you want to. It's all right to cry.'

Mum told me to get into bed, so I did, and then she went next door into her own bedroom and I could hear her sobbing. I didn't cry. I just lay there wondering how long I should stay in bed. I took a note pad and some pencils out of my bedside cabinet and I started to draw. I drew a map. I remember that map, though I don't know what happened to it. I drew an island. The island had a canyon, like the Grand Canyon, and a river, like the Amazon, and forests and dark caves, and in the middle of the island there was a deep mine filled with diamonds. But the mine was protected by a ring of fire that never went out. And the island was surrounded by a great ocean. I drew the waves, and a little boat sailing towards the island and, in the corner, a compass rose.

*

It was a boy. It was a boy walking through the ring of flames. It was me.

Dad was still shouting out 'Lady Diana! Lady Diana!' as the boy stepped through the fire and took his hand. The noise of the baby crying, and the car's engine, and the tyres sizzling and screeching, and the horn, and the crackling of flames, and the dog barking, and Dad's voice, were all getting louder. And suddenly I realised that I was shouting, too. I was screaming at the top of my voice, 'Who are you? ... Who are you? ... Who are you?'

The boy led Dad down from the podium behind the lectern, stopped and turned to look at me. His mouth opened but he didn't speak. He turned again and walked back into the flames, holding Dad's hand and, at the other side, the other side of the flames, I could see someone else waiting for them. It was the woman and her baby.

I held out my hand to Mum, who wasn't crying any more, and she took it, and we put our arms round each other. When we let go, the *Fifteen to One* studio was gone, and we were standing at the edge of the reservoir with Lady Diana. I turned to get my bearings, and as I did, I suddenly found myself standing in front of the mirror in my bathroom, holding the bottle of clove oil. I went into the bedroom and looked at the clock. It was half past four in the morning, so I pulled back the covers and got into bed, exhausted.

*

Dad had a heart attack. He was driving the hearse, and he had a heart attack at the wheel. The car spun out of control and there was nothing Uncle Terry could do. He tried to grab the wheel, but he wasn't quick enough. The car went straight through a red traffic light, veered onto the pavement and crashed into them: a young woman, a young woman pushing a pram with her baby boy in it. She had a dog with her too. Uncle Terry was the only survivor, apart from the dog. Dad was brought back from the hospital to the garage. People came to see him there before the funeral, but I wasn't allowed. He was cremated a week later, but I didn't go to the funeral either. Mrs Gill looked after me. She told me that she'd lost her dad when she was young, and that she knew how it felt. She took me for a walk in the park and bought me an ice cream, and then we watched television.

Uncle Terry didn't talk about the accident for a long time, but I remember going to the pub with him after Princess Diana was killed. He got drunk, and then he told me about it. He said he still felt guilty about not being able to stop it. 'I should have gone too, like every bugger else,' he said. 'I mean, if you saw it on television you wouldn't believe it, would you? In a hearse, for Christ's sake! A man driving a hearse has a heart attack and crashes into ... I mean, what are the odds? You couldn't make it up. Bloody nonsense.'

Mum cried her eyes out when Princess Diana was killed. She was never a royalist. She didn't watch the wedding on television or go to any of the street parties. She said they were 'for flag wavers.' But she still cried.

*

A few days later I had another strange dream. I dreamt that I was on a boat with Mum, a funeral barge, and we were crossing a river. There was the sound of tropical birds in the trees, and it was very hot. In the centre of the barge was a huge black coffin on a platform, but I didn't know who was inside it. I asked Mum if she knew who was in the coffin but she started to cry, so I decided to

155

climb up and look. I slowly pushed the heavy lid to one side and saw that it was Dad, but as soon as the coffin was open he started to fall apart, to peel away like an onion. Skin after skin came away from his face and flew up into the darkening sky, and I fell backwards onto the deck of the barge. When I looked up again, the coffin was in flames and the barge was moving towards the shore on the far side of the river. The flames started to spread, and I thought we were going to sink, so I grabbed Mum and jumped into the water. The barge carried on moving towards the shore and I held onto Mum and started swimming away.

I woke up crying, but strangely, I felt better than I had done for a long time. Even my toothache seemed much better. It's coming out tomorrow, anyway. Since the dream, I've not watched *Fifteen to One* and there haven't been any more telephone calls or strange dreams, or anything. There won't be now. It's over. I've thought about Mum a lot since that dream, which is why I'm going to see her. I haven't been for nearly a month. I don't know if she's got long left to live, and I want to make sure I say goodbye. I'll buy her some flowers, and perhaps take her out for a walk round the gardens. She can sometimes be quite clear-headed, if you stay long enough and stroke her hand. It soothes her, and she closes her eyes, and sometimes she quietly hums a tune, and seems more like her old self.

The Heart and the Feather

Every day, I travel on the Underground from Plaistow to Holborn. I work in ticketing and information at the British Museum. Vincent is the reason I'm here, of course. It may seem foolish, but I feel quite sure that one day I'm going to find him. I watch for him every day, as I walk from my bedsit to the station, as I stand waiting on the platform, as I make my way through the busy streets from Holborn to the museum. There are so many faces. The odds, I know, aren't good. Sometimes I think I see him. A sudden glimpse of a familiar gait, a similar profile, a head of red hair. Occasionally, I've followed people. When I need to assure myself that a resemblance I've noticed is nothing more than that. When I need to make sure that the person I've glimpsed in the crowd is only a stranger, and not Vincent. My greatest fear is that I'll see Vincent on the Underground, but that he'll be standing on a platform as I watch helplessly from a moving train that I can't get off; or that I'll be the one on the platform, watching as he flashes past me on a train, and away into the darkness. Sometimes, at those moments, I don't look, just in case, but often I find I can't help myself. I'm going to keep looking, because I believe that one day I'll see Vincent again. If he were dead I'm sure I'd feel it. Isn't that what's meant to happen, with twins?

*

When we were thirteen, Mum and Dad took Vincent and me up to London on the train for a day out. We lived in Lewes, in East Sussex, so the journey took less than an hour. It was a beautiful summer's day. We went for lunch at a little Italian restaurant near Marble Arch, and after we'd eaten we took the Underground to Holborn to visit the British Museum. The Underground was uncomfortably hot and airless, and Mum made us hold her hand, because there were so many people and she was worried we might get lost.

We found the right platform and worked our way through the throng of waiting passengers until we reached a space where we could all stand comfortably together. After a few minutes, there was a rumbling sound and the ground beneath our feet seemed to shake. A light appeared from deep inside the black tunnel at the far end of the platform, and the train approached. It clacked and shrieked out of the tunnel and into the station, and came to a screeching halt. We waited with the other passengers for the doors to open. When they did, a wave of people came spilling out of the carriages onto the platform. As they moved off, we squeezed onto the train. There were still lots of passengers in our carriage, but we managed to find four seats together.

'Thank goodness for that! What an awful place!' Mum fanned herself with a city map she'd picked up at Victoria station.

'Yes. Terribly efficient, though.' Dad sank into his seat and folded his arms as the doors closed and the train set off again. He pointed out Tottenham Court Road and Holborn on the map displayed above us, and told us about the old British Museum station. 'It closed years ago. It's still there, between Tottenham Court Road and Holborn, but it's not on Beck's map any more, of course. There are lots of them. Abandoned stations. Ghost stations. Nearly fifty, apparently. After it closed it was used as an air-raid shelter during the war. A lot of the Underground stations were. Nice and safe down here, I suppose.'

When we got to Tottenham Court Road, Mum said we should see if we could spot the old platform, so as the carriage doors closed and the train moved away again, we turned round in our seats and looked out of the grimy window. We couldn't see anything but blackness and the reflection of the passengers on the seats opposite us. One of the passengers was a young man, probably in his thirties. He was dark-skinned, with thinning, greasy black hair and heavy stubble. He was wearing a rust-coloured suit that looked as if it had seen better days, and he was holding a pen in his right hand, between his thumb and forefinger. It was an old-fashioned fountain pen. As I watched him reflected in the window, I saw him slot the pen into his breast pocket, untie his shoelaces and take off his shoes. He put his shoes on his lap, and then he sat with his eyes closed and his lips moving as if he was talking to someone. Nobody took any notice of him.

Dad said the British Museum station was supposed to be haunted. 'I read about it once. The ghost of an ancient Egyptian. There's meant to be a tunnel somewhere down here as well, leading straight up to the Egyptian room at the museum. There was a story about someone disappearing from the platform, I seem to recall.'

Mum was still fanning her face. 'Yes, well I'm sure there are plenty of ghosts down here. Think I'd prefer something a bit more traditional if I were a ghost, and a bit cooler. A nice Scottish castle maybe. It's so hot down here, isn't it?'

We saw nothing of the abandoned British Museum station. The train emerged out of the darkness of the tunnel into the stained, fluorescent light of Holborn, and again screeched to a standstill. We stood up and waited with the other passengers for the doors to slide open. Everybody seemed to be staring into space, nobody making eye contact with anyone else. 'That's how it works down here,' Dad whispered to me.

I looked round at the man with his shoes on his lap. Our eyes met, but he looked away immediately. His lips were still moving, and I wondered if he was praying. I remember thinking that he looked sad, but that there was something kind about his face.

*

Vincent and I loved reading about the Egyptians, and we had shelves of books at home on life in ancient Egypt, the Pharaohs, the pyramids, mummification, hieroglyphs and Egyptian gods and beliefs. We'd been to London once before, when we were younger, but we'd never been to the British Museum, and Dad had promised he'd take us to see the Egyptian collection there. We emerged from Holborn station into dazzling sunlight and a powerful, swirling current of pedestrians. Dad had planned our route, so he led the way. I walked immediately behind him with Vincent, whose arm was slotted through mine. Mum followed at our backs, her bag thrown over her shoulder. She gripped the napes of our shirts as though we were kittens.

We took a side road off New Oxford Street, which was less busy and joined Great Russell Street, where we first glimpsed the imposing façade of the museum building with its ionic columns and sculpted pediment. Dad said it was, 'more Greek than Egyptian, I'm afraid.' We crossed the courtyard and climbed the bank of steps leading up through the colonnade to the visitor entrance.

We stopped for a rest beside one of the columns. Mum poured two cups of tea, for Dad and herself, from a flask she'd brought. 'Not really tea weather, but there you go.' She gave us bottles of orange juice and packets of crisps. Dad took out an old museum guidebook he'd brought from home. 'You could spend a lifetime in here and still not get to the end of it. That's human history for you though, eh?'

Mum smiled and sipped her tea. 'Well these two will be heading straight for Egypt!'

Dad lounged on the stone steps, flicking through the guidebook. 'That's fair enough. You can't argue with a civilisation that lasted three thousand years. Not sure ours will make it that far.'

'It certainly is a long time.' Mum nodded and raised her eyebrows. 'And a lot of pharaohs too, I imagine. How many pharaohs were there, anyway? And which one of them was drowned in the Red Sea?'

Dad looked up from the guidebook. 'Ah, not sure. Aren't we conflating myth and history there?'

'Yes, probably. I always felt a bit sorry for those Egyptians. It seemed a bit harsh to me. I mean they did take the Israelites in, didn't they?'

'Well, that's God for you.'

We sat in the hot sunshine, beneath a sky of unbroken blue, drinking our juice and eating our crisps while Dad looked at the museum floorplan in his guidebook. The heat was building, and I could feel a patch of sweat beginning to develop between my shoulder blades.

'We'll head for Egyptian sculpture on the ground floor, then up to the first floor for life, death and the afterlife. Death and the afterlife! That's what we really want to know about, isn't it, boys?'

Vincent leant against Mum, his head on her shoulder and his arm resting on her leg. He traced a repeating figure of eight on her bare knee with his forefinger. 'Mainly the afterlife.'

'That's where all the mummies will be, I imagine.' Mum finished her tea. 'Poor things. Not quite the afterlife they imagined, I suppose.'

Dad got up, checked his watch and looked towards the museum entrance. 'C'mon then, let's get on.'

Vincent accidentally kicked me as he got up, leaving the dusty imprint of his sandal on my trouser leg. 'I'm sorry, Edward. I didn't mean to.' He put his arm round my shoulder, and we made our way up the steps.

*

It was cool inside the cavernous entrance hall, and the lighting was dim. It was busy, but not uncomfortably so, and there was a continuous murmur of hushed, echoing voices. Dad looked at the map in his guidebook and led the way to a long, high-ceilinged room that was dominated by a colossal red granite head. 'There we go, boys. Amenhotep the Magnificent. Quite something, eh? Let's take a closer look.'

We made our way towards the statue, past groups of visitors looking at some of the other exhibits. Vincent and I stood at the foot of the huge stone plinth and stared up at it. I'd never seen anything like it. Its monumental scale was disorientating, almost dizzying, but I couldn't draw my eyes away from it. It wore a crown bearing what I recognised as the Pschent, the double crown of Upper and Lower Egypt, with the two emblems of the cobra and the vulture. Its face was all smooth lines, with no sharp angles to jaw, lips or nose. Mum said she thought it was a serene face, but that there was something frightening about it too. Perhaps it was those blank, bald eyes that seemed to see everything, and yet nothing.

Dad and I walked round the plinth. He read from the guidebook as I continued to study the head. 'It's part of a statue of Amenhotep that was originally sited at his mortuary temple on the banks of the Nile. Apparently, there's an arm and a hand too. Imagine that! What he must have looked like when he was in one piece, not just a head!'

We rejoined Mum and Vincent, who were still looking directly up at the face. Dad stood at Mum's left shoulder. 'It says here that when they moved him from Karnak to Luxor, before he was brought here to London, it took them eight days to get him one mile! The weight of history eh, boys? Literally!'

Vincent whispered something to Mum and then came to stand next to me. He put his arm round my shoulder again. Mum stepped to the side of the plinth to read the object label accompanying the statue. 'It's not Amenhotep. Well, it is, but it isn't. It says that it was common for pharaohs to usurp the statues of earlier ones. They'd have them resculpted to look like themselves instead. So, originally this was Amenhotep, but then it was altered to resemble Ramesses the Second.'

'Is that so? Well, talk about reworking history!' Dad rolled up his guidebook and folded his arms.

Mum turned to us. 'So, he's Ozymandias, King of Kings.' The three of us stared at her blankly. 'Shelley. Percy Bysshe. He wrote a poem about this one, Ramesses. But he called him by his Greek name, Ozymandias.'

Mum read poetry all the time at home. Sometimes she read us poems that she'd memorised. She often sat with a book in her lap, silently reading. Then she'd close it, using her thumb as a bookmark, and try to remember the words. Her lips would move slightly as she recalled them, and then she'd open her eyes, and the book, to read on.

'What happens in the poem?' Vincent asked.

'Well, it's about this great statue in the desert. A statue of Ozymandias. It gradually falls into ruin and gets buried in the desert sand. It's about nothing lasting forever, I suppose.'

*

The Egyptian room on the first floor of the museum was smaller and busier. It was crammed with large glass cases containing sarcophagi and mummified bodies. As well as human remains, one of the smaller cases contained various other mummified creatures. There was a cat, a hawk, a crocodile, a snake and a bullock's head.

'They certainly went in for this mummification in a big way, didn't they? Stand still too long and they'd have the bandages out, eh, boys?' Dad had put his guidebook away and was peering through the glass at the bullock's head. The cloth wrappings, woven into a geometric pattern on the animal's chest, were still clearly visible. Its horns were small, and one of them looked as if it had separated from the head. It was hanging down at a right angle, held in place by the wrappings. It had two huge painted black eyes.

Vincent stood next to Dad. 'The Egyptians had lots of sacred animals,' he said. 'They were often sacred to particular gods or goddesses. They lived in their temples.'

Dad nodded. 'Interesting. So, what about this fella here then, Vincent?'

'Apis was a sacred bull. She was the mother of the sky god Horus and the sun god Ra, and she helped the souls of the dead in the afterlife.'

'She looks like she's seen better days, doesn't she, Edward?' Mum bent down to take a closer look. 'Those black eyes are a bit disturbing, aren't they?'

As we moved on, Vincent came and stood alongside me. 'Look, Edward. It's Gebelein Man.' We'd read about Gebelein Man, one of six naturally mummified bodies dating from around 3,500 BC. They were excavated at the end of the nineteenth century from shallow sand graves near Gebelein in the Egyptian desert. The heat of the desert sand had quickly dried and preserved them.

'Remarkable.' Dad shook his head. 'He's quite something, isn't he? You can see the skin, the fingernails – and look, there's even some of his hair left!'

Vincent bent down at the side of the case to look more closely at the head. 'It's ginger. His hair. That's what they nicknamed him. Ginger.'

The body was sealed inside a low glass case, in a reconstructed sand grave, with various clay pots and bowls surrounding it, common grave goods of the time. It was lying on its side, with its knees pulled up to its chest, but at the same time facing the ground, so that we could see the whole of its back. Its hands were held up to its face, but the features were still quite clearly visible.

Mum was standing on the other side of the case. She was resting her hand on the glass as if she wanted to touch what was inside 'There's something terribly sad about him, don't you think? He looks so sad. So vulnerable.'

And he did. Perhaps it was the foetal position of his body, which made it seem that he was trying to protect himself from something. But it was his frailness too, the mottled ochre and purple of the skin clinging to his bones, and the way his twisted hands were held up to his face, as if he was weeping, or trying to hide from our gaze, or from something terrible that couldn't be escaped.

*

We spent most of the afternoon in the museum, and afterwards we walked to Russell Square Gardens. Mum and Dad bought us ice creams, and while they sat on a bench, Vincent and I lay on the grass behind them. There were lots of people sitting or lying in the sun, or in the dappled shade of the trees, and there were others passing through, some meandering slowly and some walking briskly along the park's broad pathways. Dad had bought each of us a book and a leather bookmark in the museum shop. Vincent's book was Wallis Budge's *Egyptian Ideas of the Future Life*. Dad rested his arm along the back of the bench behind Mum, and tilted his head towards us. 'So, tell us the basics, Vincent. What can we expect from the future life? If we take the Egyptian understanding of things?'

Vincent was leafing through the book, his head propped up on his arm. 'To be accepted into the afterlife, the body had to be preserved. That's why mummification was so important. The ka, the soul, leaves the body after death, but it can only survive if the body is kept intact. If the body becomes unrecognisable through decay, then the afterlife isn't possible, and that person is lost.'

'And what does the ka get up to in the afterlife?'

'It's led by Anubis on a long journey through the underworld. Eventually, it reaches the Hall of Final Judgement and asks for entry into the afterlife. Osiris is the chief judge. The heart of the soul is weighed, together with a feather. If the heart is heavier than the feather, then it's eaten by a monster called Ammut. There wasn't a hell for the Egyptians – not existing was the worst thing for them.'

'I see. Well let's say the heart isn't heavier. Is there a happy ending then?'

'Then that person crosses a lake of fire, on the boat of the god Ra, to the kingdom of Osiris and the Field of Rushes.'

Dad laughed. 'Good heavens. And what's that like?'

'A kind of paradise. You'd be reunited with people who'd died before you. Your family, even your pets. Your home. Your favourite things.'

Mum put her sunglasses on and rested her head on Dad's arm. 'So, what makes the heart heavy?'

Vincent sat up and closed the book. 'Things that the person did, or didn't do, during their life on earth.'

Dad turned to Mum and smiled. 'Well, fingers crossed for old Gebelein Man, eh?'

We sat quietly in the sunshine for a little while longer, and then we walked to Holborn station to take the Underground back to Victoria, for our train home.

*

It was late afternoon, and the station was busy again. As we descended the escalator, the heat and the stale air seemed even more uncomfortable than they had been earlier. 'Here we go again.' Mum pursed her lips and blew out. 'Back down into the underworld.'

Dad was on the escalator step in front of me and Vincent was on the step behind, followed by Mum. Dad called over his shoulder, 'Which of your gods is in charge down here, Vincent?'

Vincent replied, 'Anubis, I suppose. Or later it was Osiris.'

Mum had found her street map again and was fanning herself. 'Isn't Anubis the black dog?'

Vincent turned round to Mum and nodded. 'Sometimes a dog's head, with a man's body.'

Dad navigated to the right platform and we waited. 'So, have you enjoyed yourselves, boys?' He checked his pocket to make sure he had our train tickets for home. We said we'd had a wonderful time. Vincent said he hoped we could come back.

'Yes, well I'm sure we can, can't we dear?'

Mum smiled. 'Yes, of course. There's lots more we should see and do.'

As we waited, more and more people began to arrive on the platform. We moved through the growing swell of commuters until eventually it thinned to a few smaller groups, couples and individuals, some talking and laughing, some reading or just standing quietly. A couple to our right seemed to be having an argument. I tried to hear what they were saying, but I could only catch the occasional word. The man was doing most of the talking, gesticulating with his hands. He kept talking about 'denial' and 'denying'. The woman had her arms crossed and was staring down at her feet. As I watched, I suddenly noticed that beyond them, not far from the tunnel entrance, was the man I'd seen earlier in the day. The dark-skinned man in the rust-coloured suit. He was leaning against the tiled wall of the station. His eyes were closed, but his lips weren't moving now, and he'd put his shoes back on. It seemed extraordinary to me that he should have reappeared so many hours later and that, with all these people moving around the city every hour, we should find ourselves back at Holborn station at the same time as him.

He stepped forward and began to walk slowly in our direction. He was looking straight ahead, and his steps were short and slow at first. I could see that he was holding something in his hand, and I remembered the pen. I could hear the rumble of the train approaching, and when I looked towards the opening of the tunnel I saw a light in the blackness. The man continued towards us, his pace quickening now. He glanced back at the tunnel. I could see that Vincent was looking in the man's direction too, but I assumed that his eyes were focused on the tunnel, and that he was watching for the train.

I felt the first tremor of the train's weight and movement passing through me as it drew closer. The man was about to pass behind us, and I thought he must be heading up the platform to board the train. He walked with purpose and concentration, as if he was late for an appointment. He was gripping the pen in his right fist. The sound of the approaching train grew louder. As he passed us, the man glanced back at the tunnel again and began to walk noticeably faster. As he did, he opened his clenched fist and dropped the pen, but continued to stride away from us. Suddenly Vincent stepped in front of me and walked towards the man.

'Excuse me!' Vincent called out to him. 'Excuse me, you've dropped something.' Vincent bent down and picked up the pen from the platform. He called out to the man again. The man didn't stop, but continued to walk away from us, pursued by Vincent. I looked back towards the tunnel, which was now filled by the front end of the train as it moved quickly out of the blackness and into the station.

'Your pen! You've dropped your pen!' Vincent was shouting now, but his voice was barely audible above the noise of the train.

'Vincent, stop. Stop.' Mum ran past me after Vincent.

I felt a blast of hot air as the train swept into the station, slowing, but still moving quickly. It almost knocked me off my feet. The man turned and looked towards the train. Vincent was just a couple of metres behind him, still holding up the pen. Then the man looked back one final time, veered to the right and fell forward, away from the platform, towards the rail track and the train. As he fell, he held his hands up to his face. There was an ear-piercing squeal as the train braked hard. It hit him, and threw him back in the direction he'd come from, towards the platform. He bounced between the edge of the platform and the train, trapped, until eventually his body was broken into a shape that allowed it to drop to the side of the track. Vincent dropped the pen and it skittered across the platform.

Vincent was standing immediately beside where the man's body had fallen. The train came to a halt, and people were running towards the scene of the accident, including Mum and Dad. One or two of them were kneeling down to see if the man could be helped, while others were recoiling, holding their hands to their mouths. Vincent stood at the very edge of the platform, staring down to where the man was lying. As Mum reached him she put her hand over his eyes and led him away. Dad put his arm round them both and walked them back towards me. As they approached, I could see that Vincent's face was white, his expression blank and his eyes wide but seeing nothing. Nothing but the man, and what had happened to him.

*

That night, when I eventually got to sleep, I dreamt about the man, and about Vincent. We were all on the train. Mum and Dad, Vincent and me. We were sitting, just as we had been on our way to Holborn station that morning. The man was sitting opposite us, but there didn't seem to be any other passengers. He had his shoes on his lap and was holding the fountain pen. His eyes were closed and his lips were moving. The train began to slow down. It stopped, but everything was dark outside, as if we were still inside the tunnel. I watched the man's lips move. I was trying to work out what he was saying, but I couldn't. The doors of the train slid open, and I realised that we weren't inside a tunnel; we were at the old British Museum station. I could see the edge of the platform illuminated by the light from the train. I looked down at my hands, and noticed that in my right hand I was holding the man's fountain pen. It was a beautiful pen. It looked as if it was made from tortoiseshell. I was frightened that Mum or Dad would see that I had it, because I knew I must have stolen it. I heard the sound of the train doors closing and I looked up. As I did, I could see that the man and Vincent were both standing out on the platform, and that the train was going to move off, leaving them there in the darkness. I got up and went over to the door. I was pulling at the rubber seals and hitting the glass to try and make the doors open, but they wouldn't. The man and Vincent were just standing there, and they didn't seem able to see me. I turned and shouted at Mum and Dad to help me but they didn't respond either. It was as if I wasn't there. They were just staring into space. And then the train started to move away from the platform, and the man and Vincent were gone.

*

Vincent disappeared just after we'd completed our A level exams, so we would have been almost eighteen. Just a few days before it happened, we'd spent the day down on the beach at Shoreham. We often went there as children. It had been one of our favourite places in the summer. Mum said it was quieter than Brighton or Eastbourne, and Dad was always saying he wanted to buy one of the houses on the edge of the beach so that he could swim every day of the year. We used to spend the whole day there, until our skin was tight and prickly with sun and salt. We'd take a picnic and sit on the warm pebble beach, paddling, and later swimming and floating in the shallow water on our air beds. There was a little shop just a short distance from the beach, and Vincent and I would walk there to buy cans of drink and ice creams.

On this particular day, Mum had given us a lift in the car. We'd brought bread, cheese and grapes and a large bottle of lemonade in a beach bag. We lay on the pebble beach for as long as we could bear the heat of the sun, then we swam to cool down, then let the sun dry us and swam again. Then we ate. Vincent had started smoking, and he had a tin with a small pouch of Old Holborn tobacco, cigarette papers and a lighter inside it. He smoked, and picked strands of the loose tobacco from his tongue. I knew that Vincent had been having difficulties, though he hadn't spoken to me about them. He'd been spending most of his time alone in his room, listening to music. He barely spoke to Mum and Dad any more, and there'd been regular arguments because he hadn't prepared properly for his exams and had been missing school. It was hard, because I didn't want to be seen to be siding, either with Vincent or with Mum and Dad. It felt as if something had come between us, and we weren't as close as we had been.

'The older we get, Edward, the more things we have to hide. To protect ourselves. It's a shame, really it is.' He sat with his legs crossed, hugging his knees to his chest and carefully tapping the ash from the end of his cigarette. 'Even you and I. We have to hide things from each other. We bury stuff, but it goes off and does its own thing when we're not looking.'

I asked Vincent what kind of stuff he meant.

'Oh, you know, stuff. Things we do wrong. Things we don't do. Things people can use against us.'

I told him he didn't need to hide anything from me. He drew on his cigarette, smiled and put on his sunglasses. 'Do you remember the heart and the feather, Ed? The more stuff you hide, the heavier your heart gets.' He extinguished his cigarette, burying it in the pebbles. 'It can become your enemy, I think. Your heart.'

As the afternoon drew on, the heat intensified and we had to swim more often to keep ourselves cool. Vincent pointed out a buoy that was a couple of hundred metres from the shore and asked me if I'd swim out to it with him. It looked a long way to swim, but the sea was calm, and the buoy would provide the opportunity for a few minutes' rest before we swam back to shore. We ran into the water and began to swim out steadily towards the buoy. I kept looking back to the beach, which was shimmering in the heat. As we reached the midway point between shore and buoy I felt nervous, but I followed in Vincent's wake as he pushed on through the water. When we eventually reached the buoy, we held on to the big orange globe and laughed, our feet touching as we rested them against the chain holding it in place. As we clung to the buoy and looked back towards the beach, I felt closer to Vincent than I had in a long time. But I felt bad for him, because I wanted him to be happy.

'How far down do you think that chain goes then, Ed? How deep do you reckon?' I looked at the surface of the water. I said I thought it was hard to tell, but pretty deep. 'Yeah, we're not going to be able to touch the bottom, are we? That's for sure!' He laughed. 'What about diving? Wonder if I could make it to the bottom and back.' I said that there was no way, that it would be too deep. Maybe it was talking about the depth of the water, and our distance from the shore, but suddenly I felt our smallness and our vulnerability.

My hands were on top of the buoy. It was slippery, and I was finding it hard to hold on. Vincent readjusted his hold and put his hands on top of mine. He was on one side of the buoy and I was on the other, and so we could barely see each other. 'You know, Ed, sometimes I think about that day when we went to London with Mum and Dad. To the British Museum? And that man who fell in front of the train on the Underground?' I replied that it was understandable – not an easy thing to forget. 'I think about him a lot. Like I want to know who he was, how his heart got so heavy and how he ended up down there. Why he did it.' I thought about it too, sometimes. And about what Vincent had seen that I hadn't. 'You know Mum and Dad never talked about it. They never said a word about it, did they?'

Vincent was right. Mum and Dad never had spoken about what had happened, and nor had we. I knew that, somehow, nothing had ever been quite the same again after it. But I couldn't find the words – none of us could – to start understanding why.

'I feel like there's something of him with me all the time, Ed.'

I was about to reply when Vincent's hands released themselves from mine and he began to swim away from the buoy and towards the shore. 'C'mon then. Let's see if we can make it back.'

I followed him. Swimming out had seemed easy, but our progress back to the shore was slow. Vincent remained ahead of me, and eventually we made it. We lay on the pebbles at the edge of the water, closed our eyes, and let the outgoing tide suck at our toes.

*

If Vincent had planned to disappear, he'd given no indication of it. He said nothing, he left no explanatory note, and there wasn't even any evidence that he'd taken clothes or any of his other belongings with him. It was, of course, a terrible time. Mum and Dad were beside themselves. Dad asked me over and over again if Vincent had said anything that might provide a clue to where he'd gone. 'Are you positive he didn't say anything at all to you about where he was going, Edward? Try and think. Even a hint.' But he hadn't.

At first the police didn't seem overly concerned. I suppose teenage boys must go missing all the time and then turn out to be perfectly all right; staying with a girlfriend or sleeping on a friend's floor. But after a few days that changed, and there were police officers in our house all the time. There was a public appeal for information, and Vincent's face appeared in the newspaper and on local television. There were posters in the railway station and around the town. Local people organised a search, too, walking the Ouse and the Downs. There was speculation that Vincent might have taken the ferry across the Channel to Dieppe, or even that he might have been abducted. But all along, I felt sure that Vincent had gone to London, though I couldn't understand how he could have left without saying anything to me. The police clearly thought that London was a possibility too, and told us they were actively pursuing that line of enquiry.

Contact with the police continued, but over time things died down, and that was what was intolerable for Mum. As long as there was a police liaison officer in our home, or coverage of Vincent's disappearance in the press and on the news, there was hope. But as the intensity of those first weeks dissipated, so a sense of hopelessness consumed her and she became a ghost of herself. When she wasn't in bed, she sat in an armchair in the living room, staring weepily into space. Yet she was also prone to furious outbursts, often directed at Dad. She couldn't bear any attempt to re-establish domestic routine. Something as simple as Dad offering to prepare a meal could provoke her, and she'd accuse him of behaving as if Vincent had never existed. Otherwise, she rarely spoke, or left the house. I think it was the not knowing that she couldn't cope with, and the fact that there was nothing she could do – no practical action she could take to try and find Vincent.

And so, home became a place that was no longer home.

*

The chance to leave for University came as a great relief. It troubled me that Vincent hadn't tried to make contact. I couldn't understand it, but I felt I needed to be in the place where I might find him, so I went to London. I studied Anthropology at University College and worked nights in the kitchens at a hotel overlooking Russell Square Gardens. It was exhilarating to be back in London. Mum and Dad had been a couple of times soon after Vincent's disappearance, as part of the Police effort to locate him, but they'd felt it best that I didn't go with them. I suppose they imagined they were protecting me.

I'd ride round on the Underground for hours. I travelled the whole of the Piccadilly line of course, from Uxbridge and Heathrow to Cockfosters, taking in Covent Garden, Holborn and Russell Square. I rode the Central line, from West Ruislip to Epping and yes, I watched for a glimpse of the British Museum station between Tottenham Court Road and Holborn. But I also took the Bakerloo line, from Harrow and Wealdstone to the Elephant and Castle, the Northern line, from Edgware to Morden and all the way back up to High Barnet, and the Victoria line, down to Brixton and back up to Walthamstow Central. I took the District line from Ealing Broadway and Richmond to Wimbledon, Kensington Olympia, Edgware Road and Upminster, and the Metropolitan line from Amersham, Uxbridge, Chesham and Watford to Aldgate.

And I looked for Vincent.

I felt sure that, if he'd run away to London, Vincent would visit the British Museum at some point. So I made regular visits to the museum, to walk round the galleries but also to enquire after vacancies. Eventually I got a job as a part-time attendant. Occasionally I would work in the Egyptian galleries. I found it strange to be in such close proximity to Amenhotep's head and

171

Gebelein Man, and all of the other treasures, and to think of everything that had passed since that day when we'd visited together. And I looked for Vincent – always. Amid the stream of faces passing through the museum, I looked for him. And I still do, every day. I look for him in the museum, on the Underground, and, occasionally, on the platform at Holborn station where that young man fell onto the tracks.

*

In *The Book of the Dead*, there's a spell that's said to prevent the heart of the deceased from opposing him in the underworld, and preventing him from entering the Field of Rushes.

O my heart which I had from my mother, O my heart which I had upon earth, do not rise up against me as a witness in the presence of the Lord of Things; do not speak against me concerning what I have done, do not bring up anything against me in the presence of the Great God, Lord of the West.

I often read it, because it reminds me of Vincent. It reminds me of what he said about the way we hide things – the more stuff you hide, the heavier your heart gets – and how your heart can become your enemy. It reminds me of the young man at Holborn station too. I miss Vincent terribly, but I think I started to miss him before he disappeared, perhaps from that very moment on the platform at Holborn. I long for those summer days on the beach at Shoreham, when we were without cares, when our hearts were lighter than any feather. And even though I know it isn't really possible, I suppose that's why I'm here, looking for Vincent. To recapture it, that lightness of heart.

Sometimes I sit on the train in the Underground, hoping that someone will smile, reach out a hand or touch my arm and ask if I'm all right. I imagine telling them about Vincent, and I imagine the tears running down my face as they hold my hand and listen to my story. But then sometimes I think that my longing for Vincent has become who I am, and that I don't want to share it with anyone, because I'd be lost without it.

And so, I'm alone, but on the whole it feels right to be so. It feels safe.

The Colossus

It's just after seven o' clock, and Lillian is awake. She's listening to the sound of the radio, but it doesn't seem to be working properly. There's no music, no voices, just a monotonous hushing sound. She reaches over and fiddles with the tuning wheel but can't seem to find a station. She turns the radio off, wondering if there's a problem with the transmitter. She lies back, and pulls the covers over her head. She feels the heaviness in her limbs and recalls the storm of the night before. It had kept her awake, the wind howling round the house, the rain battering at the windows, and the cold air creeping in under her duvet.

Normally, after she gets out of bed, Lillian makes herself some coffee and toast and sits by the window in the living room. She switches on the television and watches the breakfast news while she waits for the post van to arrive. She watches the starlings as they sit and preen on the telegraph wires and in Arthur's guttering, and she watches out for Arthur, who lives opposite, setting off for work. She always gives him a wave. Then she settles down to work at her computer, where she spends much of her day. Lillian is a writer. She writes articles for magazines, brochures and catalogues.

She usually looks forward to starting work in the morning, but today, as she pulls back the duvet and the coldness grips her, Lillian feels tired and uninspired. She flicks the light on and shuffles round the bedroom putting her clothes on. She has two cats who usually jump on the bed while she's still sleeping, impatient for their breakfast. They sniff at her nose, or rub their heads against her cheek, or wash themselves noisily beside her ear. But this morning they're noticeable only by their absence. Lillian puts on her slippers and goes downstairs, calling them, but by the time she's got to the kitchen, filled the kettle and placed it on the hob they still haven't appeared. She checks that the cat flap hasn't become accidentally locked, but no, it's open as usual. She decides that they'll turn up when they're hungry, and sets about making her breakfast. When she switches on the television, the screen just fuzzes noisily. She picks up the remote control and flicks from channel to channel, but they're all the same. She switches off the set. Perhaps the storm has damaged the aerial, she thinks.

She sits by the window. There are no starlings on the telegraph wire today, because it's come loose in the storm and lashed itself round the pole. She looks up at Arthur's gutter, but they're not there either. She finishes her coffee and toast and waits by the window for the post van, but it doesn't come. She looks at the clock hanging above the fireplace and wonders what could have happened to Arthur. He's nearly eighty, but still leaves the house at eight o' clock every morning to walk the two miles into the village and catch a bus into town, where he has a little shop that sells model aeroplanes, trains and ships. But this morning, as Lillian looks out of the window, there's no sign of Arthur. His curtains are still closed, and the house is in total darkness. She goes upstairs and looks out of her bedroom window. Leaves scuttle along the lane and the sky looks dark, as if another storm is on the way.

*

As Lilian opens the front door, a paper bag whirls round the yard and drifts up into the bare branches of the sycamore tree behind Arthur's house. There's a dampness in the air, and Lillian feels a spot of rain on her face. She leans out of the door, looking to see if the cats are hiding in the coalbunker or under the bushes. She whistles, and rattles the door handle, but they still don't appear. She steps out into the yard so that she can see to the end of the lane and the field beyond. She notices Mr Dawson's car outside his house next door. The driver's door is wide open. Mr Dawson's front door is also ajar, as if he's perhaps forgotten something and run inside to get it. Lillian waits, but Mr Dawson doesn't emerge. She looks out towards the field at the end of the lane. Mr Atkinson's tractor stands motionless in the middle of the field, which is half ploughed brown earth, half stubble, but there's no sign of Mr Atkinson himself. Lillian can see the farmyard as she moves towards her gate. There's a row of white garments thrashing about on a washing line, but that's all. As she turns back towards the house, she notices the empty milk bottle she left on the step yesterday. Mrs Atkinson would usually have collected it by now, and delivered a fresh new bottle with a shiny green top.

*

Lillian goes back inside, takes off her slippers and puts on a pair of shoes and her coat. She steps out into the yard, closing the front door behind her. She walks across the lane towards Arthur's house. She glances at her watch. It's now nearly nine o' clock. She goes to his kitchen window and tries to peer in, but the heavy curtains are tightly shut, so she goes to the door at the side of the house. There's a porch, which she steps into. She looks through the little pane of glass in the door. She can see into the kitchen, where the table has breakfast things still set out. A plate with some leftover crusts, a knife, a butter dish and a jar of marmalade, a cup and saucer.

Lillian can see into the hall at the other side of the kitchen, where she notices that the telephone receiver is hanging loose from its fixing on the wall. She rings the bell and waits, but no one comes, so she decides to open the door and check to see whether everything's all right. She turns the handle and the door opens. She steps in and quietly closes it behind her. She calls Arthur's name, but there's no answer. She goes into the hall and picks up the telephone receiver. There's no dial tone. She places it carefully back on the wall. She calls Arthur's name again, as she walks through the hall and into the sitting room. It too is empty. There's a battered leather armchair with an open newspaper on it. Beside the chair is a small table. On the table there's a glass ashtray with a cigar balanced on its edge. The cigar has a short stub of ash where it's burnt itself out. She can still see a fading ribbon of smoke up near the ceiling. Beside the ashtray is a blank sheet of notepaper, on top of which is a fountain pen. The lid of the pen has been removed, as if someone was about to write something on the sheet of paper. To the right of the chair there's a fish tank. The filter is gurgling softly, but there are no fish.

Lillian calls out again, but still there's no answer. As she leaves the living room and re-enters the hallway, she notices a picture hanging at the top of the stairs. It's a painting, by Arthur, of a ship sailing in a stormy sea at night, beneath a full moon.

*

As she crosses the lane again, Lillian notices that the door of Mr Dawson's car is still open, and that Mr Atkinson's tractor is still standing motionless in the field. She decides to walk to the end of the lane and see if she can spot any of her other neighbours. She looks in at each window but sees no one. Reaching the fence at the edge of Mr Atkinson's field, she looks across the valley to the road that leads into the village. She waits and she watches, but no cars pass, no joggers, no dog walkers; nobody. She can just make out the gates of the crematorium, which appear to be closed. She walks back home, shutting Mr Dawson's car door as she passes.

Once inside, Lillian flicks through the television channels again, but there's still no reception. She picks up the telephone and listens, but there's still no dial tone. She decides to walk into the village. She puts on her scarf and gloves. She gives the cats one final call before locking the door and setting off. She walks down into the valley, towards the beck and the old bobbin mill. It starts to rain and the noise of the drops hitting her hood mingles with the sound of rushing water in the millstream. As she passes the mill, Lillian looks in to see if she can see anyone, but nobody seems to be there either. She presses on up the hill, towards the main road. The rain begins to fall more heavily. It slants and drives into her face and she opens her mouth to taste it.

*

The crematorium is set back from the road behind a green, wrought-iron fence. The small chapel building and the caretaker's house are partially concealed by bushes and fir trees, but nothing can hide the stone chimney, disguised as a bell tower, that rises up above even the tallest of the trees. Just as she'd thought, the gates of the crematorium are closed and padlocked.

As she reaches the first houses on the outskirts of the village, Lillian notices that there's no sign of movement in any of the driveways, and nobody at the windows. Not a soul. As the slope in the road evens out and the height of the drystone wall to her right drops, she also notices that there are no sheep in the fields. There's a green at the centre of the village, around which houses, shops, the church and the pub are arranged. It's normally busy at this time in the morning – parents with push chairs heading back from the school, people out shopping, a steady stream of cars passing through – but today it's deserted. She looks at her watch again to check that it is really Monday morning, just after ten o' clock.

The rain continues to fall as Lillian cuts across the green to Selkirk's newsagents. She's encouraged by the appearance of a light inside. Outside, there's an abandoned bicycle leant against a lamp post, and an A-board showing the latest headline from the local newspaper – "FLOOD CHAOS CLAIMS MORE LIVES!" The sign on the door announces that the shop is open, so she enters. The light is on and a gas heater is fluttering and glowing in the corner. On the counter the cash register stands open, and beside it there's a mug of cold-looking tea. On the floor there's a carrier bag with a carton of milk and a loaf of bread in it. But there's no sign of even a single shopper, or of Mr Selkirk. Lillian thinks about calling out but decides not to. She walks round the shelves, takes a tin of pineapple chunks and puts it in her pocket. Then she moves towards the stock room at the back of the shop. Through the half-open door she can see stacks of beer tins, canned goods and toilet rolls, but still there's no sign of Mr Selkirk.

*

As she leaves the shop, Lillian finally realises that everyone has gone: Arthur, Mr Dawson, Mr and Mrs Atkinson, Mr Selkirk, her cats - even the starlings and the sheep. She glances at the church on the far side of the green and remembers an American girl called Amy she'd once met while on holiday in Scotland. Amy had been staying in the same hotel as Lillian, with a group of Christian young people. One day Lillian had got talking to Amy over breakfast and they'd gone for a walk together. Amy had talked about Jesus, and God, and how she believed that the world would come to an end during her lifetime. She'd told Lillian about the end times and the 'rapture' when God would remove all true believers from the earth, prior to seven years of trial and tribulation, famine and plague. As the church bell strikes the half hour, Lillian remembers Amy saying that this would all happen in the twinkling of an eye.

The rain is stopping, and patches of blue sky are beginning to appear. Lillian pulls off her hood and sets off for home, still thinking about Amy.

*

As she retraces her steps homewards, Lillian puzzles over her calmness. Even though some cataclysmic event seems to have taken place, leaving her like a shipwrecked sailor on a desert island, she feels no panic. Strangely, there's even a sense of relief. Halfway up the hill to the crematorium she stops for a moment, thinking that she can hear a bird singing. She holds her breath and waits, but no, she hears nothing. She wonders if the nothingness is inside her own head, if the rough, slimy stones in the wall she's leaning on, the sharp tang of slurry from the farm, the rivulet of icy rain coursing down her back, are all somehow imagined. Perhaps she's hallucinating, or at the point of death, and all of this is some elaborate unfolding of her dying consciousness. She imagines huge black rents appearing in the brightening sky, and crevices suddenly rupturing the pavement beneath her feet. She imagines everything that she can see disappearing like a reflection in disturbed water.

By the time Lillian arrives home the clouds have gone, the sky is blue, and the sun is shining. She puts the key in the lock and opens the door. When safely inside, she takes off her coat and shoes and goes into the kitchen. She opens the tin of pineapple chunks and begins eating them with a fork. She sucks slowly on each chunk, gauging whether the stringy texture, and the sharp sweetness, are somehow different, somehow fraudulent.

*

Lillian sets about washing the dishes from last night's supper. Pulling on a pair of rubber gloves, she fills the basin with hot water, and gazes out of the window above the sink as she scrubs. The window overlooks a rutted track leading to the Dene.

She's thinking about her mother, and that long hot summer the year after her father's death, when they'd often gone down to the Dene together, to picnic and search for fossils amid the limestone scree. They'd visited a local museum that summer too, where there were pictures showing what the Dene would have looked like hundreds of thousands, or was it even millions of years ago. The Dene had been created by a glacier, which had then thawed into a huge expanse of water, a lake in which all kinds of strange prehistoric creatures had once lived. They'd found traces of them too, in the scree; delicate fanned shells imprinted on little shards of stone. Lillian had collected them, and carefully arranged them on the ledge at the end of the bath.

She unpeels the rubber gloves and drops them onto the draining board. It's been several months since she last visited the Dene, but she feels a sudden compulsion to see it again, as if she might find some clue there, as to why she's woken to this empty world.

*

The track is muddy and there are deep trenches of standing water carved by Mr Atkinson's tractor. Lillian wishes she'd worn her wellingtons. Eventually, she reaches a densely wooded area of crags. Through the centre of this runs a small stream, one of the many tributaries feeding into the beck at the bottom of the Dene. The descent through the crags is steep, and she struggles to keep her footing as she edges down sideways, trying with each step to dig her shoes into the slippery mud. At last the path evens out and the

178

trees begin to clear. She wraps an arm round one of the tree trunks and rests for a moment, breathing heavily, and looking back to where she's come from. She savours the sweet taste of rotting mulch and watches her breath solidify in the damp air.

When Lillian reaches the gate that leads into the Dene, she unhooks the length of chain from the fence post and opens it. Even though there appear to be no sheep to keep in, she closes the gate behind her, and loops the chain back over the post. She walks across the huge, flat expanse of grass towards the edge of the beck, surveying the steep slopes of woodland and scree. She sits on the bank and watches the water flowing past, a glittering thread – all that's left of the prehistoric lake – almost narrow enough here for her to step over. But the water is deep and flows quickly towards the packhorse bridge that leads to the other side of the valley. Lillian lets the bottom of her muddy shoes touch the surface of the water.

*

She'd spent many hours alone in the Dene that summer too, sunbathing and reading while her mother was out at work. She hadn't liked to be in the house on her own. It was on such an occasion that she'd first experienced one of her seizures. She'd had them all that summer. They always began with a light-headedness, then a sensation of paralysis and that strange feeling that she was rising slowly out of her body. A sort of waking dream would follow, in which she was floating upwards, looking down at her body on the grass below. As she continued to rise, her body became smaller and smaller, and she could see over the wooded edge of the Dene, right across the surrounding hills and valleys, the villages and towns. She was sure that she could even make out the sea on the horizon too. And then she'd begin to drift back down to the ground, but as she did, she'd see that her body was no longer lying on the grass below. Instead, there was someone else; a body, but no ordinary body.

It was huge, lying in the valley bottom on its side, curled in a foetal position. It filled the whole of the Dene, right to the edge of the woods and the scree slopes. It was naked, and although Lillian couldn't see the face or the genitals clearly, she could tell from the body's frame and musculature that it was a man. The skin was pale and smooth, like marble, and there was no body hair. As she traced its lineaments, there was something about the body's sweeping

179

planes of torso and limb, its peaks and crevasses, that made her think of a landscape; a great empty wilderness.

The enormous spine stretched up towards the smooth uplands of the shoulder – which reflected the sunlight as Lillian descended, blinding her momentarily – and down to the domed buttocks and the long, high ridge of the right thigh, the knees pulled up towards the chest. The calves were in deep shadow and the feet seemed far removed from the main land mass of the body. Only one was clearly visible, resting on the other, the immense arches and mounds of the sole ending in an archipelago of toes. The left arm was hidden too, the right plunging down from the shoulder into the dark chasm between torso and thigh, the forearm stretching back up towards the head, the rocky terrain of its hand covering the face almost completely. The headland of the index finger pushed out into an ocean of red curls and, as she drew closer, Lillian marvelled at the ear, a complex labyrinth of whorled bays and coves.

She couldn't help feeling that there was something familiar about the body, this mysterious continent. But there was something else it called to mind. An ancient religious monument like Stonehenge, the pyramids, a sphinx in the desert, or some colossus from antiquity; laboured over, carved, polished, honed and perfected as an acknowledgement of greatness, an object of worship, or some long forgotten ritual purpose.

*

Back at home, Lillian lights the fire and pulls the sofa closer to the hearth. She waits until the coals start to glow, then separates and spreads them with the poker. As the fire establishes itself, she suddenly feels very tired and decides to lie down on the sofa. She watches the flames, hardly able to keep her eyes open, and when they close she sees the body again. She sees those red curls of hair unfolding, not cushioned on the warm grass, but undulating in the waters of the prehistoric Dene. She's flying over it, looking down into the water which is crystal clear, like a fish tank. And the body's there, in the same foetal position as it was before, except that now it's lying at the bottom of the lake, surrounded by strange creatures. Crocodiles and sharks, and strange looking fish that Lillian doesn't recognise, swimming round in the water. There are other creatures too: crab-like bottom feeders scuttling over the torso, suddenly emerging from the tangled red hair, dropping from the darkness of an armpit and the cleft between the buttocks. And there are raw craters in the skin, wounds from which strands of dead flesh drift upwards, because these creatures are feeding on the body. As she flies over the lake, she knows that soon she'll be able to see its face, but that it will be gone, eaten away, and that there'll be a black emptiness there. And she feels afraid. Afraid of this great, drowned colossus and the blackness inside of it.

*

The following morning Lillian wakes late, after ten o' clock. She gets up, pulls the curtains open and looks across the lane to Arthur's house. There are still no starlings. She listens, wondering if the events of the day before were, after all, a complex hallucination or a richly drawn dream, but the same silence rises to meet her. She goes downstairs, makes some coffee and sits at the table by the living room window. When she's finished her coffee, Lillian finds her rucksack. She goes into the kitchen, opens the fridge and takes out a block of cheese and some ham and makes a sandwich. She puts the sandwich in a plastic tub with an apple and slots it into the rucksack. She goes into the living room, takes a throw from one of the chairs and packs that as well.

When Lillian leaves the house, everything is just the same as it was the day before. She doesn't bother to lock the door. As she walks along the track at the back of the house, she looks up at the clear sky, thankful that the weather is fair, despite the cold. She's heading for the other side of the Dean where there's a designated picnic area. As she reaches the woods, she turns right and continues upwards instead of descending through the crags. To her left is a wooden fence with barbed wire hammered along its top, which normally keeps the sheep in. But now there are only a few wisps of dirty fleece fluttering on the sharp twists of wire. This path is less muddy and so Lillian walks quickly and makes good progress.

It's some time since she's been this way and she's forgotten that the path turns sharply away from the Dene before sweeping back round, down and then up again to the grassy plateau where the picnic area lies. She feels glad of a longer walk, a chance to clear her head. As she walks, she visualises the body again. She tries to imagine what its face might look like. She dimly recalls reading a poem at school about a colossus – the ruin of a man that someone is trying to piece back together. She's sure that she still has the book at home.

181

Eventually, Lillian reaches the final ascent to the picnic area. She feels the muscles in her legs begin to strain and has to stop half way up to catch her breath. The ground is thick with pine needles. Lillian likes the smell even though they make the ground soft and difficult to walk on. She pushes on towards the ridge where the trees stop, and finds two wooden picnic tables and also an information board showing an artist's impression of what the Dene might have looked like when it was a prehistoric lake.

Now that she's reached the summit, Lillian can see the full expanse of the Dene for the first time, empty and bathed in sunlight. She opens her rucksack and takes out the throw and her sandwich. She lays the throw on the damp picnic bench and sits down. As she eats she feels, for the first time, a sense of grief and fear at this suddenly being alone in the world. She senses that there's a blackness behind everything she can see, and that this blackness is the only thing that's real. She puts down her sandwich and looks down at the empty Dene again. She feels empty too, and thinks for a moment that she's going to cry, but doesn't.

*

Later, when Lillian is back at home, she looks along the bookshelves in the living room, but she can't find the book with the poem about the colossus in it. She goes to run a bath instead. As the hot water blasts into the tub and steam fills the bathroom, she sits on the edge of the bath. She wonders if everything will be back to normal tomorrow. If her cats, and Arthur, and everyone else will return, as if nothing has happened. But she isn't sure whether she wants things to go back to normal. Yes, she fears the blackness beneath this sad, emptied world, but there'll be such freedom too, the freedom to only have to look back – to remember

She turns the tap off and begins to undress, pausing before she steps into the water to wipe away the condensation on the mirror and pin her long, red curls into a knot.

The Accident

I remember the accident in every detail. The car swerving gracefully across the icy road. The trees in the headlights parting in front of me and the blackness beyond. The unattended steering wheel, my hands held up to my face, Julia's voice screaming and the car lurching upwards, twisting in mid-air, turning the world upside down between my fingers. And the waiting. I remember that too. Waiting for the impact. The explosion of glass and the smashing, crunching of metal, which seemed as if it would never come.

We hit the tree straight on. I wasn't wearing my safety belt and was catapulted through the windscreen. I fractured my skull, an arm, a collarbone and two ribs. I needed over a hundred stitches to my face and arms. The doctors said it was a miracle I wasn't killed, that it was touch-and-go to begin with. But they're pleased with my progress and they think I should make a full recovery. Julia was lucky. She walked away from the accident with just a few cuts and bruises.

It happened just after New Year, and now it's spring. I can see buds on the trees outside the hospital windows. Soon I'll be able to go home, but things will never be quite the same. I recognise my name on the plastic wristband that I wear – Miriam Morris – but when I look in the mirror I'm a different person. The life I have now is not the one I had. I've been destroyed, torn apart and pieced back together again – sewn into a patchwork of ugly scars. But in a strange way, it's as if I finally recognise myself now, in my new body. The wound I carried around deep inside of me for so long, is now written into my flesh for all to see. And that's how it should be. I mourn, but my tears have been wiped away, I'm dead yet alive, buried but risen.

*

I'd only passed my driving test six weeks before the accident happened. I bought the car two weeks later, after seeing it parked in Tremain's farmyard while I was out walking in the woods. It had a sign stuck in the window: 'For Sale. Price £1,500.' Beech Farm, always referred to as Tremains, lies about three miles outside the village, between Holling End reservoir and Holling Wood. Holling End was once a cluster of farms and labourer's cottages on the outskirts of the village, until the valley was flooded as part of the construction of the reservoir. The car was a Morris Traveller, just like the one we'd had when I was a child. It was the same creamy colour, with identical chestnut leather upholstery. Dad used to joke that the car was made especially for us – 'Why else would it have our name?'

Mr Tremain said the car was in good working order, though it did need a thorough clean inside and out. I offered him £1,200, which he accepted straight away. 'Shame to see it go really, but we can't afford the luxury of two.' He nodded over to a mud-spattered Volvo parked in front of the house. There was a chicken roosting on the bonnet. Mrs Tremain, whom I recognised from the village, emerged from the barn carrying a large wicker picnic hamper. Julia, her daughter, appeared in the doorway of the house. Mrs Tremain passed the hamper to Julia, who took it inside.

*

I knew about the Tremains through Morag. I got to know Morag soon after moving into the village. That was about ten years ago. I rented the house that she and her ex-husband were trying to sell after they separated, and over time we became friends. Morag was born in the village and went to school with both of the Tremains, whom she knew as David and Carla.

Morag said that the farm had been in David's family for generations. 'It's a millstone round their necks. They're drowning in debt. It's killing David and he's dragging Carla down with him if you ask me. And then there's Julia of course ...' Morag said Julia had suffered from mental health problems for a number of years. 'Sometimes she's manic, and other times she goes down into a depression. Once she thought she was the Virgin Mary. She's ended up in Greenacres a few times. She'll never be right. It's so hard for Carla. She feels guilty, because she thinks it's their fault, her and David, and the farm.' Greenacres was about ten miles from the village, an old Victorian asylum that still functioned as a psychiatric hospital.

Morag was always joking that Carla was a witch. She once told me that Carla had persuaded her to join in with a séance. 'It was just the three of us – Carla, me and Julia. We were all sat round the kitchen table. David was in a rocking chair by the range, holding a crow in his arms. It was wrapped up in a towel, like a baby. It had broken its wing. He was feeding it little pieces of bread dipped in milk and rum. Anyway, we were all a bit drunk, and Carla got out this Ouija board. There was a whiskey tumbler turned upside down, and we all had to put a finger on it. The glass moved round the board to different letters and numbers, but you couldn't tell if anyone was deliberately pushing it or not.' Morag said that it seemed as if the letters and numbers were random, to start with, but that when they looked at them more closely they realised that they made up the Volvo's registration number.

'That crow used to hop about the farmyard and sit on the cows. But David ran it over with the tractor. Julia buried it under an apple tree behind the cowshed.'

*

I picked up the Morris a couple of days after agreeing the price with Mr Tremain. I took the keys and the paperwork from him and I got into the driver's seat. Then he told me to hold on. He walked over to a lean-to shelter by the barn. 'Here, I'll throw in a Christmas tree for free.' He took a tree from a pile in the shelter, opened the passenger door and placed it carefully on the back seat. 'Merry Christmas.' I thanked him, and drove straight over to Morag's to show her the car. As I arrived, she was filling a coal scuttle from the bunker in her yard. She looked up and laughed as I pipped the horn and waved.

'Well, here's a surprise! I must say, it kind of suits you.' Morag skirted round the Morris and trailed her finger along the roof trim, nodding her head. 'Needs a good old wash but yes, it's definitely you. So, c'mon then, how about a spin?' She dropped the scuttle, opened the passenger door and jumped in.

We drove through the village and round the back of the reservoir. It was a cold, clear day, but Morag insisted on winding down the window to let the wind blow through her hair. When we reached the top road, above the reservoir, we stopped and got out to look over the water and across to the village. Morag said that there were stories about being able to see the old church spire poking up out of the water, and people hearing the church bell ring, during drought years. She laughed, and said that when they were kids she and Carla had fished there in the summer holidays. 'Sometimes we'd sit here for hours. Never realised there weren't any bloody fish!'

We walked towards the sloped concrete bank and tossed stones into the water. Morag held a finger up to her ear. 'No church bell today anyway.' I said that the reservoir must be deep to swallow a whole village. 'I suppose it must be,' she replied, 'but there's something so inviting about it isn't there – deep water? I always fancy a swim when I'm up here, even when it's cold. Dangerous though, I suppose.' A teenager had been drowned in the reservoir a couple of summers previously.

Morag lay on the bank, closed her eyes and folded her arms across her chest. 'They say your life flashes before your eyes when you drown, don't they? I read this piece in the newspaper a while back. It was some study that had been done with people who'd died and been resuscitated. Lots of them had these flashbacks – sometimes intense emotional things that had happened to them.' As I listened to Morag, I watched the surface of the water stir with a change of direction in the wind, so that it suddenly seemed to be rushing towards us. 'Anyway, it said that the part of the brain where memories are stored is the last part to die. And there was this theory that the brain's searching through all those past experiences to try and find an answer, a way out – an escape from death.'

Morag sat up and shook her head. 'Sweet Jesus, will you listen to me! You'll be throwing yourself in there if I keep this up. And when we should be celebrating.' She stood up and pointed back towards the Morris. 'The Miriam mobile over there! That car's going to change your life, girl.' She laughed and got up. 'Just think, day trips to the seaside, city shopping trips. The possibilities are endless.'

It was cold, so we walked back to the car and, as we did, I told Morag about the Morris we'd had when I was a child. How my dad used to sit me on his knee and let me hold the steering wheel when he drove it into the garage. He'd work the pedals and I'd turn the wheel. And I told her about our annual summer camping trip to Cornwall. I used to love those early morning starts. The chilly half-light, the cold leather seats, the hum of the heater, the empty roads. Mum would read the map and always get us lost, and Dad would play his music on the cassette player. He liked the big bands – Duke Ellington, Benny Goodman and Tommy Dorsey were his favourites. I used to fall asleep on the back seat, under a patchwork blanket that Mum had made specially for me.

We drove back to the village through the woods. 'I suppose it's like going back to a house you used to live in, and finding that nothing's changed?' Morag gestured towards the dashboard. 'The numbers on the speed dial, the sound of the indicators, the smell of the seats. They'll bring all sorts of memories back for you.' As we approached the village, we saw Julia walking along the side of the road. Morag wound down the window and asked if she wanted a lift. Julia smiled and shook her head, so we carried on. I saw her figure receding in the rear-view mirror. She lifted an arm in a lethargic wave, crossed the road and set off back through the trees towards the farm.

Morag said that she was meeting up with Carla later that afternoon. 'We're going for a walk together. Does her good to get out of the house for a bit, things being what they are. Though she's okay at the moment. Julia seems well. Touch wood.' Carla had told her that Julia had met a young man from one of the farms a few miles out of the village. 'He went for tea with them, apparently. Carla thinks it'll be good for Julia. To have someone. You know, someone special?'

*

When we got back to the village, I asked Morag if she wanted to come in for a coffee. We turned into the lane, and as we passed the leafless oak tree on the corner two crows lifted from its uppermost branches into the pale afternoon sky. I parked the car in front of the house and we went inside. As we sat drinking our coffee I showed Morag a photograph of the old Morris, taken during one of our holidays in Cornwall. In the photograph, both doors are open and the windows are wound down, with my head poking through one and Mum's through the other. We're both laughing. It's a beautiful, sunny day and we're in Zennor. Behind us is St Senara's Church. Mum loved old churches, and each year we would visit at least one we'd not seen before. She said St Senara's was named after a princess called Asenora. Asenora had been married to a king who threw her into the sea in a barrel while she was pregnant. She was visited by an angel, and gave birth to a son out at sea, before being washed up on the Cornish coast.

Morag held the photograph up close. 'I see what you mean about the car. Could almost be the same one. You look so like your mum. What a lovely picture of the two of you.'

I'd found the photograph a few days before, when I'd been in the attic getting the Christmas decorations. I poured us some more coffee, lit a fire and asked Morag if she wanted to help me put up the decorations. 'Sure! why not? You got any Christmas music we can put on. You know – Bing Crosby, Perry Como, Phil Spector?' I told her about dad always playing Tommy Dorsey's 'Santa Claus is

Coming to Town' when we put our Christmas tree up. I said that I didn't have much of a music collection and that she'd have to make do with a mince pie.

We opened the boxes and took out the decorations, which were wrapped in newspaper. I'd left Mr Tremain's Christmas tree in the yard. I brought it in and wedged it into a wooden garden tub with some old bricks, and we hung the baubles, tinsel and lights on it. Some of the baubles were almost as old as me, bought by my mum when I was a baby. The oldest one was a battered little silver bugle, the kind an angel might have. When we'd finished the tree, we made paper chains, licking and sticking the strips of brightly coloured paper together. As my chain grew longer, I wrapped it round my shoulders.

'I wear the chain I forged in life!' Morag said, in a booming voice. 'Go on. Who said it?' I knew, of course, that it was the ghost of Jacob Marley from *A Christmas Carol.* We hung the paper chains round the room and then I switched on the fairy lights. We agreed that it made the place look very festive. I asked Morag if she wanted to see some more of the photographs I'd brought down from the attic, and she said she'd love to see them. I laid them out, in chronological order, on the living room floor. We turned the cellophane-covered pages. There were old pictures of Mum and Dad and pictures of me as a baby, faded holiday Polaroids and school photographs. Morag laughed at the pictures of me as a toddler. 'You were a proper little cherub, weren't you? Look at those curls and those rosy cheeks.'

'So, who's this one?' It was the last album, and Morag was pointing at a photograph of Martin, wearing a hat from a Christmas cracker and holding a cocktail shaker.

*

Martin was my first real boyfriend. We met at college, and were together for a couple of years, although we lived separately. We'd spent the whole of that Christmas holiday in the flat Martin shared with two other students. They'd gone home, so we had the place to ourselves. Martin had bought me a beautiful old copy of *A Christmas Carol,* and he would read it to me in bed, sometimes before we went to sleep at night, or sometimes as we lay in bed in the morning drinking tea. On Christmas Eve we made cocktails and got drunk. We watched *It's a Wonderful Life,* then later we decided to go to the local church for the midnight service. I'm not sure whose idea it was, since neither of us came from churchgoing families. We entered through a small wooden porch with little leaded windows. The church was candlelit, and the choir was singing unaccompanied at the back, beside an elaborately carved stone font. We were given service sheets and hymn books, and we had to sit in one of the pews right near the front because all the rest were full.

Directly in front of us there was a brightly polished brass lectern on which a huge Bible stood, resting open on the outstretched wings of a fierce-looking eagle. Above it hung an embroidered banner depicting Mary and Jesus. At the other side of the nave was a crude nativity scene housed in a large, painted case which was meant to look like a stable. All the characters and animals were different sizes, and they didn't match each other. We sat quietly listening to the choir at first. Then Martin leant over and whispered in my ear, 'Do you believe in God, Miri?' He sat back and smiled. 'I can't believe we've never asked each other that question. Isn't it one of those things we should know about each other?' I said I wasn't sure, and he laughed when I told him that a church wasn't the place to discuss it. He held my hand and looked into my eyes. 'I think I love you, Miriam Morris.' I squeezed his hand and teased him that if he only thought so, then maybe he didn't really. He rolled his eyes.

The vicar announced the first carol, 'Once in Royal David's City', and the crucifer led the choir up the aisle to the stalls as the sound of the organ filled the building and the congregation sang. We read the words from the service sheets, sang and listened to the vicar's sermon. Some people went up to the altar for communion, but we didn't. When we said the Lord's Prayer, Martin bowed his head and held his hands together in his lap. I remember thinking how beautiful his hands were.

After the service we walked back to the flat sober, went straight to bed and made love. Martin feel asleep soon after, but I couldn't. I lay beside him, wide awake, listening to the Christmas revellers passing on the street below. And as I did, I found myself thinking about the embroidered banner in the church. Mary and Jesus, each of them crowned with golden halos. Mary holding Jesus close, so that their cheeks touched, and Jesus reaching out an arm to embrace her, seeming to look up into her face. Mary's head bowed protectively over Him, but her sorrowful eyes not seeing him, seeing something else. And behind them, a tree on a hill, in the distance.

I thought too about Martin's question. 'Do you believe in God Miri?' I had sometimes wondered, and occasionally found myself thinking that God must exist. After all, how could it be possible to long for something so much, if it didn't exist?

*

The night of the accident was Christmas Eve too. I fell asleep on the sofa in the afternoon, as evening began to bleed across the sky and the first stars flickered and brightened – and I had a dream.

I dreamt about Holling End, and about the old farmhouses that had been drowned by the reservoir. In my dream it was night, and there was a huge moon in the sky. I was sitting in a field with Julia, and behind us was Tremains. All the windows of the farmhouse were lit up, but they were barred, like prison windows. In front of us were Mum's patchwork blanket and the wicker picnic hamper that I'd seen Carla Tremain carrying when I was up at the farm. Julia opened it, and inside there was a fish, mouthing the air as if it were still alive, but I knew it was dead. I was trying to speak to Julia, but either she couldn't hear me or she wouldn't reply, and I could feel myself getting angry with her. At the other side of the field I could see a tree. I knew it was the oak tree in the lane, but there was something not right about it. I couldn't work out what it was at first, but then I was standing in front of it and I saw that it was upside down. Its gnarled, withered roots were sticking up into the blackness of the night sky, while its branches and leaves were buried beneath the ground. I could hear a noise in the distance that I knew was the sound of rushing water, and I knew too that the valley and the farmhouse, and the tree, and Julia and I were all going to be swept away and drowned in the reservoir. And I could feel the panic rising in me, because I needed to speak to Julia. I needed to ask her about Manasseh.

*

At first, I didn't think anything of it. A late period wasn't so unusual, but then I did the test, three times, and I knew for sure. I was too afraid to tell Martin. I can't say that I was happy to find myself pregnant, but there was no question in my mind that I would have the baby. As complicated as the situation was, I could never have considered a termination. I had no idea how Martin would react, but I hoped that he'd feel the same way. Although we weren't in an ideal position to start a family, I felt that we might be able to make it work, if we both wanted to. But before I had the opportunity to tell him and to talk it through, everything was turned upside down, when Dad died. Mum said he was washing the Morris one morning and had a massive heart attack. I took the train home on my own. Martin didn't come with me. I told him it was best if I went by myself. I stayed with Mum for almost a month, until after the funeral. It was a lovely service, and they played all Dad's favourite music. Mum was in a terrible state, but as the days and weeks passed, she gradually began to recover. I didn't tell her about the baby of course. I couldn't. I spoke with Martin on the telephone almost every day, but as time went by I felt more and more uneasy about telling him.

Eventually, mum said that while she loved having me at home, it was perhaps time for her to start getting used to being on her own. 'It's going to be a different life, Miriam, without your dad, but I need to start living it. And you need to get on with your life too.' I'd helped her with some of the practical things that needed to be taken care of, and she had the support of nearby friends, so any uncertainty I felt about leaving was more to do with facing Martin than being worried about how mum would cope. And so, a few days later, I returned to college.

Martin met me off the train and, after I'd dropped my things at my flat, we went for a long walk along the river. I felt it would be easier to talk outside, in the open air. I could tell that he was shocked when I told him. More shocked than he wanted to appear. 'Oh my God Miri, that's ... amazing! I don't know what to say. It might just take a bit of ... well, I guess we'll need to talk.' He kissed me and held me. 'But it will be ok.'

But it didn't feel ok. It immediately felt different from before. Martin was different, as if he was constantly searching for the right things to say and do, rather than being honest about what he thought and felt. And so, as the days passed, I sensed a door closing between us, and our relationship growing more and more shallow, just at the time we needed to be completely open with one another. At first, I was encouraged that Martin seemed to recognise that we needed to talk, but we didn't. Or, more accurately, Martin talked, perhaps more than usual, but about anything other than what we needed to discuss. He talked out of fear, to avoid the silence that might demand a response to the situation from him, to ensure that there was no possibility of us having to look beneath the surface of things. It was extraordinary, unreal – and there were moments when I wondered if I'd imagined it all.

I thought about the best way to begin a conversation with Martin, to get him to think about what we were going to do, but in the end I just came out with it. Martin had borrowed his flatmate's car and we were driving through town into college. He was talking about the dinner he and his flatmates were having that evening, and a cherry soufflé he planned to make, when I suddenly found myself cutting across him, saying that I wanted to have the baby and that I wanted us to be together, and that I needed to know what he was thinking. He gripped the steering wheel and continued to look straight ahead. At first he said nothing, and I could sense his panic as he calculated whether there was a way to avoid, or defer, a response. He frowned and struggled with each word as he spoke. 'I think ... It's like ... I don't know what I think Miri. I feel. I'm sorry, but I don't know what I feel. I can't ...' I waited, but this was as much as he could say. We sat in silence for the rest of the journey. When we arrived at college and Martin parked and turned off the engine, he said again, 'I'm sorry ... I'm sorry, Miri' – still without turning to look at me.

I didn't see him the next day and I just kept wondering what to do, as if Martin's inability, or unwillingness, to acknowledge what was happening was contagious. And then, quite suddenly, it was all over. I started to bleed. I was sent to hospital, and it was over. Martin came to see me when I got back to my flat. 'I'm so sorry, Miri. This is awful for you. Whatever you need me to do, just say.' He hugged me as if I'd just fallen over in the playground and grazed my knee. I could see the relief on his face, and the guilt too, perhaps. This hadn't happened to us, but to me. 'We can think about the future when you're feeling better. You need to concentrate on getting better for now.' I didn't tell him, but I'd already made arrangements to go to Mum's.

I don't know if it was a boy or a girl. I was only ten weeks in, so it would have been too early to tell, I imagine. I think it would have been a boy though. I felt such a great sense of loss, as if some huge, dark place had opened up deep inside of me and I'd fallen into it and would never be able to get out. I wanted to. I wanted to escape from this terrible thing that had happened, but at the same time, I wanted to stay in the dark, to keep feeling my wound, the loss, because it seemed as if it was the only thing in the world that was worth feeling. Maybe I felt guilty too, that somehow, what had happened was all my fault. As if, secretly, I'd wanted it to happen.

*

Manasseh was a mystery from my childhood – a name carved into a piece of stone embedded in our garage wall. Behind the garage there was an old fence, and behind that was a churchyard which had once extended into our garden. I found it all a bit creepy. I couldn't help thinking about the dead people buried underneath our garden. You could see some of the graves through the holes in the fence. They were ancient-looking things, covered in moss, so that you could barely read the inscriptions carved into the crumbling stone. Some of the graves had sunk, leaving only the curved tops of the headstones above ground level. Our garage was built from some of the old stone that had once formed part of the churchyard wall. It had been covered with a mortar render, inside and out, but over the years patches of it had fallen away to reveal the stones beneath. In amongst the roughly hewn stones, there were smoother, dressed pieces from gravestones that must have been removed and broken up at some stage. When Dad drove the car into the garage at night, you could see one of them in the headlights, bearing the name, Manasseh.

Dad had once taken me into the garage with a torch to take a closer look at the stone carved with Manasseh's name. 'It's an unusual name, isn't it? Probably from the Bible.' I said it seemed a shame that the stone had been smashed, and that because it wasn't standing in the churchyard it was as if Manasseh had never existed at all.

'It is, I suppose. But then he probably lived a very long time ago. And we think about him every time we get in the car and see his name, don't we?'

I often wondered about Mannaseh, about who he was, and what he looked like, whether he'd had a family and whether his life had been a happy one. And I wondered how old he'd been when he died.

*

When I woke from my dream it was almost half past nine, and pitch black outside. I had something to eat and watched the television. I knew that, after sleeping for so long, there was little point in going to bed early, and so I decided to go out for a drive. I

193

put on a jumper and my coat, and went out into the yard. I unlocked the car and got in. It was freezing cold, and I realised I'd forgotten my gloves, but I couldn't be bothered to go back inside to fetch them. I pulled out the choke and turned the key in the ignition, and the engine coughed into life. The windows were covered in frozen condensation, so I turned the knob on the dashboard that controlled the heater, which was soon humming and whirring noisily.

I revved the engine to warm it, turned on the windscreen wipers and waited for the condensation to melt away. After a few minutes, a clear patch appeared at the bottom of the windscreen and slowly spread upwards until I had a clear view of the yard. I put the car into gear and manoeuvred it carefully out into the deserted lane. I drove past the oak tree on the corner, through the village, and on towards the reservoir. I could see a frosting of ice beginning to form on the road in front of me and, as the reservoir eventually came into view, there was a perfect reflection of the moon in the water.

I followed the road round the reservoir and back into the woods. I must have driven for about half an hour before the narrow road began to widen and the trees gave way to open fields. There was a long, steep turning to the right, and as I reached the top of the incline I noticed a farmhouse, and then a tiny black figure walking towards me at the side of the road. I slowed down as I got closer to the figure, and as I passed, I realised that it was Julia. I wondered why she was out walking so late, and I decided to turn round and offer her a lift back to the village. I reversed the car into a gateway, unwound the passenger window and turned back into the road. As I approached, Julia carried on walking and didn't acknowledge me. I slowed the car, stopped alongside her and called her name out of the open window. I asked if she wanted a lift home.

She turned and looked at me, and for a moment I thought she wasn't going to reply, but simply continue on her way. But then she spoke, so quietly that I could barely hear her over the sound of the engine. 'That's kind. Yes, please. Thank you.'

She unfastened her coat, opened the car door and clambered in awkwardly, her left arm cradling her abdomen, which I could quite clearly see was swollen. I stared, shocked, for perhaps only a second or two, but then I looked away quickly. Julia busied herself with her seat belt, pulling the metal latch plate to extend the belt under her swollen belly and then fixing it in place with a sharp click. I ground the gear stick into first gear, released the handbrake and we set off. I felt Julia turn and look at me as I drove on. She stroked her bump with her open palm. 'Mum and Dad don't know,' she said, 'I'm not sure how to tell them.'

I kept my eyes fixed on the road and searched frantically for a response, but before an awkward silence had time to develop, Julia had changed the subject. 'It's freezing isn't it?' She reached forward and turned the heater up. 'You don't mind, do you?' I said it was fine, but added that the heaters weren't terribly effective. She rested both of her hands on her belly now, and leant back in her seat. 'It's very kind of you to stop and give me a lift. I walked further than I thought.' I said it was no trouble and that I'd driven further than I'd meant to. I glanced across at her and added that perhaps she shouldn't be walking so far, in the cold and the dark. I stopped myself from adding, 'in your condition'. 'Yes,' she replied, 'but it's so clear up here when it's like this. The stars are beautiful, don't you think?' She paused, and then raised a hand up to the windscreen, pointing up at the night sky ahead of us. 'You see shooting stars up here too. Lots of them. They're falling out of the sky all the time.'

The road began to close in on us as we drove back into the woods, and Julia turned to me again. 'This was Mum's car, wasn't it? You bought it.' I told her about the Morris we'd had when I was growing up, and how it was almost identical. 'I remember Mum driving me to school in it,' she continued. 'I came home from the hospital in it too, Mum says, when I was born.' I said that it was probably older than both of us.

We didn't speak again until we approached the fork in the road that led to the farm one way, and to the village the other. As we did, I slowed the car and asked Julia if she wanted me to take her up to the farm. 'That would be perfect,' she replied, 'if it's not too much trouble.' I indicated left, and as we swept away from the village road, I looked at my hands gripping the steering wheel and had the strange sense that I was looking at Martin's hands.

*

The farmhouse was in darkness, except for a security lamp at the far end of the building. I pulled up beside the house, where the Volvo was usually parked, and switched off the engine. Julia asked me what time it was. I looked at my watch. It was half past eleven.

She got out of the car and walked over to the front door of the house. I thought I'd better wait until she got inside. She opened the door, leaving it ajar, and switched on a light. I waited and watched as different lights came on, first downstairs and then upstairs, but after a few minutes Julia had still not reappeared or closed the door. I didn't want to leave without making sure that she was all right, so I decided to go in and check. I got out of the car, walked across the yard and called to her from the front doorstep. There was no answer, so I went inside.

I walked through to the kitchen, in the middle of which was a large farmhouse table. It was strewn with dirty pots, empty bottles and stained correspondence. On one side of the room was a wood burning stove, with a pile of ash on the hearth below it. Above the fireplace was an old framed photograph that I recognised as Holling End before the reservoir was built. I called Julia's name again, and heard her coming downstairs. She appeared in the doorway to the left of the fireplace and looked round the kitchen. She barely seemed to notice that I was there. I asked her if everything was all right.

'They're not here.' She walked quickly over to the table as if she was looking for something that might provide a clue as to why the house was deserted, perhaps a note that she'd missed when she came in. 'Where can they be? They should be here.' She picked up a handful of papers from the table and looked through them, and lifted a tea pot to see if there was anything underneath it. I could see that she was agitated, and so I tried to reassure her, suggesting that maybe they'd gone out to the pub, or to church, with it being Christmas Eve. I said that I was sure they wouldn't be far away.

Julia went back out into the yard without answering. She strode across to the cowsheds and looked inside, and then to the gateway that led down the track to the road. I followed her over to the gate and put my hand on her shoulder. I told her that I'd wait with her until they got back, and persuaded her that we should go inside and make a cup of tea.

As we walked across the yard, we seemed to stop simultaneously. We stood and listened. There was a low rumbling sound, hardly noticeable at first. It was difficult to work out where it was coming from, but as we stood there together in the cold stillness of the night, holding our breaths to listen, we each realised that it could only be coming from the old stable building on the other side of the yard to the cowshed. It had a pair of large black wooden doors, and Julia ran over and began pulling at the metal latch to open them. By this time, I think we both knew that the rumbling sound was the noise of a car engine inside the stable.

As Julia pulled open one of the doors, a great plume of acrid exhaust fumes spilled out, forcing us back into the yard, coughing and spluttering. After a few moments it cleared, and we moved forward again. I swung the other door open and there inside I could see the rear of the Volvo, with a rubber glove and a length of garden hose attached to its exhaust pipe with gaffer tape. The exhaust was vibrating with the dull throb of the engine, as were the swollen fingers of the glove. The other end of the hose had been pushed through the passenger side window, which was sealed with a towel.

I could see the car was filled with fumes. Julia was crying and shouting. I forced her back out into the yard and told her to wait, then hurried back into the stable. I went to the passenger door, but it was locked, so I moved round to the front of the car. The bumper was up against the wall and so I had to crawl over the bonnet. As I did, I could see David and Carla Tremain inside the car. The driver's door wasn't locked, but as soon as I opened it I was forced back again by the fumes, and stumbled towards the doors blindly, barely able to breath. I unfastened my coat, pulled my jumper over my nose and mouth and turned to go back in.

As I leant down and turned off the Volvo's engine, I accidentally touched Mrs Tremain's hand. For some reason she was wearing her safety belt, and I struggled to free her from it while the fumes continued to drive me back. At last I managed to unclip the strap and heave her out of the car. I took hold of her under her arms, dragged her out into the yard and laid her down as gently as I could on the frozen, rutted ground. I went back inside for Mr Tremain. He was much heavier, and it took me several attempts before I was finally able to pull him free of the car, drag him across the stable floor and get him outside.

I had no idea if they were alive or dead. I knelt beside each of them in turn, looking for signs of life. I wondered whether I should try chest compressions or mouth-to-mouth resuscitation, but was afraid of making things worse. When I looked up Julia had gone, and I wondered if she was inside phoning for an ambulance. I called out for her, but she didn't answer, so I ran inside, found the telephone and rang for the ambulance myself.

I found Julia in the clearing behind the cowshed. She was sitting hunched against the apple tree under which she'd buried her father's crow. The cows huddled by the shed gate, watching, wreaths of warm breath streaming from their nostrils. I went over and sat down beside her. She cried quietly now, and wrapped her arms around herself while we waited for the ambulance. We seemed to sit there for a long time, and when the ambulance arrived I said that I'd drive us to the hospital in the Morris.

*

We must have hit a spot of black ice. The car spun and swerved away from the icy road, the trees in the headlights parted in front of me and then there was blackness. The unattended steering wheel, my hands held up to my face, Julia screaming and the car lurching upwards, twisting in mid-air, turning the world upside down. And the waiting. Waiting for the impact. The explosion of glass and the smashing, crunching of metal, which seemed as if it would never come. And in those long seconds, as I held my hands up to my face and then closed my eyes tight shut, I saw them. I saw them all. Mum and Dad. Martin. Morag, David and Carla Tremain – and Julia with her swollen belly. And then I saw the inverted tree in the headlights of the car, and the starless blackness beyond. It was the black ice. There was nothing I could have done.

*

Morag came to see me a couple of weeks ago. It was the first time I'd seen her since the accident. She told me that Julia had been discharged from hospital the day after the accident. Morag said that she'd taken her under her wing. 'She needs someone to put their arms round her. Carla was always there for me, and now I've got to be there for Julia.' Morag's been staying with Julia at the farm. There are a lot of debts, but she seems to think Julia will get to keep the farm, or be able to sell it and have enough for a place of her own, once the debts are settled. I'm not sure whether Julia's young man is still around.

'She was so lucky. You both were. But Julia could easily have ...' Morag looked at me closely, monitoring my responses. I asked her if everything was all right. She nodded. 'David and Carla didn't know. If they'd known, then maybe things might have been different. She's due any day. She's convinced it's a boy. She's going to call him David.'

Morag didn't stay long. She didn't seem comfortable. She didn't even ask when I'd be coming out of hospital. She's taken Carla's death badly, which is understandable, but it's as if she thinks the accident was my fault. But I was the one that was helping Julia. I was there when she needed help too.

*

I've been thinking a lot about David and Carla Tremain. And I've been thinking about Martin and my baby, who never really was at all, the baby I think of as Manasseh. I sometimes wish I'd kept that old chunk of stone, as a memento. After Dad died, Mum decided to sell the Morris and the garage was demolished. I found the stone beneath the rubble, much bigger than I'd imagined, though giving no further clues as to who Manasseh was. Above the carved letters of his name there seemed to be a fragment of an angel's wing and a bugle, though maybe I was imagining that.

And what do I imagine now, removed from the world, here in my hospital bed? Well, I imagine Holling End on a glorious summer afternoon. I imagine a field of sweet-smelling grass and wild flowers, surrounded by trees in full leaf. In the distance I can see the old cottages and the church spire. I imagine a huge picnic laid out on mum's patchwork blanket, and smiling, laughing faces. I see Mum and Dad, and David and Carla Tremain. I'm there too, and Martin and Morag. In the background are the cows from the farm, one of them carrying a crow on its back. The patients from Greenacres are making daisy chains, and Julia is there too, of course, cradling her baby in her arms. And amid all of this, at the very centre of it, is a reed basket with a sleeping baby inside. The baby I call Manasseh.

We're all happy, and I know that this is how it will always be, because it is a wonderful life. And Dad is winding up a portable record player and putting on one of his old records, and people are starting to dance. But I'm sitting beside the reed basket, watching Manasseh sleep and listening to the words of the old Tommy Dorsey song, 'Imagination is funny, it makes a cloudy day sunny ...' The words make me smile, and my feathered wings flutter, feeling the warmth of the sun.

Ashes to Ashes

The older I get, the more I miss my parents. I think about them every day, and I want to go back to when I was a child. I want to go home.

I close my eyes and I imagine it.

The sun's shining and I'm walking down the track that leads to the farmhouse. It's a long winding track, lined with hawthorn and cow parsley – or 'dead man's oatmeal', as my mother always called it. I strip a fistful of the little white flowers from the cow parsley, release them into the warm afternoon air, and watch as they drift away. The track turns to the left and opens out into the farmyard. Grass sprouts up from between the cobbles. There's a rusty old rotavator and a stack of tyres outside the barn. On the other side of the yard there's a blue tractor, and Harris, our border collie, is sitting in the cab. The house is a simple red brick farmhouse, with a thatched porch to the centre, where the swallows nest each summer, and a heavy oak door with a cast iron door knocker in the shape of a fox's head. And the door is opening. I see my father standing there inviting me in, and over his shoulder, my mother waving to me from the kitchen.

It's all gone now of course.

The house is gone, and so are my parents. But I think about it, and I think about them, more with every passing day. And even though it's all such a long time ago, I feel as if I'm drawing nearer to my childhood, rather than moving further away from it.

*

The place where we lived was remote, and I think I knew from a very young age that my parents' life on the farm wasn't easy, that they had to work hard to make ends meet. I had few, if any, friends of my own age, but I never felt lonely or unhappy there. I loved the farm and the countryside around it, the trees and the flowers, the animals and the insects. And there was nothing I enjoyed more than spending the day roaming free with Harris. I think my parents did love each other, but they'd drifted apart, maybe because of the demands of the farm, but also because of what had happened to my father in the war.

The farm had been in his family for generations, and my mother had come as part of the Women's Land Army to help my grandparents work the land. I still have some old photographs of her as a land girl, helping to 'dig for victory'. All the girls in the photographs are young, and 'strapping', as Uncle Jim would have said, with their hair worn up and their big, white smiles. But it's my mother, slim and radiant, who catches the eye. Uncle Jim said she was the spit of Rita Hayworth.

My father was a navigator in a bomber squadron, and so he didn't meet my mother until the war was nearly over. He was discharged from active service on medical grounds, a year or so before the fighting finally stopped. The war had scarred him very badly, and he never fully recovered. He suffered from nightmares and I remember him sometimes crying out in his sleep. Meeting my mother helped him to forget, for a while. They were married, and after my grandfather's death, they ran the farm together. I was born a couple of years later, and although it wasn't obvious to me as I was growing up, my father was often sullen and withdrawn.

Uncle Jim was my mother's brother. He lived in town and used to drive out to see us every weekend. He would often bring a bottle of whiskey, and he and my father would sit up drinking and talking, late into the night. Jim told me about some of the terrible things my father had seen in the war. He said he wished he'd been there too, but that he couldn't serve because of his bad heart. 'He saw some bloody awful sights did your Dad.'

*

Uncle Jim told me that my father used to dream about a terrible fire.

'It was Nuremberg that he kept on about. He said the problem was the moon. It was a clear, moonlit night and the bombers were picked off by the German fighters.' Jim said my father described the tracer fire from the fighters lighting up the night sky and burning aircraft plummeting to the earth below, exploding and showering debris like flaming confetti. 'Before they could unload their bombs, they were hit with a cannon shell. There was a terrific clatter, your father said, blue flashes and flames from the electric circuits, and burning shrapnel ripping through the fuselage.'

Jim said my father described what followed as total confusion, the plane rocking and shaking, plunging down through the night sky, and filling with oily black smoke. Voices barked and crackled over the radio, gradually dying down as the plane levelled off. All but one of them, that is.

'We're burning! ... We're burning!' The words came again and again, the voice getting louder, shouting, then screaming. 'Your dad said he was in shock, kept checking that he wasn't dead, that he hadn't been hit, that his bloody arms and legs were still there. And then he heard it, that voice – "We're burning! ... We're burning"!'

'He said he scrambled through the smoke towards the back of the plane. The voice was coming from one of the gun turrets, the tail gunner. Only a young fella apparently. Anyway, the poor bugger was on fire. He was strapped in. Couldn't get out. Your father watched it, the whole thing. Nothing he could do, he said. By the time they got the fire out he was burnt to a bloody cinder. Somehow, they managed to get out of there – weave their way back through the searchlights and the flak batteries. They got back home on three engines. Five hours it took them, with that poor young fella in the back. Your father used to dream about him, the tail gunner. A nightmare. He said he used to see his eyeball pop, with the heat, and that's when he'd wake up.'

I wish I could have known about all this then, been old enough to know, and understand. Because it should have been my father who told me these things, not someone else – not Uncle Jim.

*

When I wasn't at school, I was either out in the fields and the woods, or else helping my mother. She always seemed to be in the kitchen, and we spent a lot of time there together. There were often dead things hanging around: rabbits, pheasants and even, once, a lamb. I remember my mother skinning it, peeling back the wiry fleece to reveal the slick, glistening body underneath. Uncle Jim took one of the lamb's eyeballs out and lodged it in its anus. 'There!' he said. 'It's the spitting image. It's your bloody father.' Jim was funny like that. He used to make me laugh. The other thing I remember about that kitchen is the huge blackleaded range. We used to sit round it to eat breakfast. The kitchen was the warmest room in the house, and we virtually lived in it during the worst of the winter months. 'Better feed the beast,' my mother used to say, as she shovelled coal into the range. It frightened me sometimes – the clank of the doors and those black ovens I couldn't see to the back of.

By the time I was ten years old, my father was in his mid-fifties. To me he seemed very old, compared to Uncle Jim and, of course, my mother. He used to wear a long trench coat that was always muddy round the bottom. I can see him now, his grey head bowed and his hands deep in his coat pockets as he moved slowly round the farmyard. My parents never seemed to argue or say unkind things about each other, but I remember my mother once saying that Dad needed to 'pull his bloody finger out or we'll lose the farm.' As time went by his silent, black moods became more and more frequent and I grew frightened of him. I wanted him to love me, but I think he found it hard to be close to anyone. There were times when he seemed to be less morose and more willing to accept my company, when he'd let me help with the animals. The pigs were my favourites. They used to make me laugh, because they looked sort of human, with their pasty skin, their eyelashes and their crumpled snouts. He told me that cannibals in the Pacific islands called human flesh 'long pig'. He used to make them squeal for me. He'd chase them round the yard, hitting them with a stick. I didn't like that, but it made him laugh.

*

I'll never forget that day. It was a very hot summer's day, and Uncle Jim had offered to take me to York, to have a look round and go to the pictures. He'd just bought a car, something not many people had then, and I remember he came trundling slowly up the farm track, honking his horn as he pulled into the yard. My mother and I stood watching, waiting beside the porch. Harris ran alongside the car barking at it. When Jim finally reached us he stopped, jumped out and hugged my mother. 'Hello, gorgeous! Isn't she beautiful?' My mother shrugged, and Jim started to polish the farmyard dust off the bonnet with a handkerchief. 'Are you ready then, face ache?' I nodded, and got into the passenger seat. As we drove down the track towards the road, Harris ran after us, still barking, and then I saw my father step out from the trees. As we drove past him he waved to us with his stick, and when I looked back, I saw him walking with Harris towards the house, where my mother was still standing by the porch. I didn't know it at the time of course, but that was the last time I'd ever see them.

Uncle Jim insisted on showing me the sights. He took me to see the Minster and we walked along the Shambles. We climbed to the top of Clifford's Tower and Jim showed me where Guy Fawkes had gone to school. Then we went to the railway station to see the engines. I'd never seen a railway engine close up before. There was one in particular that I remember, standing on the tracks outside the station. It was huge, and we stood on the platform, close to the footplate, and watched as the fireman shovelled coal into the firebox. I jumped when the whistle blew and the blower sent a fierce blast of steam out of the chimney. We walked down to the river and had some sandwiches that Jim had brought for our lunch. After we'd eaten the sandwiches, Jim bought ice creams and we cooled our feet in the water while we ate them.

After lunch, we went to a matinee at the pictures. I was so excited, because I'd never been to the cinema before either. Inside there was a great sweeping staircase with a thick red carpet and a brass handrail. Uncle Jim bought me some sweets and we went into a dimly lit auditorium where there was a huge pair of curtains that slowly opened to reveal the screen. Jim lit a cigarette, and when the house lights went down I could see the smoke drifting and coiling in the light coming from the projector behind us. And then the film started – it was *King Kong*, one of Jim's favourites, he said. It was hot, and I remember being uncomfortable because the seat covering prickled the backs of my legs and made them sweat. But the film was incredible. I felt sorry for King Kong at the end, as he hung from the Empire State building with Fay Wray, swatting those buzzing little fighter planes as though they were insects. When the film finished, Jim made us wait until everyone was gone, and that's when he touched me. He rubbed my leg and my private parts. He told me not to worry, and asked me if I'd enjoyed the film.

*

I pretended to be asleep on the way home, and it wasn't until we were nearly back that I opened my eyes and yawned. Jim didn't say anything, and nor did I. It was nearly dark by the time we turned onto the track that led to the house. I was looking out of the window at the hedgerow whizzing by when Uncle Jim broke the silence. 'Jesus bloody Christ almighty!' His mouth was wide open, and his gaze fixed straight ahead. I looked, and I saw that there in front of us, at the end of the track, the farmhouse was on fire. Flames were leaping from the roof and the windows, and there were thick clouds of smoke too. I remember seeing the black outline of a bird swinging across the illuminated sky above us, and smelling the smoke as we got nearer.

The fire was out of control. Uncle Jim found a bucket, filled it from a trough in the yard and tried to get near enough to the fire to throw it, but he tripped and spilt it. He ran back to the trough, refilled the bucket and tried again, but the water didn't even reach the window he was aiming for. It was hopeless. I started to cry, and I ran round to the back of the house, and into the barn calling for Harris. I couldn't find him anywhere. I ran back to the house and Uncle Jim had to hold onto me because I got too close to the flames. My eyes were full of tears and I was struggling to get loose from him, shouting and screaming for Harris. Jim was shouting too, saying that we had to get help. He dragged me to his car and drove us to the next farm where Mr and Mrs Brook lived. I waited with Mrs Brook while Jim and Mr Brook went to the village to ring the fire brigade. But it was too late, the house must have been destroyed completely by the time they arrived.

I stayed with Mr and Mrs Brook that night. Mrs Brook made me up a bed and brought me a mug of cocoa. I kept asking her if she knew what had happened to Harris, but she didn't answer. She didn't mention the fire either. Mr Brook came back late and I heard them whispering to each other in the kitchen. I knew that something terrible had happened, but there was also a part of me that imagined going back to the house the next day and my mother and father being there, and everything being back to normal. As I lay there, wide awake, I couldn't stop thinking about Harris and where he might be – and longing to have him in my arms.

*

I never saw the house again, or whatever was left of it, and I've never been back. It was decided that I shouldn't attend my parents' funeral. I suppose that was what people thought back then – that it was best for children not to experience such things. I was packed off to stay with my grandmother on my father's side. I didn't know her very well, since we hadn't visited her often. It was a while before I saw Uncle Jim again. To begin with he didn't talk about what had happened, about the visit to the pictures or the fire. Then one day he took me out for a drive in his car. He parked beside a huge field of wheat. As we sat there together at the edge of the field, I was worried that he might try to touch me again, but he didn't. He picked some stems of wheat and started to show me how to make a corn dolly. Then he began to talk about my parents. He told me that my mother had nursed him when they were children, because he'd had scarlet fever, and he said how much he missed her. I felt sorry for him. He said my mother and father had made a 'handsome couple' when they married.

'He was a good-looking fellow was your father. It was tragic what happened to him. Tragic. But I still can't believe that he would do such a thing.' I didn't know what he meant at the time. Poor Dad, and Mum. I wish I'd been with them, instead of with Uncle Jim.

*

I had a dream last night, about the farmhouse. It was dawn, and I was standing in the porch outside the front door with Harris. The door was open and my father was standing there, inviting me in, and over his shoulder my mother was waving to me from the kitchen. They were both badly burnt, but I could still tell it was them. I went inside and Harris followed, into the old kitchen, with the dead things and the ovens. My father picked up a container and poured petrol over me, then himself, and then my mother, and Harris too, who was lying at my feet. I could smell it in my nostrils and taste it in my mouth. It was sweet. I took some matches from the drawer, lit one and dropped it into the pool of petrol on the floor. We all held hands as we burst into flames, a ring of fire. I could feel the heat and smell the burning. It was sweet too. It was cleansing away all the bad things, burning them away forever. Our hands were fused together, and I could feel that my eyes were about to explode into flames. And that's when I woke up.

Acknowledgements

Thank you to Madeleine O'Beirne for being a critical friend and patient editor, and to Grainne Slavin for equal patience in the preparation of cover designs.

Most of all, thank you to Dee and Gabriel, for your love and encouragement, and for much shared laughter.

Printed in Poland
by Amazon Fulfillment
Poland Sp. z o.o., Wrocław